I0628238

The Memoirs of Emperor Velzanar

Volume One: Attack of the Rockoids

By Gene Steinberg and Grayson Steinberg

MAKING THE IMPOSSIBLE

ToadHall Press

This is a work of fiction. All the characters and events portrayed in this book are fictional, and any resemblance to real people or incidents is purely coincidental.

ATTACK OF THE ROCKOIDS

Edited by Karen L. MacLeod

Cover art by Michael Cox (www.michaelcox.com)

Published by
Making The Impossible, Inc.
14747 North Northsight Boulevard
Suite 111-168
Scottsdale, AZ 85260
(877) 405-3185
Fax: (480) 661-8009
and
Toad Hall Press
Laceyville, PA
Email: sales@rockoids.com

ISBN: 1-893407-07-1

Seventh printing: June 2012

Printed in the United States of America

"The father-son writing team of Gene and Grayson Steinberg have written a marvelous, fast paced story of interstellar warfare and star-crossed love. The battle scenes are so descriptive, you can see the space ships explode and be consumed by gigantic balls of flame...Fans of *Star Wars* and *Star Trek* will enjoy this story and look forward to many more adventures of Ray and Zanther."

Brenda Gill, Sime~Gen, Inc.
(science fiction Web site)

"Though filled with scenes of action, heroism, intergalactic political intrigue and high drama, the soul of *Attack of the Rockoids* lies in its heart and passion for building a convincing tale of a love that spans the galaxy. A thrilling story!"

Robert Simpson, former *Star Wars* and *Indiana Jones* fiction editor

"If you like Golden Age Science Fiction then you need to grab a copy of this book!"

Teresa Roebuck, Just Can't Resist
(book review Web site)

He Sees Her in His Dreams!

What inspires us?

Where do we get the ideas for a new invention, a novel, or a hot-selling computer game?

Ray Perkins, military drop-out, lives a reclusive life in a Northern California cottage. He writes computer games that have been praised worldwide, and have become best-sellers. But he has never told anyone but his very few closest friends the source of his inspiration for those stories: his dreams.

Almost every night since he was a victim of a strange accident during a secret military mission in the Middle East, he has had those dreams. Horrible dreams. Of spaceships and bloody battles in outer space above a far-off planet.

And then there is she!

Her sad-eyed, beautiful face and figure dominates those dreams. She seems to call him, beckoning him. Two lost souls searching desperately for each other.

One day a chance glance at a small newspaper story about rumors of alien landings in Nevada strikes a nerve, that maybe there's a kernel of truth behind those frightening dreams. So Perkins sets off on a foolhardy mission to find the truth. And it is a terrible truth indeed, a truth that spans time and space. In our future, over 200 years from now, the alien woman of his dreams really exists.

And she, too, has dreams, dreams about him.

But it's not just a story of two would-be lovers trying desperately to find each other. It is a story of imminent danger and a threat to our way of life, for this woman is also the commander of a huge armada of spaceships that are coming here to destroy the Earth!

Will Ray Perkins' impossible journey in search of his one true love and the terrifying truth behind the dreams that obsess him come to a sad, tragic fate?

Attack of the Rockoids is not just the story of one man's incredible search for the meaning of his own life. It is an exciting, spell-binding story of high adventure in the grand science fiction tradition.

Dedications

*I'd like to pay special thanks to my "muse"
(she knows who she is) for always helping me find
the right things to say and the means to say it.*
—Gene Steinberg

To my mom, who taught me that miracles are possible.
—Grayson Steinberg

About this Book:

It all started as a game played by father and son.

And then it became an idea for a story.

And a novel.

And then a full-blown series of magical, mystical adventures.

The book you hold in your hands is just the beginning of a great journey. There is much more to come.

Please let us know what you think about this first episode of the Rockoids saga.

Send your e-mail to rockoids@rockoids.com.

Or visit us on the World Wide Web at www.rockoids.com.

Gene Steinberg
Grayson Steinberg
June 2012

Chapter 1

There are moments in history when destiny and chance intertwine to alter the face of the universe forever. These are times when an action, a word, a movement, is the very catalyst for an entire series of events difficult to stop once set into motion.

No one can ever tell when such moments are about to occur. They simply happen, where the right circumstances are in place at the right time. Only then does the unstoppable avalanche begin. Whether the fall of the Roman Empire or the outbreak of the Second World War on Earth, a rush of events converged as one significant incident transformed all that subsequently came to pass.

In the recent past, the unfathomable hand of fate struck yet again, this time altering history on a galactic level in a way no one would ever realize for years to come and completely changing the lives of every intelligent being, including two completely unrelated individuals, separated by a wide gulf of space and time, who quickly found themselves at the very center of the crisis.

And that was only the beginning of the story...
Volume One, The Memoirs of Emperor Velzanar

* * *

In the blackness of space, thousands of light years from Earth, the eternal calm was rudely disturbed as two opposing fleets of spaceships approached each other thousands of kilometers above a planet of huge cities and gorgeous landscapes.

Beneath the armadas, millions of beings went through their daily routines, oblivious to the threat from space that would change their lives forever. Royal guests were present on that scenic world, on a well-deserved vacation, engrossed in planning a royal pageant—so much work, so little time.

On one of the ships, the situation was especially tense.

"We can't do this, sir!" protested one of the senior officers. "By firing on the alien ships, we violate one of our most sacred edicts. It could be considered grounds for a court martial!"

The expansive flagship's bridge exhibited an ocean of modern technology and industrialized architecture, rectangular shaped, with a vaulted ceiling, and a huge flat-paneled video display in front. Brightly lit control panels lined each side. The huge craft's navigators were seated in a single row at the center.

The onlookers were stunned at the severity of the argument.

The commander's steel blue eyes narrowed. Though their leader's face remained couched in shadow, the crew could sense its dark, ominous look. The voice was husky, battle-worn. "If we do not fire, they will destroy us. Would you risk genocide? How dare you even suggest..."

"Sir, you're not listening..."

"That's enough! If you continue with this insubordination, I will remove you from the bridge and throw you into the brig. Is that clear?"

Sweat poured down the officer's face. His eyes widened, and his face twitched nervously. After tense seconds ticked by, he responded with almost no expression at all, "Yes, sir."

"Excellent, I'm glad you see it my way," the commander said

with the hint of a sneer.

The immense vessel moved slowly, deliberately, to the head of the fleet, and closed in on what appeared to be the enemy flagship. Without a sideways glance, the command was given in a loud, imperious voice, "Weapons officer, target the primary enemy ship and fire!"

The officer, nervous for a second, nodded and complied with the order, tears streaming down her face. She could barely contain her fears about the consequences of her actions.

In seconds, lasers of bright green and yellow shot forth, hitting their targets relentlessly. Explosions began to dot the space between the great warships, illuminating evidence of mounting casualties.

Fighter craft tried desperately to destroy the weapons batteries on massive, oval shaped vessels, but their impotent, ineffective firepower only made their enemies pause momentarily. The blasts simply rebounded off the large craft's powerful shields and struck the fighters instead.

In this battle, it was difficult to separate the enemy from the defenders. One moment images would be vivid and intense, becoming vague, shimmering, as if viewed from a pool of water.

Suddenly the oval craft resumed fire with even greater intensity. The individual beams from the laser guns of the ship coalesced into a single, immense blast aimed straight at an enemy cruiser. The crew of the warship struggled desperately to prepare their escape pods for evacuation, but it was too late. Within seconds, a huge explosion engulfed the cruiser, and thousands of metal fragments spun wildly off into space.

The crew of a nearby cruiser, witnessing the destruction of their comrades, felt angered and frustrated at the same time. The tide of this battle had to be turned quickly. Fighters were immediately deployed to stage another attack on the impregnable laser guns, in the vain hope they would inflict some damage before any more of their ships were destroyed.

As the enemy fighters approached the deadly oval fortress, hundreds of fighters emerged from several openings within the craft. Enemy ships were outnumbered and within minutes, most of them erupted in dazzling fireworks of fire and smoke, the death cries silent in the infinite depths of space.

On the surface of the planet below, huge balls of smoke and fire filled the night sky as the battle continued, bearing mute testimony to the -conflict.

Millions of frightened inhabitants fled to protective shelters; panic-stricken females, witnessing the destruction that rained down upon them from space, sought to protect their whimpering offspring—to no avail. The planet's death toll mounted as a result of the destructive power wrought by the horrible rain of death, the terrible bombs and intense, burning lasers. Debris from the battle above poured down without passion or prejudice. Hundreds...thousands...millions of beings perished in the wake of the onslaught. For endless moments, their death cries seemed frozen in time, as if the universe itself was about to explode.

Rather than accept the succor offered by the planetary governor's palace guards, the Emperor and Empress chose to stand beside their fellow beings so they could all confront their fates as one; silently, bravely.

As the piercing wail of their death cries sounded across the small planet where the great battle raged overhead, on a world thousands of light-years away, a female with haunting violet eyes, delicate face—one seemingly crafted by the galaxy's greatest sculptor—and an exquisite athletic figure, slept soundly in her bedroom.

Her bedclothes consisted of a dark blue, shimmering tunic bearing an insignia on the shoulder: a bird-like creature with wings outstretched, surrounded by a large circle.

At first, her slumber was not the least bit disturbed by the unfolding tragedy in that far-off star system. Yet, as wave after wave of sadness and pain swept over her, images of fire, destruction, and death entered her mind. She sensed the agony of all those who died at the hands of the ruthless alien murderers. She could barely contain herself; the agony was so intense her whole body shook. Tears streamed uncontrollably down her face.

Just as she thought the awesome, terrible pain was about to subside, the agony grew even worse as she sensed the death of those closest to her, the final cries uttered by the royal family of her people...her parents. Her heart felt as if it was bursting and melting away into nothingness. Her entire body seemed to be on the verge of collapse.

Suddenly, she opened her eyes, awakening from the terrible nightmare, screaming words of longing and pain in a language no human had ever uttered. Yet one human did hear the screams of agony, a man separated from the woman by a vast gulf of time and space.

Though the words were incomprehensible to him, the man could clearly decipher their meaning and could sense her agony. For a moment, time and space ceased to exist. She called out to him, pleading with him to save her from the terrible ordeal. Her anguish and longing enveloped him until he, too, cried out loud, screaming at the top of his lungs, "No, no, no!"

* * *

The alarm went off and the tall young man awakened in a cold sweat. Ray Perkins threw off the bed covers and slowly, painfully, rose to a seated position. He remained thus for a moment, and put his hands to his head and slowly brushed away the hair from his eyes. His throat felt dry, his voice hoarse, as if he had been screaming aloud for a long time. Though he was desperately drawn to the beautiful, violet-eyed woman, Ray Perkins was weary of the toll these dreams always took. While he'd managed to turn these dreams into moneymaking computer games, he didn't know how much more he could tolerate.

After a few minutes he tried to stand, but fell, nearly knocking over his end table and clock in the process. He got up and assessed his condition, grumbling quietly to himself over his carelessness. Seeing he was uninjured, he staggered into the bathroom.

The bedroom was large, comfortably furnished with thick gray shag carpeting, two polished wooden end tables, and a long dresser. Atop the dresser stood a single small lamp, as well as several picture frames, displaying events from the past now only distant memories in Ray's mind.

Once in the bathroom, he took a deep breath, coughed again a few times, and walked over to the mirror, staring at his unshaven face. His piercing blue eyes were bloodshot. His slightly long, curly brown hair was unkempt. The brown stubble under his chin had slowly become almost beard-like, evidence of not having shaved in a week or so. There was just the suggestion of gray about the sideburns, though otherwise Ray's face remained clean, smooth, barely marked by lines and creases of age; quite handsome in conveying an inner sense of character, though Ray never really considered himself to be particularly attractive. His physique was thin but muscular, the product of a regular and strenuous work-out regimen.

Oh, great, now I'm starting to look like my father.

He tapped some cold water onto his face, but wasn't satisfied. In frustration, he just splashed it on in torrents. He still wore the old, faded jeans and baggy T-shirt he put on the day before.

Ray slowly walked out of the bathroom and made his way to the front door. He undid a couple of security locks and opened it with a slight squeak. He bent down, picked up the newspaper, and closed the door.

He remained extremely groggy, and he shook his head a few times to clear the cobwebs.

Ray finally began to feel awake, but figured it would take a strong cup of coffee to make him fully alert. He entered the small kitchenette area located adjacent to the living room and sat down on a dark enameled metal chair. He reached across to a long shelf and turned on the coffee maker. As the morning beverage brewed, he opened the newspaper and glanced at the headlines.

Ray passed up the spicy details of the latest lurid political scandals and haphazardly turned pages until a single small headline atop page six caught his eye. He stared at it for a moment. Long-dormant memories poured into his mind.

"This is damned unbelievable," Ray murmured to himself, half in disbelief, half in near shock, as he began to read the article.

* * *

Government Denies Existence
of Alien Bodies at Area 51:

The U.S. government has again denied a growing number of claims that it is harboring aliens from a spaceship that crashed on Earth more than sixty years ago.

On this subject, U.S. Air Force spokesman James W. Moseley argued, "Those tabloid papers and cult magazines have been raving about this stuff for years, and it's just not true!"

Mr. Moseley emphasized the point by pounding his fist on a nearby table. "There is absolutely not the slightest chance that the Air Force is hiding alien bodies. The very idea is absurd. There are no gray aliens!"

Mr. Moseley, a public information officer for the Air Force intelligence group in Washington, was responding to the growing clamor for Congressional hearings into the activities of the military research establishment that has become known as Area 51.

Ignoring most reporters' questions, Mr. Moseley concluded, "There is just no reason to hold hearings on this stuff. There's nothing to it and enough government money has already been wasted on fantasies."

Some so-called UFO scholars have long contended that the government captured beings from another planet many years ago and has kept them at the Area 51 facility for scientific research.

Kenneth J. Alpert of Atlanta, author of several well-known books on UFOs, claims to have evidence that extraterrestrials exist. He alleges that their bodies have been kept in a state of suspended animation at a top-secret laboratory inside Area 51, deep below the surface, in a chamber known as "Level S4."

Responding to Mr. Moseley's statement, Mr. Alpert said, "Of course they'll deny it. They've been doing that for sixty years. It's time Congress began to investigate to find out what they've been hiding from the people!"

Alpert added, "But I agree with them. There are no gray aliens. From what I can determine, these stories about gray-skinned, insect-like creatures are all just a smokescreen. The real aliens look almost like us, except for some minor genetic and physical differences."

* * *

The article had been illustrated with an editorial cartoonist's rendering of an unearthly being in a dark uniform, with a distinctive emblem affixed to its left shoulder. The alien was the classic hairless gray-skinned, bug-eyed entity that one read about in all those UFO stories. The creature wore a striking uniform bearing an insignia that consisted of a bird-like creature with wings outstretched, surrounded by a large triangle. Underneath was a caption: "UFO researcher believes reports of aliens are based on government misinformation."

Ray put down the newspaper and tried to dismiss rising thoughts. He shook his head—the idea was outrageous, but those nasty dreams and the images they portended came back over and over again.

Ray looked at the rendition of the supposed alien creatures a couple of times and thought, absentmindedly, *Gee, they didn't really get that face right at all. This alien looks nothing like the way she was in my dream.*

The images began to form again in his mind: the beautiful alien woman, her penetrating violet eyes conveying the most incredible sensation of understanding, compassion, and agony he ever felt. For a moment, Ray looked upward with a start, feeling she was staring down at him at that very moment. The vision was so vivid, he gasped. Plain as day, he saw the gleaming insignia that adorned her uniform.

He looked at the picture again and stared and stared...

The emblem—it's a circle, not a triangle!

The vision ended, jolting him back into the real world. The vividness of the images and their sudden appearance stunned him to his very core. Ray lost his grip on his porcelain coffee cup, which fell out of his hand. The cup shattered, and the remnants of his morning beverage spilled across the floor. He stared at the carpet, unable to shake the dream's image from his mind.

After being drummed out of military intelligence as a "burnout," following a "routine" mission in the Middle East, he'd dreamed about the alien woman and that devastating battle in space nearly every night. The visions thrust him right in the middle of the action, almost as if he was there with a camera. He felt the death cries of millions, and saw the haunting image of the most glorious woman ever, so human, yet alien. Ray just couldn't get her out of his mind. At times, even when he was awake, he could almost feel her looking at him and he'd abruptly turn around, but she was never there. The dream had become an obsession.

On a whim, he decided he might as well put those dreams to some use. After his military career came to a screeching halt, Ray took advantage of the knowledge of advanced computer technologies he acquired at MIT before he joined the military to please his father, and accepted odd jobs as a computer programmer. He created a computer game, "Attack of the Rockoids." Of course, nobody but his analyst and a few close friends knew it was based on those recurring nightmares. The details were so clear, so compelling, all he had to do was write them down each morning, and weave them into his game.

The game ended up being so successful, he was contracted to create another, which he dubbed "Return of the Rockoids."

There was one aspect he changed, though; the description of the aliens. Ray made them look insect-like, in keeping with modern folklore.

The psychiatrists thought writing that program was good therapy—eventually he'd stop having those terrible dreams. Every analyst he visited offered basically the same conclusion, except, of course, for the ones who thought he should be locked away in an institution. Once he found a way to use the dreams as inspiration for productive work, they said he was cured.

Of course, the dreams never stopped.

Maybe he should just get out more and seek some real female company for a change. He hadn't called his girlfriend, Patricia, in weeks. Well, his publisher needed another game, and there was that deadline....

The more Ray thought about it, the more he realized it was just a silly excuse. The dreams weren't going to disappear, no matter how many computer games he wrote.

"I have to get to Area 51!" Ray exclaimed aloud in a deep voice that bore just a suggestion of his Georgia background. Of course, the very idea of breaking into a top-secret government agency, assuming the place really existed, was absurd. The chance of success was slim at best. If he dared, he'd probably find himself arrested and left to rot inside a government prison.

The obvious dangers of this reckless venture should have been enough to dissuade him, but he couldn't let the thought go. The look in his eyes turned grim. *Oh, what the hell...If I don't try, I'll never know what's really going on.*

With renewed determination dominating his thoughts now, he absentmindedly swept the broken cup away and poured himself more coffee—this time in a paper cup—and quickly gulped it down.

Ray hurried over to the phone and punched out a number on the automatic dialing keypad. He heard a few rings and a man with a gruff voice bearing a slight trace of a Latin accent answered the phone.

"Hey, Colonel Gonzales, it's Ray Perkins."

"Hey, Ray, nice to hear from you again. It's been a while, hasn't it?"

"Yeah, I guess. Sorry, I meant to stay in touch. Guess I got side-tracked after Dad died," said Ray, as he briefly, sadly recalled his father's death two years earlier in a plane accident. His mother took the tragedy especially hard; she died the following summer after a short, painful illness.

Ray sighed. He wasn't one for casual gossip, but knowing Gonzales wanted to be brought up to date, he steeled himself for the questions, which came just as expected.

"You know, Ray, it's really bad, you living out in the country all alone. You really need to find someone, settle down...."

"Manny, I was married. It didn't work out. It happens."

"Yeah, it didn't work out because you left on that two-year tour of duty in the Middle East and never wrote or called her."

"Oh, that..."

"Yeah, and didn't Sharon run off and start screaming on mountaintops after she left you?"

"It's called primal scream therapy, Manny, and it's supposed to cleanse your psyche."

"I bet it did. What ever happened to her?"

"After she got all that screaming out of her system, she went off to Alaska and did some go-go dancing. Last I heard, she got involved with some guy who runs an oil drilling company. Lives in the lap of luxury, with her two-point-two kids or whatever."

"Are you seeing anyone now?"

"Oh, yeah, Patricia. Tall, beautiful, great body. She's lots of fun, when I get around to seeing her."

Although Ray couldn't observe Gonzales' reactions, he learned later what the old soldier thought about the situation.

Stop the chitchat and get to the point, Ray. You and I know you didn't call just to pass the time of day, Gonzales wondered as he nervously began to pace his living room floor.

"Ray, women need attention. You can't keep up relationships like that..." He hesitated a moment. "I know you didn't call just to bring me up on local gossip. What's up?"

Gonzales sat down again. His wife, Anna, always got bent out of shape when he drummed his fingers on the table; this time, he couldn't help it. His well-honed instincts, earned during a long stint as an intelligence officer, made him suspect Ray was about to say something he shouldn't be saying.

"I just read this story in the newspaper about aliens in Area 51...."

"Oh, that stuff," Gonzales laughed. "Hell, they've been making claims about that shit for years!"

Ray's voice became a little louder now, revealing a trace of anger and frustration. "Please, let me explain. I don't know if it's true or not. Something about it sounds real. That's what the dreams are telling me."

Gonzales just sighed a couple of times. He had heard about those recurring nightmares in excruciating detail, over and over again. He tried to be understanding, but sometimes Ray became too annoying and he'd impatiently end a call, pretending there was something that needed his immediate attention elsewhere. When Ray started writing his first computer game, basing it on his dreams, Gonzales thought Ray should promptly check back in with the mental hospital...until Rockoids became the hottest-selling computer game in the country less than a year later.

* * *

Ray remained uneasy, not knowing what Gonzales was up to. At first he was seated during the conversation, but now he got up and paced the floor.

"I don't know what the hell I'm gonna find, but I've gotta get in that place. I feel there's something...something important out there...something I gotta find. If you don't help me, I'll find someone who will."

Gonzales kept silent for a moment, and sighed audibly. "Ray, this is nuts. There's nothing weird over there. They just test new weapons, that's all. There are no gray aliens."

"Manny...."

"You just want to get it on with this alien chick." Gonzales laughed aloud, but had a strong feeling he was going to regret hearing what Ray was about to say.

"Damn it, Manny, just listen to me already! She's calling out to me. She's somehow involved with that war in space I keep dreaming about. Her anguish, her pain, I feel it. Sometimes I even feel she's here when I'm awake. I have to find her...I have to.

"Besides, these aliens aren't gray. They look like us."

* * *

Gonzales gasped. His mind raced a mile a minute.

Damn you, Frank, his thoughts turned to Ray's late father, as if thoughts could be read in the afterlife. *I can't believe you told him that! After all we went through when we first saw that place. How could you?*

Gonzales thought better of it. There was no way Ray's father, himself a skilled intelligence professional, would spill the beans. Somehow Ray just knew...

"Please, Manny! I've seen her so many times; I can remember every single detail about her. Her face, body, uniform, even this one little emblem on her shoulder..."

Gonzales paused for a long time, rendered speechless. His fist nearly crashed into the coffee table, but he held off just as he was about to strike the glass with all his strength.

"Manny, are you still there?" Ray's voice sounded urgent.

The old soldier managed to contain himself enough to stammer, "Emblem? What kind of emblem?"

"It was a large circle and inside the circle was some creature that looked like a bird with its wings stretched out."

Again that long pause, as Gonzales lifted himself out of his lounge chair and paced back and forth. His eyes narrowed, ears perked. He listened intently, just wondering if they were listening too.

"Ray, be honest with me. Have you ever been to Area 51?"

"Manny, I've been to Vegas for a publishers' convention, that's all!"

"You've never been to the Groom Lake complex..." Sweat trickled down Gonzales' face as he waited for the response.

"I swear on dad's grave, Manny, I've never been there!"

Another pause, but not so long this time, followed by an

audible sigh.

"Ray, very few people I know have ever seen that emblem."

"Manny, tell me what the hell is going on here!"

"I can't talk about it on the phone..."

"I need to know the truth. Can you get me in there?"

"We were only there a couple times...Frank and I..."

"You and dad? You knew all along, didn't you?"

"We can't talk about this now."

"Damn it, Manny! I'm on my knees here! You got to get me in that place!"

Again the silence was almost deafening as Gonzales thought hard and fast. He was in the thick of it now and there was no getting out. *Damn it all! Maybe Ray is the one to help me find out the truth, before it's too late....*

He demurred. This was absurd; he couldn't risk his pension, a possible prison sentence.

How the hell would Anna ever understand this? He thought bitterly to himself.

The memories came, flooding over him like a tidal wave....

* * *

The streets of Saigon were in chaos. The Viet Cong forces rapidly moved into the city. The sounds of air raid alarms rang out for miles around, and people ran through the streets grabbing whatever possessions they could. Nearby buildings were in flames and smoke rapidly filled the area, only adding to the pandemonium.

Gonzales stood in the middle of the tempest, looking for his beloved. He knew he had little time left before the enemy forces entered the city and he would be trapped.

Damn it, Frank, where the hell are you?

Suddenly, there she was...his beautiful Anna with her gorgeous brown eyes, long, flowing black hair, and her petite, lithe form. Next to her stood tall, brown-haired Colonel Frank Perkins, his most loyal friend. He and Anna rushed up to Gonzales, pushing through the crowd and out into the open.

Gonzales felt overjoyed, his eyes filled with tears. As Anna came up to him, they embraced. He looked at his old friend tearfully, his gruff voice barely above a whisper, "You saved her, Frank. You saved Anna!"

Colonel Perkins answered Gonzales in a hurried tone, "Yeah, yeah, you can thank me later. Now we have to get the hell out of here!"

The trio rushed toward the end of the city as part of a nearby two-story apartment building fell from above and smashed into the ground behind them...

* * *

The memories were compelling, consuming. How could he not help Ray, regardless of the consequences?

Anna will understand, he thought, misty eyed.

He owed Frank Perkins everything for returning his beloved Anna to him. By helping Ray, Gonzales would honor his old friend's memory, return the selfless favor he could never repay. That alone was a noble enough reason.

Gonzales managed to feign a smile and a faint chuckle. "Okay, okay, Ray, I'll help you. But next time you fantasize about a woman, make sure she's human."

He took a deep breath and then said, almost tentatively, "I really shouldn't do this...but I do know a way to get you in there. Damn it all, I owe your father a thousand times over for saving my life, for saving Anna...."

"Thanks, Manny. I don't think you realize how much this means to me."

* * *

Again silence filled the room. As the seconds slowly passed, Ray thought for just a moment he could hear faint crackles on the phone line and sometimes an abrupt popping sound, but he quickly dismissed the possibility the phone was being tapped. Why would the NSA be looking into his affairs after all these years? Did they suspect he might, out of the blue, want to break into a top-secret military installation?

Sweat began to pour from Ray's brow as he considered the possibilities. All those times he thought he was being followed on dark, dusty roads when he'd go out for a long drive. Those dark-suited men at the mall that time, long ago, shortly after his first computer game was released. He deliberately altered the insignia on the aliens' uniforms, but there was a hint of the reality.

Before his paranoia could get out of hand, Ray, with a strong force of will, managed to collect himself.

When he began to speak again, Gonzales' voice seemed to become a whisper. "Ray, they've got very tight security around that place. You can't imagine...never mind. I'll try to do the best I can to get them off your back. But there will be guards lurking around inside the complex, and if you get caught, it's your ass. Understand?"

"I understand perfectly," replied Ray calmly, nodding his head as if anyone could see him.

"Good. Now you have a day's drive ahead of you. Meet me there tomorrow night. I'll get you in there. Trust me," said Gonzales. He tried to sound clinical, but his voice betrayed him. "Make sure you get yourself a good night's sleep. Take a pill or something."

"Yeah, I'll remember that. Must have something here to help me relax."

Ray wasn't one for tranquilizers, sleeping pills, or intoxicants of any sort. While his military comrades got stoned every weekend during his tour of duty, he'd stay behind in the barracks studying his computer programming books and honing the obscure martial arts skills his Asian mentor taught him.

He hung up the phone and sat in his lounge chair, lost in thought.

Maybe there was something to this secret alien laboratory business. Whatever the truth was, if he got caught, he'd probably end up behind bars or at least spend time in a mental hospital. It was foolish, all right. Still, it was something he had to do. He had a strong feeling time was of the essence. He believed those awful dreams contained a message, a message he must heed—that is, if he could figure out what it was. Who was this alien woman? Why was she calling out to him?

She was so beautiful; her face, the vision of it seemed to fill his mind, overwhelm him whenever he stopped to think about it. Was she real? Or just some cruel trick of fate taking him on an endless journey into total insanity?

Chapter 2

The next morning, Ray packed an overnight bag into the small trunk of his beat-up 1966 red Mustang convertible. The car barely seemed up to the task of going to the corner grocery store, let alone a long trip through the hot desert to another state. That didn't deter him. He filled up the gas tank at a nearby convenience store, checked the oil, and took off, keeping a steady pace as he headed for Nevada.

The first time he started from a traffic light, a loud, sharp noise assaulted his ears; he looked around with a start. He saw nothing. He soon realized his car had backfired.

Worse, just about every time the car moved off from a dead stop, the awful sound repeated itself. Ray finally stopped by the side of a quiet road. He pushed open the stubborn door, got out, lifted the hood and looked inside. He should have spent a little more time learning how to fix the damn thing. He probed, squinting his eyes in the bright sunlight. All he could do was check that all visible components were connected properly.

The carburetor seemed all right, but clearly something was wrong. Well, the repair shop did say he needed a little engine work. Maybe later, if he survived this trip.

Now he'd have to keep a brisk pace to catch up with Gonzales that evening.

Maybe I should just give up...This is nuts!

Whenever the thought of quitting occurred to Ray, he saw in his mind's eye the lovely vision of that alien woman and felt her anguish, and he realized a little backfiring wasn't going to stop him.

He closed the hood, perhaps a little too abruptly, jumped into the seat and sped away.

Not before he seemed to feel that "presence" again, and he turned around, as usual, to find nothing.

Crack!

That damn backfire again!

At this point, he turned up the radio, hoping the noise wouldn't bother him so much. Now if only that damn racket hadn't caught the attention of the local highway patrol; Ray could only hope.

As the miles slowly passed, minute-by-minute, hour-by-hour, Ray began to get the nagging feeling he'd attracted someone's attention. Every so often, he could swear he saw a black car behind him, and whenever he moved into another lane, the car seemed to follow.

Ray knew that was ridiculous. Why would anyone be watching him? Surely not to see if he had plans to break into a top-secret government installation and investigate what was going on in a secret laboratory? Yeah, sure.

He only got that silly idea yesterday.

All sorts of paranoid feelings began influencing Ray's state of mind as the trip continued. He had a high security clearance when he was in the military. Maybe they'd been watching him all these years, tapping his phone, tailing him on his travels, waiting for him to do something suspicious. Ray had always lived a quiet life, hardly ever associated with people, dated rarely. Was his girl friend Patricia a spy too?

What about Manny? Could the old soldier, his father's closest friend, have betrayed him? *No, that couldn't be—not Manny!*

Ray laughed at Manny's final words—*Trust me.* Could he really trust anyone?

Ray tried his best not to think about the worst case scenario. He had a mission to accomplish.

He paid more than a casual glance to his rear view mirror. The black car seemed to be gone, or whoever was tailing him decided to be a bit more discreet.

Damn! Damn!

As night fell, Ray started closing on his destination. Feeling a bit drowsy, he pulled into the first truck stop for a quick coffee and sandwich. As he paid for his dinner at the takeout counter, Ray's paranoia began creeping on him again; he looked around furtively and saw nothing suspicious.

He got in his Mustang and took off, but kept taking wary glances at the rear view mirror just in case. The backfiring routine began getting worse. Any time he'd put his foot on the brake to slow the car down, and abruptly accelerate, it went off again—bang!

Soon he became comfortable, however, and turned up the music again—just in time to see a half dozen green lights flashing in the sky, star-like, hardly greater than pinpoints. They didn't seem to move in any particular direction, just stayed aloft without apparent motion.

After this short period of calm, the tension mounted again, so palpable Ray could almost touch it.

All sorts of ideas began to seem reasonable. Maybe some weather balloons, or perhaps the folks at the base were just testing some sort of secret weapon. Maybe they were doing an aerial surveillance of the perimeter of the base, looking for crazy folk who might get the idea to break in—crazy folk like Ray Perkins.

Again, for perhaps the hundredth time during the trip, Ray began to wonder whether he should give it all up and go home.

Once again, the image of the beautiful woman filled his consciousness and he again seemed to feel her presence, as if she were near. He felt her anguish, when she sensed the deaths of millions as if she had died herself, as she continued to call out to him—to save her? What did she want from him? Why couldn't she just leave him alone?

Ray then wondered what sort of person could sense the deaths of others in the way this woman could. Who was she? What was she? Human? Well, not quite, but that face, a face that was so glorious, so lovely. He could just imagine her walking into a restaurant, by his side, holding his hand. What would they think? Could she…would she…associate with the likes of him?

The lights were gone….

Ray breathed a sigh of relief again, but kept a careful watch in case any other strange things appeared. He was very, very close now, and the lights of the base were nearly visible. Just around the bend…

He saw it, in his rear view mirror. Flashing lights, this time just a few feet above the surface of the ground, not far behind him and closing fast. He turned down the radio, and a second later, he heard sirens wailing.

From his rear view mirror, Ray could clearly see a police car was pursuing him. He broke into a sweat and started fumbling for his wallet with his right hand. It dropped onto the passenger's seat, and he clumsily pulled it open while trying to concentrate on the winding roadway ahead.

Yes, the license was in there, and he carried the insurance and registration papers in his glove compartment. At least he thought he did; he popped open the glove compartment just to be sure.

Sure enough, the documents were there.

Ray checked the speedometer. He was always a cautious driver and rarely ventured more than a mile or two above the speed limit—at least since he left the military, where he was considered a real "hot rod"—so it couldn't be that…unless Nevada state troopers were more intolerant of slight speed liberties than he suspected.

No, it couldn't be!

Perhaps the car was from Air Force intelligence, and some military folk were going to pull him over and ask some nasty, pointed questions about why someone in a "classic" car was driving near a top-secret military base at ten o'clock at night. Ray would have to conjure up some really creative excuses to explain that one.

No sense trying to avoid it. Ray began to slow his car and looked for an emergency lane, as the police car tracked his every movement.

He found a place to face the music. He pulled over to the emergency lane and stopped. Now Ray had his work cut out for him. He mulled over every conceivable story he could as to why he was out there. The road led directly to Nellis Air Force base and he was traveling at a straight clip, not slowly, as if appearing to look for another exit somewhere. *Well, I suppose I could just tell them I got lost and act confused. Of course, then they'd think I was high…*

A flashlight blinded him as he struggled to lower the recalcitrant left window and identify his pursuer.

The beam flashed so intensely he couldn't see more than a dark shadow standing on the roadway just a couple of feet from him. Ray blinked, straining to see who was there. He saw a large, thick hand moving toward him as the inevitable request was heard in a dark, intense voice. "License and registration, please."

"Is there a problem, Officer?"

There was only silence as Ray opened his glove compartment, pulled out the papers, and handed them, along with his driver's license, to the officer.

Was this really a police officer or an agent from Nellis? His fears of phone taps and covert surveillance seemed more realistic with each passing moment.

Ray listened hard; he could barely hear the engine of the patrol car that lay motionless behind his vehicle.

The figure brandishing the flashlight had apparently retreated to his own vehicle. Ray couldn't hear the sound of footsteps over the chug-chug-chugging of his Mustang's engine at idle. He turned to peer through the car's rear window to see what that person was doing.

Between the bright lights of the patrol car, which seemed to have its high beams on, and its dark interior, Ray could only see the dark figure of someone inside. He imagined the person checking the license and registration on a mobile computer or of a dispatch station being radioed.

"Mr. Perkins?"

The voice startled him, and he nearly jumped in fright. His eyes opened wide now, a blinding flashlight shining in his eyes.

The man was apparently holding the flashlight with his left hand and his right hand, clearly holding Ray's license and registration, was suddenly thrust inside the open window.

He reached out and grabbed the papers, trying to time his movements to seem casual. His hand almost began to shake, but he managed to control the motions.

"Did you notice your left rear tail light isn't working, Mr. Perkins?"

"It's not?" Ray recovered enough to manage a smile of relief. "Thanks for telling me."

"You've got to get it fixed right away, bud. Otherwise you'll get a ticket."

"No problem. I'll have it done soon as I find a service station."

"Okay, just be sure I don't catch you this way again. You're getting really close to the military base."

"I was taking a shortcut, that's all. I'll head back to the main highway."

"Yes, it'll be much safer that way. It's pretty rough terrain without four-wheel drive, and you never know what might turn up on these back roads."

The flashlight abruptly withdrawn, Ray managed to stop squinting long enough to let his eyes recover gently. He sat in silence as the officer returned to his vehicle, which soon made a U-turn and sped away.

Ray hadn't realized how tightly wound he was. It took several minutes for his breathing to slow, his heart to stop pounding, and for the sweat to stop pouring down his face. He grabbed a tissue from the back seat and wiped his forehead.

He slowly began to drive back towards his destination, not fully satisfied the encounter with the patrol car was so innocuous. Perhaps they weren't just checking him out. He thought of that veiled warning: "You never know what might turn up on these back roads."

Maybe that policeman was really someone from the Air Force base after all. Maybe he just stopped him as a ruse to see what he was up to, and get his personal identification. Even now, Ray's military record may have been broadcast to the security team he expected to find at Nellis. Perhaps they were already warned about his arrival and were waiting to grab him.

At this point, having come this far, he just didn't care. What could they do to him that years of recurring nightmares and sleepless nights hadn't done? After all the torture he'd faced, perhaps a few years in prison would be a relief....

This is ridiculous. I've got to stop thinking that way! Depression is not going to help me right now.

Ray shook his head again, hoping to clear those thoughts from his mind, but without much success.

He could see searchlights just ahead, apparently focused on a large fence that flanked a stone wall of some sort. Both lined the perimeter of a huge installation of low buildings that surrounded what appeared to be a huge hangar, a hangar housing...what?

He imagined all sorts of top-secret craft might exist there. Stealth fighters, silent jet engines, sophisticated jamming devices, maybe even devices spawned from some sort of alien technology.

It wasn't just the supermarket tabloids that were filled with claims, gossip, and "informed speculation" about such things. Some of the legitimate news organizations got into the act.

The lights were not bright enough to pick out details, but Ray couldn't miss the large guardhouse that lay just around a curve on the road right in front of the fence.

Ray felt thoroughly exhausted, emotionally drained, and longed for a hot shower and a few hours of sleep. None of these options seemed to be on his plate for a very, very long time, even if he got out of this place without getting caught.

Ray began to look for a place to conceal his car among the bushes lining the side of the road. He switched the headlights to high beams for a split second to get a better view.

He nearly ran down a dark figure of a man who suddenly appeared directly in front of him.

He veered his car to the side of the road and kicked up a large pile of dust as he struggled to bring the vehicle to a stop before it struck a nearby tree trunk.

He gritted his teeth as his car's brakes put up a nasty squeal.

Ray was about to reach for a flashlight from the glove compartment when the figure caught up to him, a slender, bespectacled, gray-haired man of medium height, wearing old, dark-colored battle fatigues. The face was clean-shaven, with just a few wrinkles around his mouth, flashing that unmistakable grin. It was Colonel Gonzales.

Ray got out of his car, slammed the door, and said in a low almost embarrassed voice, "Damn it, sir, I could have killed you."

"And you're still a sorry-looking soldier."

"Yes, sir, thank you, sir," Ray responded with a broad smile and a sharp salute.

In a rush, Ray began to recite every irritating element of the trip, but Gonzales shushed him. "We don't have time for chitchat. Your car kicked up a hell of a fuss over there. It's bound to attract attention."

The old soldier's voice took on an unexpected note of authority, "All right, now, take a look at this."

It wasn't a request; it sounded like an order, and Ray had to obey his commanding officer.

With casual efficiency, Gonzales handed him a map; hardly more than a crumpled piece of white paper, showing a crude ink drawing of the base. Ray stared at it in the dim light of the overhead searchlights. He saw entrance points clearly labeled "Suggested Routes," an elevator and something labeled "Laboratory."

"Where the hell did you get this?"

"Ask me no questions, and I'll tell you no lies." Gonzales smiled. "I got it from the same person who made arrangements for you to get inside that base. Let me tell you, it cost me a whole lot of favors to old friends and almost ten thousand bucks."

"I can repay you...."

"No you can't...."

"I insist...."

Gonzales shook his head.

"I owe you one."

Gonzales just shook his head again. He quickly changed the subject, motioning toward Ray to look at the map. "Now listen carefully. Once you've entered the compound, walk right to the old hangar just ahead. There should be enough shrubbery around for you to stay away from prying eyes."

Ray looked at the tattered piece of paper that had estimated distances and locations noted in thick dark ink. Gonzales was nothing, if not thorough.

"Once you get inside the hangar...if you get inside, that is... you'll find a small elevator. See, it's there on the map, at the rear of the hangar. Hidden somewhere to the left of the elevator is a security panel; it looks just like the keypad on a phone. Just remember the numbers seven, fourteen, and seventy, press enter and you'll be home free. Once you're inside, it should take you down to Level S4, where the alien bodies are supposedly hidden— or at least that's what the UFO buffs think. Still want to do it?" asked Gonzales.

Ray nodded his head, took a long look at the desert and the sparse shrubs, spying his faithful Mustang in the distance. He had a sinking feeling it would be a long time before he saw any of this again, a feeling he couldn't shake however hard he tried.

He looked around and began to take a more studied look at the "infamous" Nellis Air Force Base. He had read about all those rumors about Area 51, but here was the real thing. It didn't look all that strange, at least not from the outside.

They walked slowly, almost on tiptoe to avoid kicking up dust on the gravel surface, or possibly making too much noise. They were just to the left of the base's main entrance, closing in. Gonzales seemed totally oblivious to his surroundings. The old soldier just continued a steady pace, showing no visible emotion. Ray, however, couldn't miss the unmistakable signs that his older companion was quite as nervous as he. He could clearly see the sweat dripping down Gonzales' back and face. Perhaps the veteran soldier just managed to hide his emotions a little better.

They were only a few yards away from the fence.

Ray couldn't miss the thin wires covering the fence, clearly indicating they were electrified, and he assumed other protection measures were present. Motion detectors, infrared cameras, and advanced security devices he couldn't even imagine.

"Time is short, Ray. You can look around once I get you inside."

Ray nodded, and Gonzales led him dangerously close to the fence, just a few feet away from the guardhouse. "Come. I had them shut down the power for a couple of minutes."

Without a second's thought, they walked right up to the fence. Ray trusted Gonzales enough to know the security measures had been temporarily disabled.

Suddenly, without warning, part of the fence started pulling away, revealing the stone wall and a walkway leading to what appeared to be a door.

As Ray prepared to start moving inside the compound, Gonzales held up his hand, in a warning gesture.

"Getting in there is easy. Then there's the hard part."

Ray groaned. That was not what he wanted to hear.

"The second problem—well, hopefully the security guards are mostly asleep now," whispered Gonzales. "They are on call at night, but they usually nod off by this time unless they hear the alarm...."

Gonzales stopped, took out his cell phone, and dialed a number. Ray saw a sentry enter the guardhouse, pick up a phone, and say a few words. In response, Gonzales uttered some barely understandable syllables that Ray took to be some sort of password.

Gonzales pulled out a small flashlight from his right rear pocket, turning it on and off three times. Within seconds, a couple of flashes were seen from inside the compound, evidently in acknowledgement.

The old soldier smiled at Ray.

"That's it, Manny? My freedom depends on a few flashes of light?"

"Light brings hope, Ray; maybe it's a good omen for the future."

Ray said nothing for a moment. His voice seemed hollow, as if it came from someone else, "I suppose we'd better get going."

"No, this is as far as I dare take you."

"What? You're gonna throw me to the wolves?"

Gonzales paused for just a moment. "Ray, your dad saved my life a dozen times in 'Nam. He brought my Anna back to me. I owe him a lot more than I could ever repay.

"But I have to think about my own ass too. If they catch me in there, it's a court martial, loss of pension, jail, you know the score. I've got to protect Anna. I've got to think about her and the kids for a change. I'm supposed to be getting out this year. I can't put them in danger. I've already taken a great risk getting you this far and that should be enough to get you started on this crazy journey. Once you're inside that door, I'm out of here."

"I understand."

"Don't worry, Ray, the chance of you getting caught is much less now that none of the guards will be an obstacle...at least for a little while."

"That really reassures me."

Before he could continue complaining, however, Gonzales cut him off with a glare. He knew exactly what he was doing and would brook no further discussion of the matter. "Don't think, Ray; just concentrate on what you gotta do. Now go, and Que Dios te bendiga!" Gonzales' voice stirred above a whisper, but it struck Ray sharply enough almost to bring him to attention.

Ray turned and walked right through the gate. Just as he reached the door in the stone wall, he almost jumped in fright as he heard a loud clicking sound and an even louder grinding noise as the gate entrance rapidly slid shut, trapping him inside. There was no turning back now.

Ray stared at the little door, lost in thought. He saw the alien woman's face from his dreams again, more vivid than ever. Again it seemed as if she were actually there, not a vision in his mind's eye, but flesh and blood, standing before him in the darkness, a vivid yellow glow enveloping her.

Tears welled in her eyes, she pleaded, beckoned him, and he knew he could never turn away.

Ray drew a deep breath and gingerly placed his hands on the knob. He expected it to be locked, but it opened slowly without protest. At this point, after all his apprehension about going to this place, his ease in entering the main complex almost seemed like a sick joke.

Within seconds, he walked inside the compound and weaved his way through an open field.

The oppressive blackness covered the land like a blanket. The searchlights overhead pointed to the skies and didn't do much to illuminate his surroundings, a lucky break for Ray, considering there were few possibilities of shelter in the desert sands; just a few clusters of bushes here and there.

The crickets put up a mighty chirp, as if competing against one another to make a most unjoyful noise. The sound seemed almost deafening against the otherwise ominous silence. Ray checked again, and sure enough, his trusty flashlight was hidden in his right pocket, the map in the lone rear pocket of his well-worn jeans.

* * *

Gonzales remained hidden behind a nearby rock as he observed the guards snoring away within the compound. He smiled to himself as he saw Ray disappearing among the shadows, and was about to depart.

Suddenly one of the guards started to stretch and stir around, rubbing his eyes. He looked in Ray's direction.

"Wait a minute, boy! What the hell are you doing here?" It wasn't a question; it was a demand!

The jig was up!

Chapter 3

The unexpected sound startled Ray; his throat ran dry. He looked behind him as security guards began to run in his direction.

He had to hurry. Maybe they hadn't seen him…maybe they spotted Gonzales standing outside the base. What to do? He wanted desperately to turn back and help his old friend.

For a moment, the inner conflict bubbled at the surface, and Ray seemed almost oblivious to his surroundings. He remained in the shadows around the wall lining the compound, hoping to remain invisible. For a moment, he recalled that old radio character, "The Shadow," who would instinctively locate dark corners and doorways to remain hidden from prying eyes.

He heard footsteps in the distance and loud shouts. The words overlapped each other, and Ray wasn't able to determine if they had seen him.

He had no choice, really; it wasn't safe here. He stepped up his pace, struggling to conceal himself in the darkness, shielded from the glare of the moving searchlights. Strange that the lights hadn't been aimed at the ground yet, where everything would clearly be visible, strange indeed.

Ray entered a clump of bushes, sharp cacti, trying to keep up his pace, and stay hidden at the same time. His efforts were too successful. He couldn't even see obstacles in the gravel beneath his feet and kept tripping over rocks and other sharp outcroppings.

The sharp cactus points scraped and tore at his clothing and skin as he tried to seek safety from the guards, whom Ray expected to swarm the place. A tall branch above rubbed and tore at his forehead.

Hardly a spot on his body didn't sting with pain. Ray inspected himself in the darkness and felt the cuts on his legs and arms.

His head hurt, and he fervently wished he had brought along the medicine he used to take for those terrible migraines. He slowly brushed his hands against his forehead and felt caked blood.

He must be a sight. His pants and shirt had gaping tears, but his wounds, painful as they were, were no more than deep scratches.

Ray sighed and tried to move slowly about in the close confines where he remained hidden.

I'm just getting too old for this shit.

The crickets stopped chirping, and a frightful silence momentarily consumed the darkness.

Ray heard a sound in the distance, and he strained to identify the source of the noise.

A rattlesnake! They were common in these parts, but normally wouldn't venture forth at night unless it was unbearably hot. Ray hadn't given the possibility of their presence much thought.

Ray just wanted to run, get out of there as fast as possible. He heard footsteps. Security guards, no doubt. He didn't see anyone, but he stayed hidden, again seeking the shelter of the shadows.

The apparent sound of the rattlesnake got closer, accompanied by a slithering noise in the gravel beneath his feet. His goal remained many yards distant, but the sound seemed to increase in intensity, as if something was closing in on him.

Ray began to sweat, but held his breath to a shallow rhythm, moving slowly, deliberately, cautiously, away from that horrible predator.

Closer and closer. The hangar in all its unpretentious glory wasn't far now, positioned precisely as shown on the map drawn by Gonzales.

Maybe I should just get out of here and give it up.

There was no turning back now. Something, a force he could barely understand, compelled him to press on, think logically, keep his head clear.

Some sort of security alert was definitely afoot, for he also saw a contingent of troops surrounding the structure, with no way in but straight ahead.

Ray had wanted to stay put for a while, but the racket from that creature had grown more intense; the sound of its passage almost rang in his ears.

He could turn back, perhaps, maybe wend his way back to the gate, open it and...

The doors to the hangar opened and Ray saw more soldiers, perhaps a dozen or so, coming through. Within seconds, they began to disperse, walking toward the barracks he observed to his left.

There were scattered bushes about and long spaces of emptiness between the shrubs. Ray wanted to get as close to the hangar as possible before attempting the final lunge toward its entrance. He stayed hidden, hoping by now that the slithering creature had grown weary of the pursuit and was seeking another victim.

The insidious rattling noise just grew louder, urgent, threatening, deadly...

Only a few troops were left now. Soon they'd be gone.

If only there was time.

Ray thought he could see the beady eyes of that awful reptile a dozen yards from him. He moved slowly, in a gentle rhythm, trying not to attract attention, not to show fear.

He couldn't delay any longer. Even if he managed to elude the security detail, he wouldn't fare as well with the snake.

The doors to the hangar slid together with a slow, erratic rumble. Ray could hear the large machines, the incessant grating of gears and rollers that filled his ears. For some reason, the doors didn't fully close.

What an incredible stroke of luck!

The gap between the doors remained, maybe a foot or two... just enough room for a grown man to sneak inside.

No, it wasn't a stroke of luck at all. *Thank you, Manny, thank you*. There was no time to think, just act!

Ray boldly ran straight to the hangar, not looking back for signs of pursuit. Without thinking, he squeezed between the cracks. There was just enough room for him to enter. As he went inside, the door slid shut with a loud thud, as if it had been waiting for his arrival.

As soon as he was inside, fear gripped his throat. He looked around, slowly moving his head, listening for subtle sounds that betrayed the presence of other human beings. Nobody was there.

He looked up, searching for the presence of a TV camera or some other security probe; it was too dark to see anything.

Ray reached into his pocket and pulled out a small, round halogen flashlight. It wouldn't light! He shook the instrument and heard the telltale sound of a loose filament. Why did the bulb have to fail at this crucial moment?

Ray looked at a nearby shelf, squinted and noticed a small flashlight lying there, just waiting for him.

He picked it up with his left hand, turning it on as he shielded its beam with his right. He cautiously pointed it about, examining the surroundings carefully, while trying to keep the beam from betraying his presence. He pointed it toward the ceiling, and confirmed no security cameras were present in this facility, at least none that were visible.

There was no indication of any top-secret technology here. It was just an ordinary hangar, with a few jet planes in various states of repair.

Why should he be surprised? Most of those rumors about military secrets turned out to be false. For one frightening moment,

Ray began to feel he got into the base too quickly, considering the security measures he'd expected. Could Manny's ten grand really buy his way in here so easily?

Had he been betrayed?

Realizing the need to make haste, Ray reached into his back pocket, grateful the tattered map was still there. He pulled it out and stared at it, carefully shining the flashlight over the contents, trying to pick out the small details Gonzales had dutifully entered.

A small elevator had been circled in thick black ink. He looked around, but didn't see it right away. The walls were dark, and he observed caution shining his flashlight about.

He saw it, off toward the rear left of the hangar. A small sliding elevator door, plain as day.

Ray's bruised body huddled close to the planes so he couldn't be seen; he believed there were still surveillance measures active here, and he tried to make his motions as gentle as possible, hardly making sounds at all as his athletic shoes touched the concrete floor. Ray realized none of these precautions would help if they used motion detectors, but assuming Gonzales had kept his promise, the detectors had been disabled, for now.

He passed a plane parked near the elevator, and with a start, felt something touch his shoulder.

As the slippery substance wet his tattered shirt, he smiled as he realized how silly he had been to react with such fear. It was just a few drops of leaking fuel.

He turned his flashlight back on, as another few drops fell on his shoulder. He felt something almost slimy touch his mouth, and the jet fuel left a horrible taste, but he carelessly wiped off the liquid with his free hand, trying to keep his face and mind clear at the same time.

Ray took the last few yards that had to be traversed to reach the elevator. A small wall-mounted security panel sat at eye level at the door's left. Just as Gonzales said, at first glance it looked nearly identical to the physical touch pad on a portable phone, except for a small enter key at the bottom. Ray stared at it in frustration.

Clearly it wasn't his day. His expertise at safecracking was laughable. He remembered that incident inside some nameless sheik's palace in the Middle East briefly, how he had fitted some sensitive earphones to his ear, turned a few knobs, and the alarm went off.

It was never quite the same in the field.

Ray had gotten out of there with a whole skin, but two days later there was the incident with the mysterious nerve gas, and he wasn't so lucky that time. It was something he once again fervently wished he could forget.

Ray grabbed the map and looked at it again. He thought the security panel was supposed to be outside the hangar, not inside. Could Gonzales have made a mistake? And those silly numbers—7-1-4-7-0. Oh well…nothing ventured…

With scarcely a sideways glance, numbers were pressed slowly, deliberately. Ray pressed the little enter key …and he waited…and he waited.

Just when he thought nothing was going to happen—or perhaps he'd trigger the alarm—the door slid open so rapidly, Ray jumped.

The elevator seemed positively ancient, reminiscent of the ones he saw in one of those old tenements in New York City. The walls inside appeared to be finished in deeply scratched, dark, enamel paint. Illumination was provided by a single bulb in the ceiling, conveying a shadowy, oppressive light in the small cabin, with nothing but a conventional-looking numbered panel in front of him, to the right of the door.

Before he could press a button, it slid shut.

The elevator stayed there.

Ray had never been quite accustomed to small surroundings, due to some unknown childhood trauma, they told him. His breath became ragged, he began to sweat and feel nervous, frightened, and almost overwhelmed. He tried to concentrate on the task at hand, but it took a few moments for his mind to clear, his breath to regulate itself.

His choices were 1, 2 and B—for basement, he presumed.

Ray dutifully pressed the basement button. For a second,

nothing happened; he heard a soft rumbling sound as the elevator went down ever so slowly. In about thirty seconds or so, it stopped rather abruptly, and rocked back and forth a little raggedly.

For one panic-stricken moment, Ray felt that perhaps the elevator's cable was frayed and splitting apart. *Why is the damned elevator so small?*

The door slid open so quickly, Ray almost shuddered. He took a deep breath, his ears listening intently, as he looked over his surroundings.

With perhaps a little too much eagerness, he walked out of the elevator and looked around, pointing his flashlight around the small room.

He gazed long and hard at the scene before him. Everything seemed conventional on the surface.

There were large shelves and electronic instruments. He saw tools, blueprints. He didn't pretend to understand the purpose behind all the dials and displays, but nothing looked out of place or terribly different from a conventional electronic repair station. In the far left corner was the entrance to a bathroom and a water heater.

Ray felt both confused and irritated. *Damn! This is just a wild-goose chase.*

He looked at the map to make sure he had followed Gonzales' directions exactly. He slapped his head with his left hand.

I'm so stupid!

A little scrawl next to the picture of the elevator read, "Press the basement button, count five seconds, press it again."

Ray couldn't believe for a moment that pressing the button twice would do anything. Having come this far, he figured there was nothing wrong in giving it a whirl.

Again, he sensed the presence of that alien woman, looking over his shoulder, beckoning him to continue his quest.

Ray counted out loud after pressing B the first time.

"One-one-thousand, two-one-thousand, three-one-thousand, four-one-thousand, five-one-thousand."

He obediently pressed the B button again.

For just a second, nothing happened.

Motors started churning and the elevator vibrated. The door slid shut. Clunk! More motors churned. Another pause, and Ray thought, at first, the elevator might be broken or that nothing was going to happen.

The elevator moved all right…but its motion was neither up nor down but sideways.

The rapid movement came suddenly, as Ray nearly fell to the floor; he almost lost his balance.

His head jerked back with a start, fear plain as day in his eyes. Ray resisted the urge to push the "alarm" bell for help. That would be foolish. There was no rescue for him here, only guards and handcuffs and certain incarceration.

He had to remain calm, expect the unexpected. The whir of the machinery again grew louder as the elevator's pace increased, rocking back and forth, seeming barely under control. Ray held his balance by sheer force of will.

The elevator stopped, paused, and started going straight down again.

Unfortunately, the single light bulb burned out at that moment.

He looked around; sheer blackness filled his eyes. He scrambled through his pockets for his flashlight, but he realized he must have left it back in the basement repair shop.

The elevator stopped suddenly, roughly, with Ray nearly thrown to the floor. The door abruptly opened, leading out into a long, dark tunnel.

He wondered what would go wrong next.

Ray hoped this miserable ride was over, that he was at the bottom level of Area 51, the infamous Level S4. He concentrated for a moment and meditated upon his situation.

Ray had another problem to contend with in the meantime—whenever he stood up to his full height, his head bumped into the ceiling, so he had to crouch uncomfortably. His back began to ache as he stumbled on. His muscles hurt, already battered and bruised from his fall among the cacti outside. He continued to crouch, struggling to keep a steady pace.

In a few minutes, the tunnel became brighter, and he saw an occasional recessed fluorescent light in the ceiling. At the same time, the tunnel became wider and taller, until he was finally able to stand erect comfortably. He stretched his arms, and did a few of the neck exercises his martial arts guru had drilled into him. He almost seemed to will his aches and pains to subside.

His mind began to focus on his surroundings. He was in a long, curved, dimly lit hallway, and it seemed to go on and on with no end in sight.

He knew he could not let down his guard. Any moment the base's security detail might show up to capture him; he couldn't imagine Manny's efforts to hold them at bay would be successful for much longer.

Ray couldn't help but chuckle at the notion of the guards finding him, lost in the recesses of a top-secret government facility, doing martial arts exercises. Now that was something he would have trouble explaining.

The odor came without warning; faint, acrid, a trace of a gas that seemed familiar to him. Now he remembered the odor he sometimes smelled at home right after he had those weird dreams of battling alien craft in outer space. So irritating...it slightly resembled burnt sulfur. Ray couldn't forget; it first accompanied the sighting of strange glowing lights in the sky, lights he had thought (at the time) were enemy aircraft, just before he was knocked out by that mysterious gas.

Ray tried to breathe in a shallower fashion to reduce the effects of that terrible smell, but it grew worse as he continued along the dark, curved hallway. He considered, not altogether seriously, whether he might be coming closer to these strange alien creatures that had been rumored to exist there.

The stench soon became nearly unbearable. He managed to keep going until he emerged from the hallway into a small, lighted room with...yet another elevator.

Damn it! That last elevator was enough to drive me to distraction. Is this ever gonna end?

Ray tensed for a moment and listened for evidence of human

traffic in the dark hallway.

But the layers of dust that covered the old fluorescent lamps indicated that this place might not have had visitors, human or otherwise, in years, or that perhaps, cleaning and maintenance just weren't high priorities here. His eyes stared for one long moment. Ray walked slowly towards the elevator where he pressed a large red button. The door opened, and he stepped inside.

About a dozen levels were listed, each with a red button at the right of the engraved label, and at the bottom he found it—Level S4. Strange that it should be labeled so clearly.

After all he'd been through that night, it seemed like another sick joke.

Ray braced himself for the worst, pushed the button and closed his eyes. A grating sound filled his ears as the elevator door slid shut. The deep whirring sound grew louder as it picked up momentum and went lower and lower. It sped up considerably, and it soon seemed to be moving as fast as an elevator in a large skyscraper. He held on for dear life now, expecting it to stop suddenly—or crash!

The pungent odor had faded; soon it was practically gone, as Ray became only slightly more confident of his chances for survival.

He had no idea how long he'd traveled. It seemed as if that elevator had dropped for several miles at least.

For one fleeting moment Ray thought maybe there was something wrong, that everything would soon come crashing down into a deep, hidden chamber and he'd be dead. He found the urge to close his eyes hard to resist.

After a period that seemed almost interminable, he felt a sharp jolt as the elevator stopped and the door abruptly slid open. Ray opened his eyes as he emerged into a large room. There were two large containers, which resembled fish tanks, at one end of the room. They were lit with an orange-white glow.

For a minute, Ray simply stared at what lay inside. His mouth opened wide in astonishment and he just stood there, oblivious to anything else.

The creatures were humanoid, all right, with greenish gray skin, delicately formed heads, perfect features, and big, almost hypnotic eyes with large violet or dark blue pupils. Lips were pencil thin, and noses were gently sculpted as if an expert plastic surgeon had done the work.

Their arms and legs were slim and athletic at the same time, seemingly capable of tremendous feats of strength. They were almost human, yet Ray sensed abilities that went far beyond those of humans.

Ray knew who those creatures were!

They were indistinguishable from the beings he had seen in his dreams. Their name rang like a bell, the strange word that first erupted in his conscious memory so long ago: Rockoids!

Ray stared in disbelief. The Rockoids were exactly as he remembered them, down to the very last detail. He tried to slow down his rapid breathing and calm himself, as sweat began to pour down his neck. Ray took a second to gather his wits about him, and tried to observe his surroundings more carefully. He had to use his intelligence skills to help him focus his eyes on the strange sights and sounds around him.

The laboratory was filled with plain, glowing, and blinking buttons, knobs, handles, meters, futuristic-looking machines, and tables with large bottles filled with strange-looking chemicals. Ray stepped back toward one of the non-glowing control panels and tried to avoid looking at the Rockoids. They were dead all right, but so well preserved it seemed they might come alive at any moment.

Unfortunately, Ray spent too much time examining the alien bodies, and not on what seeped forth from the ventilation chamber in the large laboratory. He became aware of the return of that gaseous smell; only this time it was more intense than ever. Caught off guard, a wave of dizziness nearly overcame him; he stumbled back, bumping his shoulder on a switch attached to one of the strange machines.

A loud click broke the silence. Almost immediately, the machines began flashing several different colors at once in random patterns.

He began to see a thick, yellowish gas floating all around him.

Before Ray could decide what to do next, he became even more disoriented. He struggled to fight the waves of unconsciousness that seemed about to overwhelm him and hurried back toward the entrance of the room.

However, as soon as Ray began running, he heard and felt a deep rumbling sound.

Legs moved faster and faster until Ray stood before the closing elevator door. Just as he was about to attempt to squeeze himself between the narrowing crack, the door abruptly shut with a resounding clang.

There he remained: trapped inside the room!

The terror of being stranded in that awful place made him breathe deeply and rapidly, and he began to cough as he inhaled the strange gas. It spread thick around him, and he could hardly see. He struggled to hold his breath, but the intense odor had already weakened him, so he found himself breathing in fitful gasps.

Ray briefly wondered if he wasn't breathing the same sort of air that those Rockoids might have breathed, and he struggled to see through the gas. Maybe he'd find a gas mask somewhere.

As he grew weaker, he stumbled around the room, bumping into tables, tripping over chairs, knocking over chemical bottles, and making one big mess. He could hear objects dropping, liquids and glass. He expected he'd soon be bleeding uncontrollably from cuts and bruises inflicted by the shattered glass.

Ray nearly overturned the transparent tanks holding the Rockoids as he staggered about. The situation had become intolerable. He tried to scream out for help (as if anyone could hear him). However, his efforts were useless. The words never left his mouth. They just stuck in his throat, and although he tried to swallow, the effort only ended up making it sore.

To Ray's surprise, the gaseous cloud suddenly dispersed. The odor remained, but in a far less pungent form. He felt overjoyed, and he was about to make his way toward the elevator when he realized he couldn't move. His limbs were paralyzed. Ray tried harder and harder, but his efforts only served to wear him out.

Suddenly everything around him began to ripple, as if he was caught in a transparent flame. He felt the room spinning around him, making him even more disoriented than before. His surroundings became brighter and brighter. Within seconds, the light became so unbearable, he thought if he kept his eyes open any longer, he would go blind.

So this is what people see when they die.

At that moment, relief was brought to Ray's eyes. Blackness suddenly engulfed the room. He first believed the intense light had blinded him, but quickly realized that every element of the room, from walls to ceiling, and the contents within, had somehow absorbed the incredible darkness in which he was now immersed.

Ray began to fall. The sensation seemed mild at first, not much different from a parachute jump once the chute had expanded. He could only think of the feeling as gentle, rolling, safe, knowing he'd hit bottom and become upright in a few moments.

Sure enough, the manner in which Ray swayed back and forth seemed reminiscent of those near-forgotten parachute jumps back in the Middle East. Gentle and swaying…comfortable.

Suddenly the pace of Ray's fall began increasing rapidly, precipitously, and he seemed to be pulled straight down, faster and faster. Startled, frightened, Ray barely had time to think where he might end up.

He simply kept falling on and on, without end, without a feeling of approaching solid ground, not knowing if he was ever going to land. Could he be dreaming? The entire scenario seemed horribly real.

He finally got the courage to look down, shocked to see the face of the gorgeous alien woman of his dreams. She had a look of deep pain on her face. He felt her anguish….

Suddenly, the eye of what appeared to be a gigantic tornado replaced the image of breathtaking beauty, a silvery mass, spinning at a speed that Ray surmised was hundreds of miles per hour. The tornado slowly drew him closer and closer into its eye, faster and faster. He could not resist; his muscles were frozen in time….

He must surrender to that incredible force of nature. Maybe he'd wake up from his nightmare, safe and sound in his bed at home... if all this were truly a dream.

Ray's whole life began to replay itself. He became a child again, back in the small but comfortable home he had lived in during his younger years. Adulthood brought him to the classrooms of MIT, where he had first learned how to program computers. A quick jump to the Naval Academy in which he enrolled to please his father, where he got the foolish idea to become a Navy SEAL, and somehow managed to achieve that impossible goal.

Ray saw his friends and watched as he, still a cadet, had to endure the taunts and abuse from upperclassmen.

His mother lay in her deathbed, tentatively clinging to her final moments of life, never the same after his dad died in that freak accident.

Before he had a chance to think about the words he couldn't utter when she was alive, he was fighting that strange, desert battle in the Middle East, a silly mission, really, just to dig up some intelligence information from a low-level official.

Ray and his crew never reached their destination. Just yards away from a huge compound, explosives suddenly burst all around them. His comrades fell to the ground, one upon another, and that noxious gas filled his lungs, making him feel he was about to suffocate, and he, too, fell to the ground.

The hospital stay wasn't pleasant. The dreams began during his convalescence. At first, just faint images of space, and the ships came; huge, oppressive, great behemoths of shiny metal, their giant laser weapons raining fire and destruction in all directions.

Above everything, Ray saw her face. The most wonderful creature he'd even seen, so close he could almost reach out to her. It seemed he'd always known her, forever apart, yet so close he could witness her private moments of agony.

He could even see what he presumed to be her counselor visiting her in her private chambers one fateful evening. The words were alien, weird and melodic, more sung than spoken; somehow he could understand their meaning: "Zanther, my princess, I bring you sad tidings."

"I know, my lord Yexin, it is my parents. I felt their death, I felt all their deaths...."

Ray sensed the alien woman's anguish, oppressive beyond his ability to comprehend. He, too, was nearly overcome with grief, a grief felt for unknown alien beings who shared nothing in common but their tragic, senseless deaths.

Just when it seemed as if he had regained control of his muscles, maybe find a way out of that horrendous, spinning inferno, everything went black once more.

Total silence ensued...

* * *

The voices were faint at first, hardly more than whispers, one here, another there. The volume intensified, as Ray heard faint notes of some indescribable melody, barely audible in the distance.

People were talking, laughing, happy giggles infusing his ears.

Ray could see nothing; it was all black. Had he gone blind?

The distinctive voice of a young child yelled out, "Mommy, who's that strange man?"

"Why, that's just a staggerhead. Ignore him."

The light returned to Ray's eyes.

Chapter 4

Positively huge, the place seemed filled with colorful lights and decorations. People with strange clothes strolled about, sometimes so fast it seemed as if they were jogging.

All the sights and sounds were crystal clear to him now, illuminated by an amazing type of recessed lighting that spread nearly uniformly from the high ceiling. It seemed like daylight. Ray squinted whenever he gazed upward, astonished at the view before him.

Ray saw dozens of people walking by, en route to various locations. All were clothed in garments exhibiting the colors of the rainbow, but most had one thing in common; their gloves and boots were all a dark brown or black, as if they were conforming to some unspoken fashion convention.

A young couple walked right by him.

The tall, red-haired man wore a blue long-sleeved shirt and pants, shiny black gloves, and boots. The somewhat portly woman at his side was dressed in clothing similar in design, except her shirt and pants were red.

Ray still felt disoriented, barely able to stand, trying to remain upright.

He almost laughed out loud at the first thought that came to him: *I have a feeling I'm not in Kansas anymore.* He stifled the laugh and instead attempted to process all the strange and wonderful sights.

Most of people nearby tried to avoid Ray, staying at a respectful distance, for good reason. He was a sight. His hands and face were dirty, bruised, with dried blood on his forehead. His jeans and shirt were torn.

The dizziness almost overwhelmed Ray as he walked outside what seemed to be the exit of this facility. He took a deep breath. As he was about to regain full consciousness, he bumped into a signpost.

The brightly lit, multicolored sign overhead read, "Thanks for Shopping at the Area 51 Shopping Mall!"

As Ray stared dumbfounded, the vertigo engulfed him once more. He stumbled back into the mall, using walls for support.

When he returned to the mall, he began picking out details he hadn't noticed before. As much as the storefronts resembled a regular shopping mall, they were quite different. Their clothing displays were as odd as the garments worn by the passers-by. The merchandise was totally unfamiliar to him and the names on the doors, with few exceptions, did not resemble any establishments he knew.

Well, Ray did see the signs for The Gap and McDonald's, but the logos had clearly undergone great changes. It seemed as if the whole world had turned upside down overnight.

What was he doing here? One moment, he was in that...that place, the laboratory, with the alien beings in those gigantic tanks! The next came that strange odor, that whirling, the falling...

Now—this! Was he truly dead?

People stared at Ray, whispered into each other's ears, and chuckled as they saw him. The fact Ray could hardly stand straight, no doubt made them feel he was a harmless drunk or a lunatic.

Ray felt so disoriented he didn't even care.

Despite his state of confusion, some things just couldn't escape his notice. Several of the people he passed were downright strange. They hardly seemed like people at all. Some had protruding foreheads, others had heads that seemed almost fish-like, complete with gills and scales. A few of the beings even resembled giant crabs. Their faces were clearly real, not a mask or outlandish costume. Every element of their appearance seemed authentic, from the odd manner of their gait, to the form-fitting uniforms, to the casual manner in which they strode around, as if they were used to each other's different appearances.

The feeling that he had been suddenly dropped into the middle of a science fiction movie nagged at the core of Ray's being.

It became a little too much for Ray. He resisted the urge to scream for help, but couldn't still a few panic-stricken cries as he staggered about, trying to get away. Nothing he'd ever seen or heard during his travels around the world prepared him for this.

Eventually, Ray found his way into a clothing store, stopping dead in his tracks to look around.

The female clerk's eyes widened with fear as Ray approached. He resisted the urge to run out of that place, but with difficulty. Seconds ticked by, and neither party said anything. He stared at her, she at him and they stood, almost frozen in their tracks, about two yards apart.

Ray had to find out where he was, how he got here, and what in hell was going on.

With renewed resolve affecting his still groggy mind, he boldly walked right up toward her and stumbled against the nearest wall.

"Where...am...I?" Ray asked, panting wildly, breathing heavily between each word.

"You're in the Area 51 Shopping Mall, ninety kilometers north of Las Vegas," said the clerk calmly, in a smooth, soft voice, as if she got asked this sort of question all the time.

"I know...that...already! What time is it?" exclaimed Ray, as he began to feel calm.

The clerk pushed a red button by the cash register—or what Ray took to be a cash register because of the distinctive drawer at the bottom of the flat-screen terminal—with her small, slim hand, and a robot-like voice said, "The time is 10:05 A.M."

"No, what year is it? What day? What month?" He tried to act as if this was all routine chitchat.

She didn't react to Ray's almost hysterical behavior (hysterical in her opinion, anyway); instead she matter-of-factly pushed the button again, and the same voice said, "The date is September 3, 2232."

"Why am I here? What is that thing?"

Calmly and slowly, the clerk replied, "I don't know why you're here, but this object is a computerized calendar."

"Who are those creatures—from space? I've never seen anything like them before!"

The clerk couldn't believe she was behaving so rationally in the face of this wild, insane man. He must be humored, to give her time to get out of this ticklish situation.

"Well, we do get visitors from all over."

The woman had quite enough of this acting job. She knew she must react fast before this staggerhead became violent, seeing as he was showing no signs of wanting to leave.

"Excuse me, I'll be right back...I need to finish checking my inventory."

She smiled briefly, a forced smile. Ray could see the fear in her eyes as she stared at him. She couldn't hide that.

Nor did Ray fail to notice how she walked to the back of the store with fearful sideways glances.

* * *

Once the clerk was back in the stockroom, she gazed anxiously at something on her wrist that looked like a watch, but sported a miniature TV screen.

The woman didn't hesitate, summoning up the courage to bark into the screen, "Get me the Las Vegas Police Department right now!"

"One moment please," replied a robotic voice.

A few seconds later, a stern-faced man with brown hair, impassionate brown eyes and wearing what was clearly a police uniform, appeared on the screen.

"Captain Gotlieb here. How can I help you?" said the man with a distinct trace of the Bostonian accent that identified his birthplace.

As he responded to her call, he noticed on his viewscreen that the caller was Laura Jenkins of Laura's Fantastic Fashions at the Area 51 Shopping Mall.

Jenkins quickly summarized the situation to Gotlieb.

"Hmmm. I guess he had a little much of the good stuff," Gotlieb replied. We'll be right over to check it out, okay?"

"Wait, what if he leaves the store?"

"Don't worry, Ms. Jenkins. A staggerhead is pretty damn easy to spot in a big crowd these days. If he's still in your store, just stall him as long as you can. Humor him, but be gentle. We don't want him getting too violent."

That was reassuring!

Laura Jenkins didn't take very kindly to such possibilities. She'd seen more than enough strange people since opening her little clothing store four years earlier. The changing tastes in fashions always presented problems. Keeping the shelves well stocked with what the customers wanted every week was a never-ending source of headaches.

And those damned staggerheads! There was a large tourist trade in nearby Las Vegas, and she never seemed to be able to rid herself of those unsavory visitors, even if their presence was largely unthreatening.

Oh well, here I go again. She nodded her head as she looked at the tiny screen on her wrist.

"Okay. You're sure you'll be here in a few minutes, right?"

"Don't worry, Ms. Jenkins. We'll be there in a flash. I'll even come myself. Thanks for calling us before this thing blew up."

"Thanks so much!"

"No problem. Goodbye."

Captain Gotlieb's face disappeared from the screen. Jenkins put her hand to her side as the image on her watch-like device changed to a faint gray glow; her calm demeanor amazed her. She returned to the front of her shop, where Ray was still waiting.

"Would you like to buy something? I mean, you don't want to look out of style," said Jenkins. She again forced a smile, trying hard to mollify this clearly crazed individual.

Young, in her mid twenties, Jenkins seemed almost too slim, with light makeup, and wearing a colorful set of coordinated slacks and blouse of shimmering reds and pinks. Aside from a set of earrings shaped remarkably like sharks, a gift from her father, and the wristview device on her hand, she remained devoid of jewelry.

She was even rather attractive in an anonymous sort of way, with a cute, upturned nose and almost pouting mouth. Her hair was dark brown, almost black, long, but held tight in a bun behind her slim head. Her slim physique seemed evidence that she had even been a fashion model at one time.

For a moment, Jenkins was lost in thought. She picked at her left earring and wondered about the whereabouts of her father, a trader of weird, unconventional goods no doubt gallivanting about the galaxy looking for trouble again.

The abrupt change in the clerk's attitude made Ray more suspicious than ever, as alertness seemed to return to him. They stared at each other again briefly, and both figured they might as well play out their roles in this little drama and see what happened next.

"Yeah, I guess. These clothes probably aren't flying off the shelves these days. Just show me the latest thing," said Ray.

Ray figured the gas in that underground chamber was giving him hallucinations, but this entire crazy scenario sure seemed realistic.

He saw the clerk walking over to a rack of clothes, looking over the selections. She chose a complete outfit that included red pants and a shirt, and selected another one that was almost the same style, except it consisted of a blue shirt and black pants. She retrieved a pair of black gloves and boots from a nearby display.

She took a quick breath, returned to Ray, handed him the clothes, and quickly returned to the cash register. She gripped it tightly, evidently to provide a modicum of security.

"Would you like to try these on?" she remarked, very casually. Clearly she knew how to handle the crackpots and eccentrics who visited her store.

Ray started to protest, but thought better of it. He was now fully aware of the rather frightful manner of his appearance and actions.

He expected to be taken out in handcuffs any time now, but he realized there wasn't any alternative other than to run and become a fugitive. That certainly wouldn't resolve his situation. He obediently strolled into a nearby dressing room, behind a shimmering, rainbow-colored curtain, and tried on each outfit separately. The room had a small, violet-colored bench, and a little counter with an object that resembled a microwave oven, with a few flourishes that he took to be control panels and meters of some sort.

Adjacent to the dressing room, he found a small bathroom, and Ray took the opportunity to take a few moments to clean himself up before donning his new duds. Inside, he was pleased to discover that a long, hose-like device sprayed a soap-like material that served as both cleanser, deodorant and, apparently, healing lotion for minor cuts and bruises.

When Ray emerged from the dressing room wearing the blue and black outfit a few minutes later, he was the spitting image of a twenty-third-century civilian.

"You look splendid," Jenkins smiled; this time the expression seemed genuine.

Consulting her cash register, she smiled with studied efficiency, "That will be fifteen hundred credits, please."

"What's that in dollars?" Ray asked.

"Dollars? What are those?" Jenkins replied, still struggling to remain absolutely casual in the face of this absurd question.

"You know! Dollars! Money! Coin of the realm!" Ray

exclaimed.

"I'm sorry, but the only means of exchange we use around here are credits. Maybe we can work out something anyway. Do you have a credit card?"

"Too many actually. Let me find one with a decent credit line," Ray remarked as he began searching for his wallet.

Fortunately he remembered to stuff the wallet into a handy pocket of his new duds (though he seemed to have a perfectly awful time squeezing it in). After a few seconds, he managed to extract it, took out his Visa card, and handed it to Jenkins.

"Do you take these?" he asked.

"I'm sorry. Those became obsolete over a century ago. Do you have anything else?" she said as she slowly handed him back his card. Jenkins hoped the staggerhead's frustration at not being able to complete the transaction wouldn't make him violent.

Where is that police officer? Why do they always take forever to respond?

Through it all, the smile remained frozen on her face and she kept her voice as level as possible, forcing herself to act friendly by sheer force of will. Inwardly, though her visitor seemed more presentable now, Jenkins feared he might crack at any moment.

Ray put back his Visa card, searched his wallet again, and found his American Express card, which he handed to her.

"Do you take these?" asked Ray.

His frustration grew, but he, too, kept his voice level.

"I'm sorry I've never seen one of those," said Jenkins, once again handing him his card back, slowly.

Ray calmly returned the American Express card to his wallet. Just as he was about to retrieve his Discover card, the only credit card he had left, someone rudely grabbed him by the shoulder.

With difficulty, Ray turned around, and saw the tall, thin man now holding him in an ever-tightening grip. The uniform was different all right, form-fitting, silvery in color, the wearer clearly a police officer of some sort. Ray caught a brief look at the mustached face and grim expression. The nametag said Captain David Gotlieb.

"Is there any trouble, Captain Gotlieb?" asked Ray.

"You should know, buddy. You're the pirate trying to plunder this lady's store like it's some damned space freighter." barked Gotlieb as he pointed to the puzzled clerk with a frozen grin, still standing, almost at attention, behind her cash register. Inside her mind, she sighed with relief, knowing this irrational intruder would soon be on his way to a nice prison cell.

"What? That's crazy! I was just trying to pay for some clothes here, but the clerk wouldn't take any of my credit cards," Ray argued.

Ray finally gave up all pretense of seriousness and added, "I guess next you'll tell me I just killed the Wicked Witch of the West, right?"

"The what?"

Gotlieb wondered what sort of person this was. He'd seen staggerheads before, but this stranger's voice remained strong, not quivering, and his gait seemed rock steady. In fact, he didn't look intoxicated at all. Gotlieb vowed to keep that in mind when he interrogated the suspect. For now, he simply decided to voice his standard spiel: "Sorry, buddy, but we're gonna have to take you to headquarters in Las Vegas for questioning."

"Questioning? Damn it, I didn't steal anything! I'm no pirate!" Ray yelled. Yet he didn't struggle. He knew that would only make his predicament worse.

The policeman ignored Ray's protests and put two ringed devices around his arms, which seemed to force them to the side, leaving them paralyzed. There was no pain at all, but his arms remained immobile. He struggled momentarily, but quickly realized the effort was futile; he had to give in and hope the authorities would understand his situation and be lenient with him.

He was directed to leave the store, through the mall to the exit. Ray felt amazed at the calm demeanor he displayed in the midst of all this chaos. One minute he was overcome by noxious fumes in a top-secret military base and the next he was walking about in a big shopping mall and someone was telling him he had been transported many decades into the future.

Yeah, sure, if this is madness, I have it in spades!

* * *

As the two men approached the mall exit, the one Ray stumbled through earlier, Gotlieb yelled to his men, "All right folks, the show's over. We got our man! Get back to your hovercars, and I'll catch up with you guys on the bright side of the moon!"

The two officers waiting outside nodded and strolled casually to their patrol cars.

"Okay, buddy, you have the right to remain silent. Anything you say can be used against you in a court of law," said Gotlieb as they walked out the door. He continued to expand upon the twenty-third-century variation of the Miranda law. There were a few new wrinkles, about the right to contact an attorney from Ray's home world if he so desired, but this was his home world, wasn't it?

"Court of law? I didn't steal the clothes! I've never stolen anything in my life!" Ray protested, ignoring the memories of those candy bars he and his pals regularly pilfered from a neighborhood grocery when he was barely in his teens.

"The questions we ask, and how you answer them is gonna decide if we hold a trial or just let you go home," said Gotlieb coldly.

"Yeah, go ahead and take me home—if you people have discovered time travel yet," Ray grumbled under his breath.

Ray now realized he was in the mall's parking lot, a place filled with semicircular vehicles with darkened glass windows and no visible headlights. The rear of these odd contraptions had sets of taillights that looked more like small rockets. The license plates were rounded, encircling glowing numbers and letters.

Gotlieb's vehicle had been adorned with a large police insignia on both sides, but was otherwise no different from any of the other vehicles. When the police captain walked up to the car, the back door slid open to the side and Ray found himself pushed roughly inside. As soon as Ray almost fell into the waiting seat, the door slid shut and two belts passed above and around him, from his shoulders to his hip, locking him in a seated position. The wrist restraints dropped automatically from his hands and he sat back, looking toward what might be a dashboard on this strange vehicle.

Gotlieb quickly took his place in the front seat. Within seconds, the front door slid shut, his seat belt encircled him, and he was safely locked in place.

The inside of this strange police car looked almost the same as the vehicles of Ray's century. However, there was no steering wheel; a long stem with a smooth, rounded top, replaced it. There were also many other strange gizmos and gadgets on the dashboard that he could not identify.

Ray sighed and pinched himself. When he realized it hurt, he began to come to the realization this was no dream. The reality of the situation finally hit him between the eyes. Somehow, that mysterious experience in the deep, dark chambers of Area 51 transported him to the future.

Or maybe he died, and went to...well...that other place.

"Okay, old man. Sit back cause this is gonna be the hardest ride you ever took," said Gotlieb, dripping with sarcasm.

"How fast can this thing go? I used to practice riding cars around racetracks on the weekends. There's nothing this thing can do that I haven't exceeded already."

Gotlieb laughed.

"You gotta be stuck in the past, old man! Our vehicles can go over four hundred kilometers per hour when they're just cruising!"

He pushed a green button, and Ray felt the car slowly rising.

"Hey, what the hell's going on here?"

"Okay, buddy, think logically here. If this car didn't fly, it wouldn't be called a hovercar, now would it?"

"No, it probably wouldn't," Ray replied, a sickly smile frozen on his face.

"Thank you. Your life's been spared because of that answer you just gave me." Gotlieb chuckled, ever the sarcastic one, but Ray didn't appreciate the joke.

"Okay, old man, here comes the fast part," Gotlieb announced, apparently proud to show off the capabilities of his vehicle.

He turned a knob, and the hovercar gained altitude with an incredible burst of speed. Had he not been secured in his seat belt, Ray would surely have been knocked about the cabin. A deep, upsetting feeling in the pit of his stomach intensified as the vehicle reached its cruising altitude.

Gotlieb turned the knob again, and made the car accelerate even faster. Ray panicked as the enormity of the situation caused his head to throb—or was that just a headache? His heart pounded, and his vision began to waver, as dizziness seemed to intrude on his consciousness again.

The hovercar sped past smooth buildings, all very different from one another; many of them were made of some sort of shiny, metallic material. Some were spiral shaped, and they rose much higher than the limit of Ray's sight. They were seemingly immersed in a sea of airborne traffic, consisting of rows and rows of speeding hovercars and even a few flying motorcycles called (as he later learned) hovercycles. The strange vehicles seemed to pass around them at uncontrollable speeds, yet the distance between them remained fixed. The logical portion of his mind surmised some sort of computerized traffic control system was at work.

"What is this? Where are you taking me?"

"We'll be at police headquarters in ten minutes. Once there, you'll be able to sit back and relax until I question you about all this crap, old man." Gotlieb laughed.

Ray tried to relax, but the dizziness returned in full force. He remained confused, unable to get a grip on what happened. Finally, a wave of unconsciousness overwhelmed him and he blacked out, his head falling slowly to the side.

The vehicle continued on, at top speed, lights and sirens flashing. In minutes, the craft slowed and began to descend. A lighted pathway stood before them as the vehicle seemed to float gently toward the ground. Finally, it came to a dead stop in front of a -parking stall.

Gotlieb and an assistant carried their prisoner out of the vehicle, and Ray was taken towards a large, cold, drab building looming ahead in the distance.

Chapter 5

Time passed slowly for Ray as he slept. That awful dream about a battle with the aliens and their huge, marauding spaceships returned again, this time more vivid than ever.

As expected, the gorgeous alien woman appeared to rise above the carnage, disconnected from the rest of the universe. Once again her expression was, at first, one of content, then it quickly turned to one of deep anguish.

She seemed so close he thought she was standing right before him. He remembered his life spinning before him as he was immersed in that tornado-like phenomenon.

He knew her name!

She was Zanther!

* * *

After a few hours of fitful slumber, Ray woke up in a cold sweat, laying on a long cot in a room lit by some sort of recessed beam of light with no visible source. The room itself had a reddish cast to it, dim and drab. He would have believed he was incarcerated in a prison cell, but for the weird sights around him.

Next to him loomed a large desk with all sorts of strange gadgets on it. He saw buttons, knobs, and glowing meters, and a helmet of some sort, not unlike one a motorcycle rider would wear. Standing in front of him was Captain Gotlieb, two other officers, and someone with a white lab coat and a stern look on his craggy, long-nosed face that Ray took to be a scientist.

"Where am I?" Ray asked with a hoarse voice, recalling he was somewhere in Las Vegas, but exactly where in that city he didn't know. He slowly sat up, his back aching terribly from the effort.

"You're in a high-security interrogation chamber two stories under the Las Vegas Police Department," replied Gotlieb calmly.

"Why?"

"The woman who called us said you were acting pretty weird and you might be violent. We can't think about letting you go till we ask some questions," replied Gotlieb again, his earlier sarcasm gone.

Suddenly Ray looked down and realized he was wearing the very garments they claimed he tried to steal from the clothing store.

"Hey! Why do I have these clothes on? I thought you charged me with stealing them!" Ray exclaimed.

"The manager took pity on you and let you keep them. What you had on before was so out of whack, you stood out in that mall like a sore thumb, according to the manager. I guess she got rid of your original garments. Quick-thinking lady, but I would have liked to have them here for evidence."

Ray smiled for the first time since he arrived in the future and said, "That's just peachy."

"Yeah, I guess so, old man, but now we have to get on with the questioning. Some of these questions are gonna seem pretty weird to you, but we have to know the true story behind all this."

"Ok, Captain. I have to tell you I'm not really myself. I'm tired as hell, and I've just had another dream."

"Dreams? Yeah, we want to know more about those too. While you were sleeping, you were crying out loud about 'Rockoids,' alien attacks and calling out for someone named Zanther. Who's that—your girlfriend?"

Ray just stared, sat back and sighed. Now everyone knew about his dreams. He figured he'd be a candidate for a straitjacket next the way he was carrying on.

"Okay, old man. First question: Do you own a hovercar?"

"No way. I never saw one of those things until you arrested me."

"Why not? Do you like walking or do you just use public transportation? Was your license revoked?"

"No, I don't have a hovercar because we never had anything like that in my lifetime."

"Trying to tell us you're from the past, eh? You really expect us to believe that bullshit? I'll tell you what—it's impossible! How could you have gotten here from the past if we're not even close to discovering time travel yet?" Gotlieb asked, almost shouting. "Now tell me the truth! Did you stow away on a spaceship? Are you trying to infiltrate Earth?"

Gotlieb thought he was laying it on a little thick, but he didn't want to put this strange fellow at ease, even for a moment. Clearly this stranger was hiding something. There was no way he could be a time traveler. Working time machines did not exist....at least there were none he personally knew about.

"Spaceship, are you kidding? Next you'll be saying a tornado in an underground lab dumped me into that shopping mall," Ray said matter-of-factly.

"Tornadoes, huh? You expect us to believe there are tornadoes underground, in a laboratory and they take you through time? You gotta think we're pretty damn stupid here, buddy! Next you'll be saying aliens abducted you from the past and dropped you into the future." Gotlieb sneered at him.

Gotlieb began to suspect they had the biggest staggerhead of all in their midst...maybe he was even on Telnon-C (a highly addictive hallucinogenic drug manufactured on a distant alien world).

At this point, the scientist came forward, glancing sharply at Ray. Gotlieb was about to say something, but the scientist raised a hand to stop him, and asked, in a very serious fashion, "Y'all were in Area 51?"

Gotlieb protested. "I'm not finished questioning the suspect, sir."

"Captain Gotlieb, I am your commanding officer, and when I feel like asking our guest some questions, I have the perfect right to do so. Now I'd appreciate it if y'all would just move aside...and that's an order!" The scientist's booming Texas-bred voice was sharp and direct as he gave Gotlieb a stern look.

The police officer started to say something, but quickly stopped himself, shutting his mouth so the words he truly wanted to say couldn't be used against him later.

"I just wanted to know if there were really any alien bodies hidden there. The idea was bothering me, so I didn't want to be... bothered any more." Ray said, not betraying his true feelings on the situation in the least.

"Who told you about Level S4 and the a—," the scientist started to say.

"Excuse me, sir!" Gotlieb interrupted, sounding increasingly irritated.

Ray was starting to believe the relationship between Gotlieb and the so-called scientist had more history that he first thought—and not a terribly friendly history at that.

After making sure Gotlieb and the scientist weren't going to argue, Ray responded to the latter's question, "Are you listening to me now?"

Ray continued without waiting for a response.

"Good. When I was in Level S4, I saw the Rockoid bodies."

"Rockoids?" exclaimed the scientist and Gotlieb almost in unison.

"Isn't that what the alien bodies you captured are called?" Ray asked.

"No. We speculated they might be Rockoids, based on what little intelligence information we had about them, but we never got a definite confirmation," replied Gotlieb.

Gotlieb stopped in his tracks and laughed. "That's really clever of you, Perkins. I didn't think you had it in you."

"In my dreams that's what they were called," Ray said.

"All right, those dreams seem to be bothering you so much, why don't you just tell us all about them?" asked Gotlieb.

"Now you're a psychiatrist too, eh?" Ray retorted sarcastically.

Gotlieb glared at Ray, but said nothing.

"All right," Ray sighed, "I'll tell you what I can."

Ray took a deep breath and began to relate the story about the onset of those horrible nightmares. He talked briefly of his military experience, his war injury, and treatment at a military hospital for problems the staff attributed to an undiagnosed psychiatric condition.

Ray told of his earliest dreams about the first Rockoid space battle and, especially, the face of that gorgeous alien woman with the haunting violet eyes.

Zanther!

Even as he spoke, he could see her face and figure. He wanted to call out to her, but held his tongue. She could only be an illusion!

There was no Zanther.

Or was there?

Ray continued talking for what seemed like several hours, interrupting his narrative only for brief periods for soft drinks and bathroom visits, and continued on in earnest.

Gotlieb and the scientist prompted the conversation with a few questions along the way, but for the most part let Ray continue all by himself.

Ray tried to recall as many details as he could, concentrating on the development of his computer game and how he wove the details of those dreams into the program. His explanation was only interrupted by a long-winded lecture on the part of the scientist, in which he told Captain Gotlieb about the "primitive" games in vogue during the early part of the twenty-first century.

As Ray finished the final part of his description, in which he told Gotlieb about the face of the Rockoid woman in detail, the captain grinned and said, "Been a long time since you got laid, old man?"

Ray's anger intensified at that remark. At this point, in his already confused and frustrated state of mind, he was on the verge of punching Gotlieb out. Galvanized for action, Ray stood up abruptly, as the policeman tensed.

Ray thought better of it and sat down again, staring straight ahead. He realized that if he became violent now, there was no chance whatsoever that they'd let him go. Then again, what did it matter? Where could he go, what could he do? If this was truly the future, he was indeed a stranger in a strange land.

Ray struggled hard to ignore Gotlieb's sarcasm and said, "Okay, Mr. Police Captain and Mr. Scientist, what do you think of all this? Am I crazy or what?"

Both Gotlieb and the scientist sat back a moment in their chairs. Then they got up and went into an adjoining room, where they talked in an animated fashion between themselves for a few minutes. Briefly, it even looked like the two were arguing about something; their mouths were opened wide, as if they were shouting at each other.

Through it all, Ray heard nothing. Evidently, the walls were efficiently soundproofed. His intelligence-bred instincts took over and he looked over the interrogation room for some means of escape. A burly officer protected the single door at the far corner; could he overcome the guard? Probably not. He imagined that folk in this century had combat abilities way beyond what he knew. For sure, he would be subdued, perhaps injured, killed. Even if he managed to escape, where would he go? No doubt he'd be caught and incarcerated again, and maybe this time he'd be put away for good.

Ray could do nothing but watch and wait. He saw the police captain uttering a few words into his wristview (as Ray later learned the device was called), waiting, as Gotlieb seemed to receive instructions. He had a grim look on his mustached face as he continued to discuss the situation.

Gotlieb returned to the interrogation room alone, and took a long, hard look at Ray.

"Hmmm. I hate to say this, Mr. Perkins, but you got us in a real bind here. Many of the things you've told us so far are true," said Gotlieb suspiciously. "Some of it is classified, meaning you're either a spy from somewhere or you've tapped into some unknown source of information."

"Yeah, you can call me James Bond...."

"James who?"

"Never mind."

"You don't think I'm a spy, do you?" Ray asked, almost in a state of shock.

"No, we don't," Gotlieb responded calmly. "All the evidence shows what you're saying is legit."

"Evidence?" Ray wondered what they knew.

"We use voice patterns to check for signs of deception, and you are definitely telling the truth—at least you think you are."

At this point, Ray figured he'd better fess up and show his trump card. He could no longer hide a certain detail of his dream that had been bothering him ever since his interrogation began. Maybe it was important, maybe it wasn't; he might as well get it out in the open in case there was any significance to his statement later on.

"All right, I left out one key detail. The aliens in my dream, the Rockoids...well...they didn't attack us first. We attacked them."

Gotlieb seemed almost shocked in his response, which was also tinged with derision. "That's impossible! The Alliance never attacks unless it's attacked first! That's a hard and fast law. It's the standard by which we operate."

Gotlieb paused for a second.

"You break it, you're thrown in the slammer for a few centuries!" exclaimed Gotlieb, almost laughing.

"Then why were all the other parts of my dreams true? Huh? Try to answer that one, why don't you?"

"Honestly, I don't have a clue. We do know that dreams aren't always literal descriptions of a real event. Maybe your own personal fears are affecting your dreams. That's something our psychiatrists are going to have to figure out."

"You mean I'm nuts, right? If that's what you think, maybe there's no point in continuing this nonsense!"

Ray stood up.

"That's it, I'm outta here. Bye!"

Before Ray could walk a single step, Gotlieb raised his hand, signaling him to stop. "Wait, Perkins! We don't want to restrain you. You're still in custody. Now calm down."

Ray seethed with nearly uncontrollable anger. His breaths came fast, as he panted and sweated. The logical portion of his mind soon took over; it took another couple of seconds for Ray to regain control, but he sat down again, slowly, reluctantly, fighting his inner demons to remain as calm as he could under these crazy conditions.

"I'm okay, folks! Sorry, but this is just getting out of hand, that's all. It hasn't been one of my better days." Ray tried to force a sickly smile that never got beyond a sneer.

"I quite understand, Mr. Perkins," the scientist, who came back into the interrogation room at that moment, said. "Frankly, we're not really sure what to make of you. We're just trying to find out what this is all about."

"Look, these dreams...I've got no control over them...none whatsoever. You tell me some of them are true, right?"

"We do know that dreams are a combination of your conscious experiences and your subconscious; it's really hard to separate the real from the fanciful."

As the scientist got into his spiel, it seemed as if his syrupy Texas accent faded and flattened. "Remember, back in your century—and for the sake of argument, let's assume you really are from the twenty-first century—there were all those reports of alien abductions. People were hypnotized and came up with all kinds of strange stories about being taken aboard spaceships, meeting insect-like aliens.

"While we do know about an alien crash—specifically concerning the beings you saw at Area 51—we never had any evidence of aliens experimenting with humans. These Rockoids are really quite human-like in most respects; you'd hardly tell them apart cept for the gray-green color of their skin. We haven't had much contact with them, but we do know they have the unique ability..."

"They are all able to sense when their fellow beings are involved in great tragedies, right, Mr. Scientist?" Ray interrupted.

The scientist's eyes betrayed his surprise that this crazy character that claimed to come from the past honed in on this key element of the Rockoid psyche. Speechless, he could only nod his head in agreement.

"You still feel my dreams about us attacking the Rockoids first are illusions, right?"

The scientist paused for a few seconds, thoughtful, but no longer skeptical. "Listen, we really don't know what the truth is. We're just gonna to have to examine you further."

"Ask me anything you want," Ray said, staring in readiness at both, with a threatening glare.

"Okay. Let's go on. Tell me again who you are, where you come from, when you were born, and your current place of residence,"

"Okay, my name is Ray Perkins, I come from Savannah, Georgia, I'm 33, and I live in Palo Alto, California."

Ray started to get agitated again.

"Why do you ask me over and over? I've told you this half a dozen times already. Hasn't it sunk in yet?"

"Here's the deal, Perkins. We got a big problem with some of your claims," Gotlieb chimed in.

"Your accent betrays a Georgia background, but the city you say you came from...well, I think something's wrong there."

"What the hell are you talking about?"

"Are you sure you didn't make a mistake? How do you know you didn't come from Atlanta?"

Ray thought it was rather funny he wouldn't be able to remember where he was born; maybe his captors believed his perceived insanity extended to his long-term memory as well.

Still, Ray decided to play along and answer. "My father took all of us to Atlanta many times for business. It was almost like a second home to me, but I'm really from Savannah. Why would that be suspicious?"

The scientist interrupted, "In World War III..."

"World War Three!" Ray shouted. "When the hell did that happen?"

"Can I please finish?" asked the scientist angrily.

Ray's mouth began to open, he sighed and nodded his head slowly.

"Okay, we're going to have to give you a fast history lesson. If you really are from the past, you've got centuries of history to catch up on and not all the news is pleasant," warned the scientist.

"I can handle it," Ray assured him.

"I hope so, but you had better take a deep breath. A lot of things have happened on this planet that may be shocking to you."

"Please, I'm a big boy now. Just spill the beans."

"Very well, Ray Perkins. Let's begin this way." The scientist took a deep breath and dove right in, savoring every carefully calculated word he uttered. "World War Three occurred in the late twenty-first century, and it was probably one of the saddest events in human history. The war and its aftermath claimed well over five hundred million people. It took decades to establish peace and complete reconstruction around the world. We are better off today, of course. The people of Earth now live in peace. We no longer have border conflicts, and we are part of a large coalition of intelligent creatures from many races and star systems."

Ray, instead of giving one of his own sarcastic comments, simply sat still in his chair, clearly dumbfounded at the incredible news.

His voice stammered slightly as he asked, "H-H-How did this all come about? Was it a nuclear war?"

The scientist continued, oblivious to his surroundings, as he relished the chance to teach someone something without being interrupted.

Ray remained utterly silent, in a state of near total shock as he continued to hear the horrible details of the most devastating war in human history.

The scientist's expression remained grave, as if the entire war were something up close and personal to him; in truth, many of his ancestors had perished in that dreadful conflict.

He spoke of awful destruction, cities laid to waste, disease, famine, death.

The scientist told Ray that the city of Savannah was devastated during the war; its shattered landscape left barren. During reconstruction, what remained of the once great city was transformed into a huge cemetery and a war memorial for the victims of the dreadful conflict

In Ray's mind, all he could see was fire, explosions, gunfire, cities in ruin, bodies strewn among debris, blood, severed limbs, images of human carnage beyond comprehension.

The scientist at last came full circle, "All right, now let's get back to the answers you gave. This part about living in California, well..."

"It's true, I swear..." Ray said. Words eluded him; a stunned look filled his eyes.

Dr. Johnson took the cue and droned on, his voice grave, his craggy face managing a deep frown.

"You see, back at the end of World War Three, in a last-ditch attempt to turn the tide of the war in their favor, the Chinese Air Force staged surprise raids over the three biggest cities of California: San Diego, San Francisco, and Los Angeles, using the bulk of their remaining bomber fleets with great success. These raids devastated the cities before the Allied forces finally drove away the Chinese. As they retreated, the enemy implanted special weapons deep within known earthquake fault lines. These weapons triggered targeted explosions that caused massive tremors so powerful they were felt halfway across the world. Much of California itself split off from the rest of the United States. The resulting aftershocks over the next few months quickly sank the rest of California, a factor also hastened by the unexpected explosion of the geologic bombs planted beneath the surface that hadn't been discovered and deactivated yet.

"Of California's entire population, one-quarter died in the

Chinese bombing raids and the earthquakes pretty much killed off the rest. Now you should understand why nobody your age could possibly have lived in California. If you still don't believe me, then you better watch this," explained Johnson.

The old scientist directed his attention to a large, flat TV screen-like device embedded against a far wall. The scientist gave a command. "Screen, open documentary: World War Three section 18, code Alpha-Delta 984."

Suddenly the screen began displaying pictures with a near-holographic reality. Ray witnessed the dreadful truth, fully immersed in the sights and sounds that assaulted his senses. The pictures depicted horrible, bloody battles that engulfed the world, waves and waves of warplanes blowing the cities of Europe and Asia into oblivion, throngs of people lying dead among the debris.

At the very end of the documentary, he saw planes bombing what could only be Los Angeles and a rather large bomb dropping on the fault line, causing a massive earthquake. As the screen faded, Ray saw images of California sinking into the ocean, other pictures showing stunned faces of people who knew, in their last conscious moments, there was nothing that could be done to save them.

The sound that accompanied these vivid pictures seemed more realistic than anything Ray had ever heard in a high-tech movie theater. The sounds of bombs, planes and cries of the injured and dying assaulted his ears as he imagined he was in the middle of the huge catastrophe. He looked around, back and forth, fearfully. The immersive experience seemed so authentic he had to constantly reassure himself he wasn't really being fired upon.

As the documentary ended, Ray exclaimed, "I did live in California, long before all this happened. I've been saying that ever since I woke up!"

"Then you should be grateful you weren't living there during World War Three—if you're telling the truth."

Ray stared at Johnson angrily, but the scientist barely seemed to notice.

"It's so strange, in the wake of such a tragedy, just a few years later, a new area of peace and prosperity would begin on Earth."

"What do you mean?" Ray asked.

"Four years after the end of the third World War, Earth decided to launch the first craft sent into space in decades. A joint effort by all the nations of the world, the purpose of this craft was to explore Mars as a prelude to its colonization. However, we weren't prepared for what happened when we reached the Red Planet."

Johnson paused, as if awaiting a reaction. When Ray just stared at him impassively, he continued as if nothing had happened. "Our whole vision of the universe was shattered in one fell swoop. Our craft encountered a cigar-shaped spaceship, belonging to a race that called themselves Cettians. They said they were part of a galactic government known as the Alliance. They radioed us their response, in English, amazingly enough.

"In just a few days another ship belonging to this Alliance arrived on Earth, and we made contact with these visitors, who were of a half dozen races or so; some similar to humans, some quite different. They had observed our progress in developing space travel since they had first discovered us, years earlier. They had also observed our seemingly endless wars, and it required our best diplomats to persuade the Cettians that we should not be destroyed in the interests of galactic stability."

Johnson's patter moved so rapidly from fact to fact, Ray barely had time to absorb the enormity of all the information being rushed at him. He struggled to listen as carefully as possible, hoping he'd have a chance to ask questions later on.

"Over the next century," Johnson droned on, "the Alliance grew into a loosely knit but powerful confederation consisting of twenty-seven different planetary governments, each residing in separate star systems, along with dozens of colony worlds. Today, petty border conflicts no longer exist on Earth, and we...well, we all live in peace now. We haven't had a war in years, and that last one was a relatively minor conflict."

"Minor! Ha!" Gotlieb rolled his eyes in disgust.

"Captain Gotlieb, you're out of line ...."

"He's gonna find out about the Jintorian wars sooner or later...."

"Oh, for Christ's sake, David, I don't think we should trust him completely yet...."

"Damn it, ...sir..."

Gotlieb and Johnson resumed their argument, and it was clear to Ray no love was lost between these two. Ray felt consumed by exhaustion, his mind almost numbed by the onslaught of strange, unfamiliar references and information. Finally he lost his cool.

"For crying out loud, guys, stop this crap right now!" Ray's face turned red with anger, hands shaking. "This arguing is getting us nowhere. Listen to me, please! Don't you realize now I'm telling you the truth?"

"That's the other thing I want to talk to you about," Johnson said. "As you've been talking, we've been scanning your brain. See that cerebral scanner on the ceiling—you know, the big light beam shining down on your head?"

Ray got up with a start and tried to escape the insistent beam. He walked from one end of the room to the other, but the beam tracked his every step, no matter how fast he twisted back and forth. He looked at his captors, fearfully, feeling like a caged animal.

"Don't worry, old man," Gotlieb spoke in a reassuring fashion. "The cerebral scanner won't hurt you a bit. It's programmed for your brain's electrical patterns and it's gonna follow you wherever you go in this room.

"I'm almost sounding like a scientist myself," Gotlieb smiled briefly at Ray, but continued to exhibit obvious rage toward Johnson. "The real use of this device is to determine whether you're telling us the truth, or at least whether you think you're telling the truth."

Ray glared at Gotlieb's obvious sarcasm, looked up again and checked out the ray of light more closely. Thin and light blue, about a quarter inch in diameter, it was perfectly focused. The device itself looked like a large lens, with strange machinery around it, but only a few recessed controls. He took a closer look at an instrument panel across the room, where Johnson peered on occasion. That was probably the control source.

Johnson seemed to forget his arguments with Gotlieb for the moment. He even managed a craggy sort of smile as he showed off the device. "This scanner does well enough to determine simple truth and belief. We really need to know more about you, though. We have a much more powerful device over at another military installation in Brussels."

"Hey, wait a minute!" Ray interrupted. "You're asking me question after question. I've got a thousand and one questions for you two. When do I get my turn?"

"All in due time, all in due time, Perkins." Johnson abruptly changed the subject. Ray grimaced, trying to hold his emotions in check.

"We will answer each and every one of your questions. I promise you. Right now, there are things we need to know about you, important things. We can only learn about them in Brussels. We've got a laboratory there where we can actually see what your mind sees. We need to explore your dreams further and find out just what's true about them and what isn't. We need to know what's causing them."

"I feel like a science experiment."

"You're quite unique Perkins. We've never had a time traveler before."

For once, Gotlieb seemed to let down his guard long enough to crack a smile.

"We need to know more about you, as much as we can anyway."

"Oh, great, and will you then take some tissue samples, put me in a cage and charge admission?"

"Please, old man, it's not like that. We just want to find out what's going on. Nobody's gonna hurt you. You have my word on that." Gotlieb replied.

"That's reassuring...." Ray remained skeptical.

"I'll tell you what. We'll continue your history lesson after we get you to Brussels. If what you say about those Rockoids is even partly true, we need to get that information to the authorities. Maybe we can even dig up some clues about what's happened to you. You'd want to know that, I guess." Gotlieb tried to reassure him once again.

"Of course. I'm still not convinced I won't wake up and find this is all a dream too."

"It's real, Perkins, trust me. Now come with us and we'll take you to Brussels. How's that sound, old man?" asked Gotlieb.

I always did want to take a trip to Belgium...I wonder if they still make decent beer.

Ray finally smiled, though reluctantly. "All right, Captain Gotlieb. I'll go. Lead the way!" Ray began to feel a little less hopeless.

As he started to get up, however, Gotlieb pushed him back down into the chair.

"Not so fast! We...well, we have to take a few precautions first."

"Precautions?"

Dr. Johnson took a strange-looking gun out of his pocket and aimed it at Ray.

Panic-stricken, Ray cried, "Wait! Wait a minute! You're going to shoot me now! Hold on! Stop..."

His military training helped him concentrate, as he looked for ways to overcome his captors, escape...go somewhere...anywhere...his paranoia, subdued in the last few moments as he began to come to terms with his situation, rose to the surface again. Sweat began pouring down his face, though he didn't care to wipe it away at the moment.

"Wait, wait. We're not going to hurt you." Johnson interjected.

"Yeah, and I suppose you shoot all of your visitors, right? Give me a break!"

"It's not like that," Gotlieb reassured him. "Relax, I told you already we're not going to hurt you. If we wanted to kill you, you'd be dead already."

"Yeah, that's reassuring..."

"Okay, this is a stun gun; it'll put you to sleep for a short while, that's all. At worst, you'll wake up with a little headache, but otherwise it's totally safe."

"Why am I not convinced?"

"Please, Captain Perkins, hear me out," Johnson replied.

"When we examine your brain, you're going to need to remain unconscious or else the process may cause serious damage to the cerebral cortex. Now if you'll just stand still, it won't really hurt at all."

"Now wait a minute! Do you really have to shoot something at me? I mean isn't there another way, like a sleeping pill, anesthesia or something?"

"I'm sorry, old man," Gotlieb said with a bit of regret. "We have our procedures, and you know a lot about many things—too much, in fact, and we have to act according to our own rules. I promise you...I assure you...it won't hurt a bit. You're just going to have to trust me. The stun gun is much less painful than a drug."

Ray sighed and stood at attention, closing his eyes to avoid looking at Gotlieb and the weapon. For a second, he almost wondered if they just wanted to kill him and not have to confront the reality of his existence. Out of sight, out of mind, Ray figured. Since he had already been to war, he assumed he could accept his death...

Ray remained lost in thought when the moment came.

Captain Gotlieb fired the gun. A green beam shot out from the weapon and struck Ray square in the head. Ray fainted, falling into the waiting arms of two of Dr. Johnson's assistants.

As Ray was transported across the world, he had no idea of the strange occurrences taking place in the dark depths of outer space...a series of events that would soon change his life and those of millions of his fellow human beings.

The massive egg-shaped vessel floated slowly through an uninhabited star system several hundred light-years from Earth. The enormous craft obscured a clear view of the small, grey planet behind it.

Suddenly a large opening appeared in the center of the vessel, conveying a dark, hollow emptiness to the onlooker. Five smaller oval ships, dwarfed into near insignificance compared to the larger ship, drifted slowly out of the opening. The small craft gained power and quickly flew off in the planet's direction; within seconds, the opening was sealed tight, with no evidence it ever existed.

The great ship that served as the flagship among this small fleet slowed down and finally stopped in space, hovering in a synchronous orbit around the planet. Instructions were sent back and forth among the members of the fleet, and the small spaceships finally landed on the planet's surface. A number of ground vehicles, circular, with thick wheels consisting of some sort of flexible material, stronger than rubber, spread out from the landed ships. The inhabitants within the vehicles were well protected from the hostile environment as they used various devices to take samples from the ragged surface beneath them.

About two timeframes later, the mineral-collecting fleet returned to the huge oval craft, each mining vessel packed with all sorts of precious natural resources.

The flagship remained in orbit. Finally, after several more timeframes, huge flashes of light appeared out of nowhere, each coalescing into an oval-shaped craft half as large as the flagship. In all there were ten of these cruisers, and as soon as they joined the orbiting craft, all but three, who were to stay behind and serve as backup, departed with courses set toward another uninhabited star system thought to have planets with vital resources.

Meanwhile, inside the flagship, Zanther, Empress of the Rockoid Empire, sat in her tapestry and jewel-bedecked throne room. She tapped her long, thin, delicate fingers on her throne, a large chair made of a shiny, dark red wood-like material that seemed almost absorbent to the touch.

Zanther's dark mood consumed her, as she paused to consider how her race had suffered at the hands of the evil marauders who killed millions of her people at a far-off colony world several kilo-timeframes ago.

While Zanther was not expected to display her emotions in public, inwardly she still mourned their deaths.

After several Earth years spent in a massive project to expand her race's war making machine, their sacred mission of vengeance was proceeding as planned, but she didn't delve upon the mundane issues of the troop and armament complement of her fleet, nor the tactical decisions she would soon have to make.

Instead, Zanther recalled the viewscreen images of powerful weapons systematically obliterating vast cities from existence. She thought of her father, the emperor, and her mother, who had, with her older brothers and sisters, gone to Dorton for a long period of recreation and meditation.

Those barbarians exterminated nearly all of her large family. Zanther and her only surviving brother were now alone, and she, the eldest, had become the ruler of her race, an authority that weighed heavily upon her after having been educated in the healing arts.

At times, Zanther found it difficult to reconcile her former role as a healer with her present role as a military leader who was expected to order the extermination of billions of living beings without passion or prejudice.

Her huge, dark, expressive eyes remained closed, and her hands gripped the armrests of her throne ever more tightly, perhaps hoping the pressure on her fingers would make the ache disappear. Zanther resisted the urge to take chemicals to lessen her pain, for she must remain alert and in command of her huge fleet. She took a few deep breaths and slowly started to calm down.

She began to think again, this time dispassionate, logical. Zanther was truly the warrior in heart and soul; she was ready for battle.

She knew it would be a completely unequal battle. The fleet of the humans and their fellow conspirators was not equipped to repel an attack of this magnitude.

It would be a revenge that, in the words of her defense minister, "would be one to savor." Yet Zanther could not help but fear the inevitable, that many of her own kind would also perish in the upcoming battle.

There were also nagging uncertainties that dulled her expectations of total success. There was little doubt the Alliance had detected the presence of her fleet by now. What sort of countermeasures would they devise?

Time after time, Zanther nearly aborted the campaign, ready to return home and attempt to resolve their differences on the negotiating table. This was the way their ancestors, in ages long past, settled disagreements with the lesser races of the galaxy.

However, that approach was obsolete; it was no longer the Rockoid way. Who was she to turn back? Would she not be regarded as a coward if she chose not to pursue this glorious battle? Would there not be chaos on her home world if its leader could not be depended upon to uphold the traditions of her race and the wishes of her ministers?

Another important variable complicated her decision: the presence aboard her flagship of Xorax, the Rockoid defense minister. Rockoid laws clearly dictated the defense minister must always accompany the emperor or empress during a major campaign.

Xorax was a member of a rival family that once ruled the Rockoid Empire many, many kilo-timeframes ago. There were growing suspicions he desired to usurp the throne and restore the glory of his now very small, but closely-knit family, as well as actively pursue their traditions of conquering other "inferior" races across the galaxy.

Despite all of her doubts, Zanther sent a telepathic message ordering her minister to convene a meeting to discuss the final battle plan before the next three hundred timeframes, equivalent to about one Earth month, had passed.

Her mind returned to thoughts of her dreams, frightening images of the night that conveyed the palpable presence of an outworlder, a human with whom she felt she was in contact, a mysterious sort of contact that existed deep within her subconscious.

The visions first revealed themselves right after the tragedy at Dorton. Those dreams could hardly be considered nightmares; they were so well detailed, she almost believed they were reflections of reality.

She tried so hard to suppress those sensations, those vivid dreams, yet as her fleet came ever closer to Earth, they suddenly intensified. At times she'd look around her, feeling that strange human stood right behind her, yet she knew nobody was there.

Try as she could, she couldn't banish those dreams from her mind.

Every single night Zanther would see that human male, the same person over and over again, involved in some strange, savage battle in an alien desert. She was quite sure the dreams were a sign that whoever this human was, he was trying to communicate with her.

She had a strange passing thought as the dreams intensified. Perhaps this human awaited her on Earth. She tried to look into his soul, but she didn't know if such a being, even if he existed, was capable of telepathic insights. Her intelligence operatives told her the humans didn't possess such abilities.

The remnants of these horribly vivid dreams continued to impinge themselves on her consciousness. Zanther couldn't keep silent any longer; she decided to speak with her counselor, the High Priest Yexin, about her concerns. She sent Yexin a telepathic summons to come to her throne room; he quickly strolled in a few minutes later.

The aged minister's wiry frame belied his great physical and mental strength. He wore the long, dark robes of his rank, but his jaunty gait and ever-present smile seemed to contradict the seriousness of his position and authority.

The top of his head was completely shaved in the fashion typical of the Rockoid male, and a fringe of thick, ruler-straight gray hair stretched from ear to ear, across the back of his head.

To him, the young Empress was like a daughter, for he had no family of his own. Yexin was also her late father's closest friend and confidant. He had dedicated his life to the teachings of the lore passed down by multiple deities that lay at the heart of the Rockoid religion. That, along with the burden of several previous failed marriages, reduced his enthusiasm for mating.

His already exaggerated grin broadened as he entered her chambers.

"Good evening, Empress Zanther. How are you feeling?"

Zanther smiled faintly back. "I can sum it up in one word, my friend: stress."

Yexin appeared puzzled as Zanther explained the dreams she had been having in the six Earth years that had passed since the battle of Dorton.

Yexin remained thoughtful for a moment. "Why have you not told me of this before?"

"Would you have believed me? I consulted the medical texts, and all they said was the symptoms were accounted for by stress and grief. I accepted both explanations. Yet the dreams persist, and now they grow stronger."

"My Empress, that is very strange. How and why these dreams could be appearing in your mind is a puzzle to me. But that is not the problem right now. You face one of the most important decisions of your young life."

"Yexin, I must know what is causing these dreams. I cannot let them haunt me or else they could endanger our campaign...."

"That is the point, Empress. You must not have doubts about this. You must keep uppermost in your mind the fact the Alliance attacked us first. We must seek vengeance, Empress."

Zanther tried to remind him, "Yexin, we did not always make war."

"They made war on us...."

"Is there not another way to resolve a conflict—the negotiating table, perhaps?"

"It is no longer our way."

"This human, I sense some of his thoughts; I feel he has a good heart."

"To think that way is forbidden; it could be interpreted as treason."

"Yexin," Zanther managed her glorious smile for a second. "I feel it."

"It is forbidden..."

"Perhaps Zeuther would have better served our people as emperor."

"Your younger brother is intelligent, crafty, a brilliant soldier. One day he will be ready to lead should Nerval-danai require it, but you are the chosen one, by right, and because there is nobody else in the Rockoid Empire who is better suited for the task."

"Oh, come now, Yexin, you do not need to flatter me thus. I love you as I loved my father; you have been with me since I first emerged from my mother's zanaka...." For a second Zanther couldn't continue, as tears filled her eyes.

"I came here by right of succession and nothing more," she finally managed with difficulty.

"Zanther, you combine Empress Zounar's beauty and compassion with Emperor Zikath's strength and wisdom, and, when you let it show, his sense of humor..." The old High Priest smiled his winning smile once again.

"Our people are counting on you to execute the war against the Alliance in the most efficient manner possible; they expect you to be merciless, to savor our inevitable victory. I trust that is what you will do. Am I correct?"

She sighed. "Correct, my dear friend."

Yexin smiled. "I will see you soon, Zanther. If you need me... you know I will be here."

The Empress smiled back.

Zanther touched Yexin's right and left shoulders gently with her open hands, the Rockoid custom for showing affection to a close friend.

The High Priest bowed slowly, respectfully, and left of the room.

Zanther felt increasingly tired. The sleepless nights, the concerns over the fateful decisions she must make; they all conspired to keep her in a near-exhausted state, despite the hours of intense meditation. She desperately needed some well-earned rest; she slowly removed her clothes and went into an adjoining room, where she took a quick shower in the huge, cylindrical bathroom. Finally, she put on her colorful but simple evening wear and was soon fast asleep.

Once Zanther's mind entered a state of slumber, the mysterious dreams returned, this time more intense than ever, still depicting the strange desert battle. However, the image that remained paramount was, once again, the handsome face of that human. She didn't want to believe it, but she feared this outworlder was becoming an obsession.

She was now more certain than ever he was trying to contact her, trying to tell her something.

Most important of all, she knew in her heart if she didn't find out what he was trying to say, a terrible tragedy might result...and her intuition was usually never wrong...

Chapter 7

R ay didn't learn about it until later, but while he was unconscious, his body was placed inside a hovercar and the entire
party zoomed off to an Alliance military base just outside of Brussels in the country formerly known as Belgium.

Less than an hour later, the vehicle landed in front of an impos-
ing-looking building, replete with multiple slim, metallic towers
with row upon row of huge windows. Ray was carried to a side
entrance and whisked away into an elevator, where he was transported to a huge room that very much resembled an operating
room.

Ray was gently placed upon a long white table. A team of men
and women in white lab coats attached his limbs to metallic straps
and conferred among themselves as to the next course of action.

"Why the hell did we bring Perkins here?" Gotlieb asked.
"Wasn't the cerebral scanner enough to show he was telling the
truth?"

"As I explained to y'all before, those scanners only give us part of the story, " explained Dr. Johnson. "We are field-testing a new generation of holographic mind probes in this laboratory."

Gotlieb stared in amazement, but said nothing.

"These holographic probes can actually replay what the mind experiences," Johnson went on. "That way we can observe precisely what Ray has seen and felt. Otherwise, we'll never know what's true and what isn't about this fellow's background."

Gotlieb took a long, skeptical look at the huge lenses poised at the ceiling of the laboratory.

"You sure these lasers won't mess with his brain?" he asked.

"Of course not. As long as the lasers aren't kept on for too long, we can scan Ray for several hours with no damage at all," replied Dr. Johnson. He smiled in his usual twisted, craggy fashion.

Gotlieb glared at him, never feeling comfortable in Johnson's presence. Too many things had happened in the past, when he was still serving under Johnson in the Alliance's military forces, things he was loath to forget.

Johnson pressed a few buttons on a touchscreen, turned a few handles, and pulled down a few switches, after which a hole opened up on the right side of the table. From this opening emerged a thin, oval-shaped device that was so tiny it could not even be seen with the human eye unless one was looking right at it. The device slid into Ray's right ear and disappeared.

"This probe will scan his brain and retrieve the information from his memories, which will be translated on the viewscreen in a form we can understand—images and sounds. Even though the probe will pass through his ears and brain, there shouldn't be any danger to his health unless he wakes up. Of course if he wakes, the probe would threaten his life. If he survived, he'd probably suffer serious brain damage," explained Johnson.

"Dr. Johnson, are you sure there isn't some other way to do this? I mean, I know you've done this before, but I don't want this guy to get killed here!" protested Gotlieb in an increasingly worried fashion.

As much as he detested Johnson personally, Gotlieb never

hesitated to look in wonder at the man's accomplishments. For years, Johnson had been a top commander in the Alliance military forces. On the side, almost as a hobby, he'd also managed to become a well-known scientist who devoted his attention to all sorts of cutting-edge technology. Although he continued to hold a military rank, he preferred to be referred to as head of the Alliance's military research division.

Johnson quickly assuaged Gotlieb's worries. "Don't you worry David; there is a ninety-nine percent chance he won't wake up during the scan."

"What about the other one percent?" sneered Gotlieb.

"Don't be sarcastic! If he starts to wake up, we'll know it. There will be plenty of time to render him unconscious again. Now let me continue with this operation. I don't want this fellow harmed any more than you do, David. Y'all just gonna have to trust me!" Johnson shouted.

"All right, all right! Please continue."

Trust, sure. Why should I trust you, you old bastard?

Without a moment's hesitation, Dr. Johnson announced to the machine, "Engage, function B2, security scan Delta."

There were a few blinking lights on the instrument panel, as the computer verified Dr. Johnson's voice scan. A soft female voice intoned, "Request acknowledged."

Ray remained unconscious and passive as the experiment began.

"The probe should reach the center of his brain in one to two minutes!" exclaimed Johnson excitedly. One would have been surprised to learn that the scientist had run this process on hundreds of patients over the years, yet never ceased to be amazed at the sort of information the scan extracted from a human's brain.

The scanning machine, in its original form, was not a product of Earth technology. It had been developed centuries ago by a humanoid race in the far reaches of the galaxy, and the technology had spread through a number of different cultures.

Exactly a minute after the probe entered Ray's ear, a three-dimensional image of his memories began appearing on the large viewscreen at the rear of the room. Dr. Johnson studied the data carefully, rapt attention on every detail. He pressed a few buttons to navigate through the thought display, in a fashion hardly different than one might navigate from one page to another in a document on a computer.

"Oh my God! I've never seen anything like this! You should see this, David! It's just amazing!" exclaimed Johnson, for once sounding almost friendly towards Gotlieb.

Gotlieb looked over at the screen. His eyes opened wide in astonishment when he saw the audio and visual representation of Ray's thoughts.

It seemed as if they had journeyed to Earth's past. Johnson scanned through the images being retrieved, and he saw ancient ground vehicles, primitive air carriers, and homes and large buildings made from wood, brick and mortar. The scenes that unfolded before them, with pictures and sounds, were so real, they could almost feel they were party to the events. The multi-dimensional images seemed to dance in front of the screen. The sounds displayed an incredible level of detail, way beyond what contemporary audio systems could produce in a movie theater.

Johnson's attention remained rapt, unwavering, as he examined what Ray saw in his dreams about the battle between the Alliance and the Rockoids.

The huge Rockoid cruisers and the relatively small Alliance warships fired multicolored beams in every single direction, sometimes even hitting "friendlies." They were even more astonished to hear the loud thunder of huge engines speeding through space. The effect was particularly troubling because everyone knew sounds couldn't be heard in space. Was it a construct of Ray's subconscious mind? Most likely, but it was indeed a strange effect, adding to the enigma unfolding before Johnson and Gotlieb.

The conflict continued, lasers flying in every direction, fighters desperately scrambling to avoid destruction by a barrage of firepower coming from either the huge Rockoid ships or the Alliance cruisers.

The battle continued for several minutes. Suddenly one of the Rockoid cruisers, which had been under fire for quite some time, exploded, blowing debris in several different directions. The force of the explosion created sufficient momentum to knock the other two Rockoid warships off course.

While three of the Alliance cruisers chased after the retreating Rockoid warships, the rest stayed behind and began bombarding the surface. As city after city was vaporized, Johnson swore he could hear the screams of millions of dying Rockoids, sending a chill right up his spine. Worse, the troubling implications of how this battle started were simply impossible to believe. Johnson struggled to dismiss what he saw as a fabrication of the mind of Ray Perkins, but nevertheless he had his doubts.

"Speak of this to nobody, Captain Gotlieb." he ordered without allowing time for a response. "It contradicts everything we know about the incident at Dorton. It can't be true. His unconscious mind is obviously creating this impossible spin on the conflict... Just remember what you learned at the academy. Bury an unacceptable theory until you have further evidence, unless it is critical to the survival of the Alliance."

Gotlieb nodded, his own doubts far more difficult to assuage. He stared, motionless, stunned, disbelief filling his tear-stained eyes. He wanted to cover his eyes and ears, stop the flow of such treasonous images, yet they were too compelling, too real to dismiss out of hand.

Soon those awful death cries become unbearable and Johnson found it almost impossible to continue the brain scan, when the gorgeous face and body of that Rockoid woman appeared on the screen, hovering almost motionless in space. She was even more beautiful than Ray had described. The very sight of her violet eyes and exquisite form kept Gotlieb and Johnson glued to the screen for a long, silent moment.

The Rockoid female's face bore an almost content expression before an expression of deep anguish took control. Her mouth started to open wide, tears flowing down her cheeks, and...everything went black.

Johnson felt deeply troubled by what he saw, even though he forced himself to ignore the implications of some of those battle scenes. For three decades, since the end of the last horrible conflict with the shark-like Jintorian race, the people of the Alliance had lived in peace. That tragic conflict surely soured the desire of humanity and its allies to fight new wars.

The five long, painful years of the Jintorian War left dozens of worlds in complete devastation, and others in economic and social disarray. A number of planets had still not recovered; the war's effects lingered for decades.

When the bitter end of the war came at last, the Alliance's painful journey to peace and prosperity seemed to have reached its fitful climax.

As a decorated veteran of the war, which claimed the lives of his father and many of his friends, Johnson experienced first-hand the conflict's awful aftermath. It cemented his cold-hearted attitude toward his military obligations.

It was that attitude that also made him dislike some of the young recruits from what he considered "privileged backgrounds" who later came under his command. He especially resented a young hotshot ensign, a recent graduate from the Alliance academy, by the name of David Gotlieb.

His thoughts returned to the present, and Johnson announced to the computer, "Experiment ended."

The computer's voice responded, "Request acknowledged." The beams slowly diminished in intensity, and soon vanished. Ray continued to sleep, a restless, fitful sleep.

Gotlieb looked skeptically at Johnson. "All right, sir. You can't hide anything from me any longer. You told me this battle was an 'isolated' incident resulting in relatively few causalities for both sides. What we've just seen from Perkins' dream totally contradicts what you said."

Johnson smiled a lame smile. "Okay, David, I suppose you might as well know the truth."

Gotlieb frowned at the old scientist, but waited patiently for his explanation.

The scientist sighed. "I know you're probably going to be upset when I tell ya this, David, but this wasn't just some isolated incident. Based on the reports from the Alliance ships present at the battle and the intensity of the firepower they were delivering, it seems entirely possible we inflicted as many as ten million causalities on the Rockoids in a matter of hours...the actual figure may be even more than that, but we never confirmed an exact total...."

"What the hell...why wasn't I told?" Gotlieb demanded.

"Don't you ever read your briefing papers?"

"Since I retired, I've been putting it off...."

Johnson didn't have the patience to explain the information was strictly on a need to know basis and he personally overruled the request that Gotlieb be informed about the incident, figuring he planned to retire anyway, regardless. That's what his wife and kid wanted, and he would be happy to be rid of that privileged pest. Now things had changed, and the situation had become critical. He was reluctant to give the order, but there was no other way. He knew too much already, and now it was time to act.

"I'm very sorry, we have to get you up to speed, David. You're going to be recalled."

He paused a second before he continued in an almost matter-of-fact fashion, "I've talked to the Secretary of Defense. The President will have to make the final decision on what to do next. I'm sure he'll want to talk with you soon, David."

"Goddamn it! You never miss an opportunity to screw up my life!"

Johnson glared at him. "You know your duty, soldier." He said nothing more. Gotlieb just glared back.

Despite Gotlieb's efforts to forget the endless conflicts with his old commander, they managed to bubble to the surface whenever the two men were forced to work together.

Finally, though, Gotlieb won at least one part of the argument when Johnson agreed that only the President had the final authority to make a decision on this matter.

Johnson added, "This character needs to be watched—he may be up to no good."

"Sir, you've subjected him to every known mental probe in the universe, and he's come up smelling like a rose."

"I don't care—maybe those goddamn Rockoids sent him here as a mole."

Gotlieb groaned. "Not that again."

"All right, all right. Remember, we still can't be entirely sure whether he's a spy or not. We have to watch him every moment of the day. Now we have a lot of work ahead of us."

The scientist strolled briskly out of the room.

Gotlieb knew what he had to do next. He voiced a few soft commands on his wristview that opened up certain security channels. Within seconds, the dark-skinned visage of President Ethan Rogers appeared in full view on the tiny screen.

The president had already been briefed on the strange tale of the man who claimed he came from the twenty-first century. It didn't take much for Gotlieb to convince him to set Ray up in a high-security presidential suite at the White Palace, the same building where important diplomatic visitors were housed during their visits to Brussels.

President Rogers couldn't conceal his skepticism about the whole screwy episode. "Listen, David, we don't know the full story here. So I am going to put a twenty-four hour security detail on him and monitor his every move. He won't even so much as blow his nose without our people knowing what came out and where he put it!"

Gotlieb laughed at his old friend's perverse sense of humor.

"No problem, Mr. President. I'll make all the arrangements."

"Very good, David. For the time being I have to call you back to active duty...."

"Come on, Mr. President, I already put in my twenty years...."

"Don't you worry, David. It's only for the duration. You're not the only one. I may have to call many more of the reserves back to duty as well."

"I don't want to sound insubordinate, Mr. President, but that doesn't reassure me."

Rogers laughed heartily. "Don't you, worry, Captain Gotlieb, I'll have you back at your comfy little police station soon enough. I need someone I can trust at the head of the security detail. Once

Perkins is comfortable, bring him to me. I want to talk with him."

With noticeable reluctance, Gotlieb nodded and switched off his wristview. He sat sadly for a moment and wondered what he'd tell his wife. Would she understand? He did tell her he had to remain in the reserve for ten years as a condition for early retirement; that he could be recalled to active duty at any time. Susan would probably understand—like hell she would! He wasn't too happy at the prospect of dealing with her anger.

* * *

While Ray remained unconscious, Johnson and Gotlieb transported him by hover ambulance to a ninety-two-story tower situated in the northeast quadrant of Brussels. It was here the president and his family lived for three months of every year. During that time, the building not only housed the presidential quarters, but his offices and those of his personal aides as well. Ten large dining centers were used for receptions to honor alien ambassadors and other diplomatic visitors. Hundreds of secured hotel rooms were set aside to provide safety and comfort for the many visitors to the city. There were dozens of restaurants with both Earthly and alien cuisine and shopping centers, both of which were visited often by tourists. Every nook and cranny of the large structure was monitored with state-of-the art security systems. In addition, a force of hundreds of officers patrolled the building day and night. Thousands of additional troops were housed in nearby dormitories, in the event military action was required.

If Ray had been awake when he arrived there, he probably would have been astonished at the differences and similarities between the White Palace and the twenty-first century architecture with which he was familiar. Unlike the few buildings he'd seen so far, this one had a classic design, in some ways similar to a skyscraper from his time, except for its smooth, circular shape, which tapered gradually towards the summit. The variety and scope of the other structures in the city were even more amazing. Yet Ray slept on, oblivious to the magnificent sights and sounds around him.

Ray arrived at his quarters in the hotel shortly after midnight.

Although the effects of the stun gun had long since worn off, he was exhausted and he slept on.

During the trip, Gotlieb called his wife, and tried to mollify her without much success. Susan yelled at him for betraying her, she began to weep, but finally began to accept his situation. "How long is this going to take? What's this all about?"

"Sorry, honey, it's all classified. You know the score. The president says it'll only be for a short time, a few weeks at most, I'm sure," he lied. "We'll still be able to take those two weeks on Drevin. Now you take care, and I'll call you back as soon as I can. Talk to you later, honey."

She couldn't resist getting in the last word. "David, I thought Ethan was your friend. Why is he doing this to us?"

Gotlieb shrugged. There was no way to win that argument. He just repeated his promise to return as soon as possible

They said their good-byes, but Gotlieb wasn't so self-assured. He had been personally recalled to active duty by the Alliance President, and he knew his old friend would only do that to him in times of emergency. And it might take a lot longer to resolve than anyone expected.

Chapter 8

The next afternoon, Ray regained consciousness. He took a moment to admire the large hotel room in which he lay before he noticed the pretty red-haired woman standing before him. She wore casual clothing. Ray stared at the woman with feelings of astonishment, for she looked hauntingly familiar.

"Where am I?" Ray asked groggily.

"You're in one of the best suites in the White Palace! I'm sure once you're awake you'll get a kick out of it," the woman replied.

"White Palace? What's that?" Ray asked, this time less groggily.

"That's where the Alliance President lives, and you're in it," explained the woman.

"Who are you? You're not..." The thought left him as quickly as it came. Barely awake, Ray felt he was about to lose consciousness again. He later learned even a single stun gun blast sometimes had such lingering effects.

"My name is Major..." she started to say, but Ray fell asleep again before she finished.

"See you later, Captain Perkins," whispered the woman. She stood there, smiled and admired the sleeping man for a moment longer.

She walked over to the door, which slid open as soon as she approached it, and almost sauntered out of the room. Once she was a few meters away, the door slid shut behind her. She nodded to a couple of sentries who stood outside Ray's room.

She strolled off to a waiting elevator at the end of the hallway, hardly trying to conceal the mischievous grin on her face.

* * *

After falling asleep again, Ray did not experience any dreams about the horrible battle in space between the Rockoids and the Alliance at first. He actually smiled in his sleep. Perhaps because the dreams hadn't returned or maybe it was because of the lovely woman who stood before him as he had briefly awakened.

As quickly as they left, though the dreams returned, and Ray noticed one added wrinkle. They were more vivid than ever, so intense he was even more convinced he was actually witnessing a real event.

The dream began, as usual, in space, above the alien world. Everything proceeded as before. As the Alliance warships began bombarding the planet relentlessly, the Rockoid woman's face appeared, first in the background, then seemingly suspended above the conflict, as if she was an observer of the proceedings.

Once again, she appeared content before her expression turned to one of deep anguish, which Ray felt yet again. If she were only real...if he could only reach out...comfort her...

Zanther, what do you want from me? He was about to shout her name aloud, in the vain hope she'd hear him, but stopped as the words were about to leave his lips.

It took several minutes before his rapid breathing and heartbeat slowed to normal. His hoarse voice convinced him that he had been shouting out loud in his sleep.

Despite its intensity, he didn't ponder the meaning of the dream for long before he realized he was very hungry. The last thing he had eaten was a sandwich and coffee, and that was a couple of lifetimes ago, at least according to the calendar. Of course to him, the actual passage of time consisted of just a few days.

Now that he was awake he was able to see all the appliances, machines, and furnishings in the room. The bedroom looked almost like the ones he'd seen in a very fancy hotel room of the twenty-first century except for one change; there was no TV, nor any device he could recognize as being one.

He didn't know how one checked out the latest news. Did anybody still read a newspaper? He really believed he would be able to find a TV screen of some sort. Perhaps if he looked harder...all he could find was the large windowpane providing an extraordinary view of the huge city in which he was staying.

He wanted food more than he wanted the latest news, so he looked for a room service menu. A large circular table with three silver-clad metallic chairs around it lay in the middle of the room.

Ravenously hungry, he practically tore apart the suite, trying to find a menu. He reached into drawers and was surprised to find they slid open at the touch. There was not a hint of a menu anywhere, nor did he find the usual colorful brochures and stationery he expected to see in a luxury hotel.

Finally, he gave up, and put everything back where it was supposed to be.

An idea came to Ray's mind. He walked to the front door of his room and gave it a quick examination. In addition to the entrance, two doorways were located to his left, equidistant along the walls. The first, a sliding door like the entranceway, led to the bathroom, which had a sink of fairly conventional appearance, but no bathtub. The only thing he found that might be a shower was a large chamber with a curtain.

Ray felt dirty, grimy. He hadn't washed in two days and figured this was the best opportunity as any to do so.

He could probably wait just a little longer to satisfy his hunger.

He took off his dirty clothes, threw them carelessly to the side, and stepped into the shower. Inside he found the enclosure not terribly different from the ones he used back in the twenty-first century. There was one major difference; it responded to voice commands, a characteristic he discovered purely by chance when he started asking questions aloud. Once clean and newly alert, he searched around and found a closet containing a whole wardrobe that fit him perfectly. Clearly this room had been carefully prepared for his benefit.

Now we're getting somewhere.

Ray chose a matching set of blue shirt and pants, and the same shiny black gloves and boots he had seen everyone wearing at the Area 51 Shopping Mall.

Once dressed, Ray set to work finding something to eat. He checked out the second door, which led to a small kitchen-like area.

Inside the room, he found a large wall-mounted screen that resembled a TV monitor. A rectangular device covered with a glass-like door lay below it, something that vaguely resembled a large microwave oven, but without timer or other accessible controls.

He looked around, but he could not find a refrigerator, pantry, or any other conventional repository of food. He commenced to panic; he was so hungry.

Ray got a crazy idea, something from a TV show. It had always worked there, whether the starship's occupants wanted a cup of tea or a full-course meal.

He finally decided what he wanted most was an old-fashioned Southern meal. He felt awkward, stating his request aloud, to nobody in particular, casually giving a long list of his culinary preferences. Not a single detail was omitted; Ray wanted to put this strange device to the ultimate test.

He waited...but not for long.

After about a minute, a light appeared in the transparent chamber. Seconds later, the chamber opened, and a large serving tray slid out. His meal was placed neatly on the tray, precisely as ordered.

A large plate was stuffed with piping hot fried chicken, black-eyed peas, and okra. Ray admired it with great astonishment, noticing the faint glimmer of steam rising from what appeared to be a sumptuous meal. Several pieces of corn bread were neatly placed on a small plate and beside it, a tiny cup with a butter-like substance in it. Next to the tray, Ray saw a full set of silverware and cloth napkins.

He grabbed the tray, left the kitchen and sat down at the table. As he tried the food, amazed that it tasted so right, so perfect, almost as good as any home-cooked meal he'd ever tasted. Then again, he was so hungry, he figured almost anything would delight his senses.

Ray downed the meal eagerly, leaving nary a crumb in the plate. Yet something was missing.

He returned to the kitchen, coming out seconds later with a large plate of peach pie.

As he downed the first bite of his dessert and savored its luscious flavor, the entrance slid open. Dr. Johnson and Captain Gotlieb walked in, nonchalantly, as if they had been invited. "Would you mind? I'm trying to finish my meal!" Ray shouted angrily.

"Sorry, but we have a very important matter to attend to," apologized Johnson.

"What kind of experiment are you planning for me this time?" Ray asked, his voice laced with sarcasm, as he lifted his fork into his mouth for a second bite.

"No, no more experiments," Gotlieb replied seriously. "President Rogers wants you at Alliance Headquarters immediately."

Gotleib's face looked stern; his eyes seemed to stare right through Ray. The latter thought the anger was directed toward him. He didn't learn until later that Gotlieb had just engaged in another loud argument with Johnson and was still trying to recover his composure.

Thinking the stare was related to something he'd done wrong, Ray gasped, nearly choking on his food.

Ray took a deep breath and sat down with a confused, quizzical look on his face.

Chapter 9

Ray remained wary of leaders, whether of companies or governments. He recalled all the difficult negotiations he'd made with his software publisher, how the greedy so-and-sos fought him tooth and nail over every penny when they worked out a royalty agreement. He recalled how the military establishment abandoned him when he was hospitalized. It seemed like he didn't exist.

A government leader? He'd only seen those from the back of a meeting room or on TV. He had never met anyone more powerful than a member of his state legislature and was taken aback, clearly stunned.

"What? Why me?" Ray exclaimed, still in near shock.

"We showed him the video of your interrogation and then a report of the 'Brain TV' probe we performed on you…he was very interested…to say the least," explained Johnson.

Ray looked around his room, hoping this was all just a bad

dream. Gotlieb and Johnson were insistent.

"Listen, I've never met the president of anything...." Ray exclaimed, sounding agitated.

"Here's your chance to meet one. Don't worry about your dessert. You can take it with you," said Gotlieb.

Gotleib's smile seemed to return, as he began to forget the tension of his ongoing dispute with Johnson.

Ray put down his fork, grabbed a napkin, and hurriedly, clumsily, wrapped up what was left of his pie, trying to grab a quick bite before he sealed it. He got up, package in hand, and said, "Let's be off."

* * *

Ray, Gotlieb, Johnson, and a contingent of security guards, were transported to the local Alliance headquarters by hover-limousine, a bizarre looking vehicle that, like its twenty-first century counterpart, had a stretched cab containing two extra rows of seats. The trip wasn't exactly pleasant. Ray still wasn't quite accustomed to the rapid bursts of acceleration one had to deal with when riding in these contraptions; his stomach was tied up in little knots. After a few minutes, the feeling of impending nausea passed and his stomach settled. He clung to the napkin containing his dessert, but didn't feel inclined to tempt the fates to consume it during this unsettling ride. Ray didn't want to dirty the upholstery; he imagined how Gotlieb might react if he vomited on him. The thought was enough to bring a faint smile to his lips.

Once Ray recovered, his gaze stayed glued to the windows, watching the various sights in the city of Brussels, which were simply amazing.

He saw buildings shaped like corkscrews, long rectangular structures stretching almost to the city limits, tall, thin skyscrapers that must have been two hundred stories high dominating the city's spectacular skyline. He saw literally hundreds of buildings of all shapes, sizes, and colors, with no time whatever to dwell on any single, incredible detail.

All the images had nothing to do with the pictures he had seen of twenty-first century Brussels. He wasn't surprised: so many other things seemed to have changed in the past two centuries. He wondered for a moment about his friends and family...they were gone for good. At best, he might locate one of their descendants. His eyes misted over a bit. Ray had never really come to grips emotionally with the strange feeling of being a time traveler...of being taken from his home, his life.

Then again, it wasn't much of a life. More often than not, he found himself cooped up in his home writing computer games. Occasionally, he felt like a hermit, or a prisoner, and longed for a change.

That change had come, all right, though not quite in the form he expected. Maybe they had counselors here who could help him cope, but for now he had to rely on his own wits.

Before he had a chance to sit back and make a half-hearted attempt to enjoy the trip, the limo landed again, the seat belts were released, and he was able to exit the vehicle.

"We're here," said Gotlieb as Ray stepped out with a feeling of great relief. "I guess we're gonna have to put that leftover pie in the fridge till you're done." Gotlieb smiled broadly.

Ray realized they were standing in front of one of the tall, cork-screw buildings he had seen in the distance from the White Palace.

Ray did not have any more time to gaze in awe at this fine example of architecture. With barely a pause, the entire group walked briskly to the building and hurried inside. Ray couldn't stop for a moment, lest he be pushed inside by the men, women and aliens who surrounded him.

As he walked on, Ray wondered if the security detail was part of standard operating procedure for visitors to the president or strictly to keep tabs on him. He still wasn't certain if they regarded him as a prisoner or guest. Gotlieb's attitude, however, seemed much friendlier since they picked him up at the hotel. *Maybe there's hope for me yet.*

When they walked inside, Ray noticed the surroundings seemed somewhat dark and dreary compared to the bright, cheerful decorations he'd seen at the hotel. Everything in the lobby was medium gray except for the well-kept potted plants at the sides of the front door, and the fine marble desk where what Ray presumed to be a secretary was working.

They walked over to the woman, who seemed totally human in appearance, with tightly coiffured blonde hair, and, for a change, a relatively short skirt revealing shapely legs. She looked up a few seconds later from her viewscreen, stared for a second, and stood up, flashing a professional smile.

"Ah, you must be here to see President Rogers. One of his advisors should be down here any minute to escort Captain Perkins, Captain Gotlieb, and Dr. Johnson to his office. The rest of you will remain here until the meeting has ended."

Amazing! How did she know his military rank? It seemed as if everybody around here recognized him, leaving Ray with a feeling of extreme discomfort. He always maintained a low profile and resented being an object of attention, even when his computer games became successful and he was widely sought after for public appearances.

He paused to ponder. Obviously they had consulted his military record while he was asleep. That was both good and bad. Good they knew he was for real, bad they probably learned about all his mental problems. Ray realized he had probably revealed many of his innermost secrets during those strange interrogation sessions, although he wasn't consciously aware of much of what occurred.

At that moment, an elevator across from the secretary's desk opened. Someone in a dark gray suit, which blended perfectly into the drab surroundings, stepped out of the elevator and came toward them.

As he came closer, Ray noticed his skin appeared to have a greenish tint to it; it looked slimy. For a second, Ray imagined this person was wrapped from head to toe in alligator skins, but upon closer examination he realized it was the being's natural skin texture.

The being came up to them, shaking each visitor's hand in turn. When Ray accepted the handshake, he noticed it felt as slimy and scaly as he had speculated.

"I am Korflen, President Rogers' chief advisor. He is expecting you. Come with me, please." The creature's voice had a slight sibilant quality to it. It also appeared that he struggled to pronounce his words perfectly, as if English was not his native tongue.

They followed him into the elevator, which closed as soon as they entered. Korflen announced, "Floor ninety-four, please."

Ray sensed his stomach lifting as the elevator climbed. He wondered how he'd ever get used to these abrupt stops and starts that seemed part and parcel of travel in this strange age.

A few seconds later, the doors opened, and they stepped out into a beautiful marble hallway that, to Ray, was a relief from the dark and dreary lobby. The thick white carpet seemed almost silky in sheen. Along the sides of the hallway, he occasionally saw potted plants, and a number of portraits lined the walls. Ray got just a brief glance at the pictures; he guessed they were probably all government officials of one sort or another.

Finally, they reached a brown door at the end of the hall, which opened when they approached, as if it anticipated the precise moment of their arrival.

When they reached the door, Gotlieb and Johnson stepped aside. Both men had smiles on their faces, and Ray was quick to pick up on their changing attitudes. Up until now, there was a decided tension between these two.

Korflen announced (it seemed almost like a command), "Enter."

"What? You mean the president wants to see me alone?" Ray protested, sounding very surprised.

"Yes, he does. He has some very important matters to talk to you about. He wants to have...what do your people call it...ah yes, a heart-to-heart conversation with you," explained Korflen.

"Now, isn't that peachy...." Ray gave a sickly sort of smile.

He stepped inside the open door and saw the president's office. The wall was plain marble, similar to what he had seen outside. There were potted plants scattered around, some familiar, others both strange and wonderful. He learned later they were imports from other Alliance worlds.

There were tables, chairs, and sofas, all clad in a shiny mahogany-tinged wood-like substance that seemed to emit a strange, unearthly glow. The room was large enough to accommodate at least twenty or thirty people, making it ideal for a conference among government leaders.

At the rear of the office was a large brown desk where someone was seated with his back toward him. The individual was apparently looking at a large, flat screen on the left side of the wall.

"Mr. President?" he asked.

"Hello, Captain Perkins! Come and sit down!" exclaimed President Rogers in a deep, enthusiastic voice. He muttered "Screen off," and the screen went blank.

Ray sat down in a convenient brown leather chair in front of the desk. He noticed it was extremely comfortable, and it seemed to adjust itself perfectly to his physical form. He almost felt relaxed, despite the nagging nervousness that began to overwhelm him.

The president turned around in his chair to face Ray. He looked for the most part like a normal African-American male, but there were several noticeable differences. His forehead bore a noticeable prominence with little ridges on it, and his fingers were longer and thinner than those of most humans.

Rogers was used to dealing with visitors. He was a gracious host with a warm smile, and Ray began to feel at ease as his host asked, "So how are you doing, Captain Perkins? How are you enjoying life in the future?"

As he spoke, Ray began to realize the motions the president's lips made when he talked were not synchronized with his voice. Ray thought for a second about the poorly dubbed kung fu movies he once liked to watch on Saturday mornings. Ray quickly responded to the president's question.

"I guess I like it here, but it's not easy to get used to. So much has changed. I guess I shouldn't be surprised, but I wish people would let me ask some questions. It seems like everyone wants something from me."

Rogers just nodded with an expression of casual understanding, as Ray paused, thinking that he might as well ask the question uppermost in his mind. "Look, I don't want to sound insulting or anything, Mr. President, but why don't your words and the movements of your mouth match?"

"Do not worry, Captain, I take no offense at all. English is not my native language, nor is any Earth tongue. You are hearing my words translated by a special language translation device. We had one fitted to you while you slept."

Ray looked up with a start, and started feeling around for some sign of the strange device.

Rogers laughed. "It's embedded in your skin behind your right ear. Not to worry, it won't bite, unless it gets hungry."

He laughed again.

Oh, no, now we have a president who thinks he's a comedian.

Ray probed his fingers nervously around his ears, managing to find a small bump around the back of his right ear, barely detectable. It was covered over with skin. *Amazing!*

"It's a great system. It's managed by a set of central computers, interfacing with each one of these little receivers. With the translator, I can converse in my native language and you in yours. We both understand each other. I do speak English, of course, but I am more comfortable speaking the language of my home world."

Ray took another look at the man's obvious alien appearance. The president smiled, and Ray saw his mouth contained more teeth than an Earth person's, each smaller sized. The smile was open and friendly.

The president said, casually, "Perhaps I should tell you a little more about myself. I was born on the planet Taucon in the Tau Ceti star system.

"It's an M-type planet about one and a half times Earth size, with somewhat higher gravity. It's located only about twelve light-years from here, less than a day's journey from Earth with our current technologies. My father was from Earth, and my mother was a member of the Cettian ruling ministry. Perhaps some day you will have the chance to pay a visit. If you like skiing, Taucon has some of the best slopes in the galaxy."

"I would love to visit your home planet and give the slopes a try," Ray replied, not knowing if he wanted to experiment with space travel yet or if he even gave a damn about skiing. He had so far managed to completely avoid anything involving sprinting across mountain slopes.

All, right, Mr. President, I've had enough of your bedside manner. Can't you get to the point?

"Now, Captain Perkins, I'm sure you've been wondering why you were called to this meeting," said Rogers, who made a quick personality change from casual to serious.

"I expected we weren't here just to get acquainted," Ray said, forcing a smile.

Now we're getting to the nitty-gritty...

"I spent the better part of last night reviewing the results of the mind probe and watching that 'Brain TV' video of you. I have to say I had trouble getting to sleep after watching those pictures."

"I often wake up in cold sweats when those dreams happen."

Rogers smiled, displaying an apparent expression of genuine sympathy.

"You clearly have knowledge no normal person could have; we are concerned about that...very concerned. You know some very dangerous facts we have kept hidden under deep security, and even worse, we've just learned that a fleet of alien ships from an unknown world has begun to gather on the edge of Alliance space."

Ray's eyes revealed his shock. "Are we going to be invaded?"

"I honestly don't know, but I have to tell you we are gravely concerned. There was an incident on a far-off world, the same one you saw in your dreams, which raises questions about the fleet's motives."

He paused for a moment as if to consider something, and continued. "Before I tell you about it, though, I need to show you something. What you will see is top-secret. Only a dozen or so people in my administration have been given access to this information."

Ray wondered why they'd bother to show him something classified; could they have believed his crazy story all along while feigning skepticism?

Rogers reached into his desk and pulled out something that resembled a credit card, but it had no name, insignia, or numbers on either side of it.

"This video flashcard is almost like an optical disc from the twenty-first century, except it can hold far more information and has much better quality when seen on one of our viewscreens. It can even display three-dimensional images. You are going to see a video that was taken by one of our scout ships near one of the Alliance's border outposts."

He slipped the card into a slot behind his desk, and a large color image of a small, grey planet practically leaped right out of the wall.

Suddenly a dark gray mass filled the screen, covering the planet behind it. Ray sat there dumbfounded as the reality of his dreams stood in bold relief before him...a massive, oval Rockoid super cruiser.

"It's the Rockoids," he whispered, barely audibly. Sweat started to pour from his forehead now, and he began to move his hands nervously.

"Yes, I know," replied Rogers calmly.

Rogers seemed to hesitate for a second before explaining himself, "About five years ago, one of our most decorated military leaders, General Elizabeth Thompson, discovered a colony of intelligent humanoid creatures in the Dorton system about 7,000 light-years from Earth while wrapping up a routine mapping expedition. This was part of the final stage of a two-year-long mission of exploration with her crew on the heavy cruiser *Star of Terra*. Seven other heavy cruisers and two battleships, the *Acclaim* and the *Reliant*, which arrived for the last leg of the mission, were to be tested in various situations, including combat if necessary, to see if they were ready to be mass produced by the Alliance Fleet.

"While in orbit over the planet Dorton, General Thompson's command ship was targeted and fired upon by three large alien cruisers. In an effort to protect her ship and the rest of her small convoy, she vigorously defended her fleet from the merciless, unprovoked assault and managed to destroy the enemy.

"Her ship was also fired upon from the planet below. Thompson attacked the colony too, taking out several military instillations. Our ships were fortunate to escape with minimal damage and casualties."

Ray sat there almost dumbfounded. He had seen some of this battle in his dreams, all right, but something was definitely wrong.

Something about those dreams didn't quite jibe with the story the Alliance president delivered so matter-of-factly, but the memory was too hazy. Maybe all those stun gun beams or drugs they had pumped into him still affected his memory.

Ray still had the nagging feeling the Alliance ships attacked first! If his recollections were real and not fantasies, it could have staggering implications for both the Rockoids and the Alliance. These doubts raged on and off throughout the depths of his soul. If only he had proof one way or the other. Maybe his dreams would eventually reveal some key detail he could use as evidence.

He swore to himself, almost audibly, but the president didn't seem to notice. He'd have to check this out soon, because he believed they actually trusted him for some strange reason. Maybe they just wanted to give him a security clearance so he couldn't spill the—beams!

President Rogers hardly paused before continuing his narrative.

"Some of the alien invaders were captured after the battle and we were able to translate a small portion of their language and learn something about them. It appears the Rockoids have visited Earth a number of times over the past few centuries, without making official contact. In fact, some of their craft crash-landed here in the late 1940's. The pilots were taken to the top-secret military base at Area 51 you discovered before you entered a time warp."

Rogers paused. "In fact, we even have a picture of one of these Rockoids to show you. This one was barely alive when we took the photo.

"Display file forty-five, picture number one hundred seventy-five."

The picture Rogers requested appeared on the screen, a close-up shot of the face of a Rockoid female. Although the creature's eyes were shut, it looked almost like a perfect copy of that anguished woman in his dreams.

Ray did his best to conceal his shock—was the creature in that photo an ancestor of that glorious alien woman of his dreams?

"Then you know how I got here," Ray changed the subject.

"We do not understand the technology. We're only guessing the means of transportation because your military never succeeded in making any captured alien devices work. They hoped the machines could somehow be used to up the ante back during the Cold War in the early 1960's. When their efforts failed to bear fruit, they gave up on the project and sealed the chamber due to the potential threat of infiltration by the Soviet Union.

"We do know there was a strange explosion in Area 51 in the early twenty-first century and the research laboratory there was wrecked, almost beyond repair. It wasn't fully restored until years later."

Goddamn it. Ray thought. *It's true. And it's all my fault...*

"Does anyone know why I have been having those crazy dreams?" Ray tried to divert the subject from his own unwitting involvement in that episode, feeling incredibly guilty over what he'd done, even if by accident. He began to add up the charges: Breaking and entering into a top-secret government installation, vandalism and heaven knows what else. For a moment, he wondered why his hosts hadn't brought him here in chains.

"This is just guesswork from our scientists, so don't take what I'm going to say too seriously. We really don't understand all of it ourselves."

Again Ray had to calm down, convincing himself the Alliance president was really trying to help him figure out what happened. Maybe he could return the favor—that is, if he could ferret out the truth about the Dorton affair.

Ray's comfort was short-lived, as his suspicions bubbled to the surface again. Perhaps this president was a smarter political animal than Ray believed and was just playing along with him, gathering information that could be used against him later. Ray watched and waited, trying to appear to accept the situation without question, but inwardly remaining skeptical of the man's motives.

Rogers continued, oblivious to any outward signs of Ray's suspicions. "The news I have to give you may not be terribly pleasant. We have spent several years measuring the incredibly powerful mental wave patterns of these Rockoids. It appears they can communicate by telepathy. It may very well be that your mind has somehow tapped into those patterns and is in sync with them. I can't say how, but you may be sharing thoughts with one of these Rockoids.

"My scientific teams will try to figure out a real answer for you, if one is available. In any case, much of what you've seen and heard in your dreams is true."

Ray's mind filled itself with all sorts of contradictory thoughts, feeling both curious and disgusted to know he was reading the thoughts of an alien creature. What of his personal experiences and innermost thoughts? Was this other creature sharing them too?

Even stranger was the feeling of intense empathy with the Rockoid woman. She was alien, maybe their enemy, but Ray couldn't control his feelings.

And her face: so indescribably beautiful he couldn't help but have his fantasies about her. These contradictions confused him.

Sometimes when he thought of Zanther, he felt he could see into her heart, where he saw only compassion and deepest understanding. The look on her face; he could see she was one used to command. Perhaps she was a military leader of some sort...maybe he could contact her and arrange...*No, that's crazy...I really am going insane.*

Rogers interrupted Ray's train of thought. "As you can see, you know secrets never disclosed beyond the inner circles of the Alliance government and military. The information you have provided for us is extremely valuable. I would very much like for you to continue to help us. Unfortunately, we know no way of returning you to your own time. We have not perfected any method of time travel, although we have reason to believe the technology does exist, somewhere in the universe."

That pronounced hardly shocked Ray. He had already given up hope he would ever return to the past.

He also wondered about his girlfriend; he had hoped that that relationship would turn serious, and she did seem to like him a lot. No doubt she gave him up for lost quickly enough and found someone else. Ray wanted to feel sad, but instead he felt almost numb.

There was the glorious face of Zanther! Ray could see it again, for a second, almost as if she were there in the president's office watching them. He resisted the urge to turn around and check.

Finally Ray had to ask the question gnawing at his mind.

"Mr. President, look I know the laws in your century are different from mine, but why haven't I been arrested for what I did to that Area 51 laboratory? In my time, I'd be in irons now." Ray managed a weak chuckle.

"Rest assured, our laws are quite as stringent as yours, if not more so, in our century. As you might gather, the statute of limitations has long since past. We couldn't charge you for your crimes if we wanted to, and you may not believe this…"

Yeah, you can say that again!

"You were drawn to Area 51 for reasons we do not understand. It is more important for us to understand why, rather than punish you for something we think was really beyond your control."

"Listen, nothing personal, Mr. President. But I did get here somehow," he protested. "Isn't there a way to reverse this process? I still have a life waiting for back in the twenty-first century."

"I honestly don't know. We haven't done much experimentation in time travel. It has some nasty consequences, we fear. How do you account for someone who might change the past and all the events those changes affect? We're proceeding very cautiously."

"I guess I'm stuck here, eh?" Ray felt surprised there wasn't a trace of sadness in his voice. In fact, he seemed almost exhilarated at the turn of events. His past life had become almost boring, routine. Writing computer games had become a long, dreary, exhausting process. Even though it proved profitable, it was a profession he'd stumbled into accidentally, a consequence of his awful dreams. He was ready to try something new—although this wasn't quite the sort of "new" something he had expected.

The president didn't hesitate to spell out Ray's choices. "You have two options, Captain Perkins. One is to become a normal civilian and blend into our labor force and way of life. If you take that path, we will have to erase portions of your memory because you represent a great security risk based on the things you know. We will have to retrain you to a new profession that matches your specific skills. That step can be risky, though. You may lose important portions of your identity as well...."

"Ouch! That's not very encouraging!"

"You worked in intelligence. You know that all governments have leaks, and sometimes information gets into the wrong hands. Let me tell you there are means to get that information that are both painful and thorough. Nobody could withstand those attempts without proper preconditioning.

"You have a second choice, though. This is the one I hope you will accept. We'd like you to take a position in the Alliance military forces and work with us to deal with the impending arrival of the Rockoids. Your special insights will be valuable, indeed."

Ray didn't feel very comfortable at the threat of having his memory altered. Even if he accepted the alternative, could he possibly achieve the lofty goals this president set for him; could he possibly survive the training? Would he just die off in the process, lost in some staged accident and eliminated before he became a real threat to this Alliance?

Damn, I've got to stop being so paranoid! Why can't I just think people actually want to help me?

Rogers appeared to be the gracious host, accepting his guest's delay at reaching a decision—and it wasn't long in coming.

Ray smiled. "I suppose I really don't have a choice here...."

Rogers just nodded, giving a smug smile of his own in return.

"It won't be easy, though. Any member of our military forces must attend the Alliance naval academy for four years. In addition, you have a couple of centuries of history to catch up on. We need to acclimate you to our time and our way of life. It's going to be difficult, very difficult. We need to accelerate the training program so you can complete your studies in weeks rather than months. I've examined the historical records of your military experience, and I think you have a good chance of getting through the training with success."

"Thank you, sir. I'll do my best."

What choice did I have? Join them or have my mind vaporized!

"Excellent! I wish I could speak with you further, but I have some urgent appointments with my security staff. I'll be checking on your progress in the weeks to come and maybe we'll get together for another conference. Right now, we have to pack you off to London. It's getting late, and you have a long training session awaiting you there, tomorrow morning."

Ray sighed. He knew it would be a waste of time to hold out any hope for some extended rest and relaxation now.

As he left Rogers' office, an almost silly thought came to his mind: *I never did get to finish that peach pie!*

* * *

The military situation was considered normal at the Mars and Europa colonies. A low-level alert remained in force, due to the reports of the presence of Rockoid ships in Alliance space.

Millions of inhabitants, who had journeyed to these worlds from across the Alliance, went about their daily routines, working, playing, eating, and sleeping, unconcerned that they might be the targets of an attack by aliens.

The two colonies were quite similar in size and construction. All were marvels of twenty-third-century technology. Several large cities were spread across the two worlds, encased in huge domes, made of a clear but impenetrable alloy composed of special minerals discovered on a far-off Alliance world. Each city was completely self-contained, with atmosphere and artificial gravity fields created by fusion generators.

Inside the domes, every effort was made to make the residents feel at home. To provide maximum comfort and security for a variety of species, they opted to fashion the cities after the typical small New England town of mid-twentieth-century Earth. There was a central shopping district in each, where one could also find the town hall.

The local government consisted of a board of elected representatives of the inhabitants called "selectmen." Day-to-day affairs were overseen by a city manager, a hired hand working under the governor of the colony, who in turn reported directly to the main solar system authorities on Earth.

Sprawling shopping centers were located at the outskirts of each city, with merchandise imported from across the galaxy, to serve the needs of the diverse population.

Hovercars were employed for regional transport. Huge oval tunnels had been dug beneath the surfaces of Mars and Europa to connect one city to the next.

An immense central spaceport served the needs of travelers from other planets. Ships from both Earth's solar system and the Alliance worlds arrived there regularly. Although the colonies were designed for heavy industry, a growing number of tourists cherished the duty-free shops, red-light districts, and casinos set up by the local governments to keep their citizens from becoming bored with their daily routines.

The major income generators, though, were not tourism. The huge amounts of money spent to build these colonies came from industrialists who set up vast mines to extract the bountiful harvest of a hundred and one minerals.

As more and more minerals were recovered from the bowels of these worlds, the civilian work force was increasingly allocated toward local manufacturing. The specialty was transportation; spaceships on Mars and hovercars on Europa.

By far, the largest manufacturer was RECOM, the Alliance's number one military contractor. RECOM's Martian shipyard/outfitting facility had not only given a boost to the colony's income, but also increased the population by more than five times in the first seven years of its existence.

However, the Alliance's efforts to disarm its military after the end of the Jintorian wars struck RECOM hard. Production quotas dropped precipitously. A freeze was placed on hiring and many older workers were encouraged to take early retirement. The future didn't look terribly bright, as the need for instruments of war seemed to lessen with each passing day.

That all changed with the arrival of the Rockoid spaceships. The local RECOM plant managers had a mid-level security clearance because they needed to keep abreast of the military requirements for their hardware. They knew what was coming, and, despite the clear danger to friends and family, inwardly hoped a war in space would help revitalize their plants and restore their lucrative bonuses.

For now, the lives of the residents of Mars and Europa continued as if nothing was amiss. Adults went to work, children to school; religious services were still held every week or at whatever time was appropriate to a particular religion. For some unaccountable reason, though, attendance at religious services began to increase. Maybe the populace sensed something was coming that would require them to secure their faith.

If the threat that existed at the edge of Alliance space was real, their way of life would soon change—forever.

Chapter 10

The London skyline easily conveyed the impression the city was totally different from the one Ray recalled. He was amazed when he saw the futuristic scenery. In fact, he noticed Gotlieb had to fly a bit higher since some of the buildings were so tall. This city was far more inviting than Brussels if twenty-third-century architecture was in the realm of one's expertise. In fact, none of the city's major historic monuments remained, having largely been destroyed in the Third World War or demolished for reconstruction purposes later on.

He did not get the chance to admire the London skyline much longer, for the two men soon reached the city's center. Gotlieb's hovercar swooped down toward the ground and stopped at a parking stall in front of a large rectangular building with some sort of fighter plane on top of it.

"Here we are, old man!" announced Gotlieb.

The seat belts released, the doors opened and they stepped out.

Ray stared at the large building with astonishment.

He thought the Alliance Naval Academy would be something spectacular, a showpiece of the latest in architecture and construction techniques. Instead, the building had the classic design of a twentieth-first-century university, with a few transparent elevators at the four rounded corners of the structure.

The architecture itself was traditional, emphasizing large gray spires and enormous glass windows that revealed the classrooms within. Dull and drab was a fitting label.

Ray looked long and hard for a signpost to indicate the purpose of the structure, but found none. There were no signs anywhere.

They walked into the academy and down a plain, long hallway with tiled floors and large, nondescript oil paintings, until they stopped at a door on the right end of the hall.

"Enjoy your training session, old man. I'm sure you'll like your teacher. She's a good friend of mine."

"What's her name?"

"She's Major Jennifer Grant; she won't mind if you call her Jennifer. Now I have to run. See you later, old man."

"See you later, David." Ray realized he just called Gotlieb by his first name. Strange the person who arrested him upon first meeting him could perhaps, some day, become his friend.

Strange indeed.

Gotlieb walked quietly and briskly out the front entrance. Ray heard the soft rumble of Gotlieb's hovercar in the distance, and the whine of its accelerators as it sped away. Ray waited until Gotlieb was gone before he walked inside the room where his education in modern military lore was to begin.

There were several dozen beige-colored metal chairs and desks with cushion-like armrests placed in orderly fashion about the rear two-thirds of the room. Some sort of headgear and a panel with strange dials and instruments on them were placed at each desk.

A large viewscreen hung from the rear wall.

At a desk in the center of the room, Major Grant stared at a small screen resembling a computer monitor.

As he got closer, he took a careful look at the woman's face. She had a strong likeness to his girlfriend, Patricia, having the same warm, penetrating blue eyes, perfect red lips, and beautiful light red hair; and, yes, the same tall, lithe, shapely physique.

Ray felt Major Grant might have been mistaken for Patricia's sister. On closer examination the illusion became all the more certain. For now, though, Ray thought he'd keep their strong likeness to himself.

He asked, as casually as he could, "Excuse me, Major Grant?"

She looked up, saw Ray, and smiled. She got up and shook his hand vigorously, evincing the impression of great physical strength.

Ray regarded her with curiosity and perhaps a bit of lust. The Major definitely looked like she worked out and he didn't fail to notice his heart beating just a bit faster and his breath becoming a little deeper.

"Ah, Captain Perkins, it's so nice to finally meet you. How are you doing?"

"Pretty well, Pat—er, ah, I mean, Major Grant."

He immediately realized his mistake, but it was too late. He didn't know why he said it.

Jennifer didn't seem to notice his discomfiture, just the comment. "Nice to hear you're doing okay, but my name's Jennifer, not Pat."

"It's just...you look a lot like someone I used to know... that's all."

"Who was this person? A friend?" She didn't even try to hide the gleam in her dazzling eyes.

"She was my girlfriend, actually." Ray trailed off for a second; he continued, with some hesitation and sadness in his voice. "We were becoming close, I think, when all this happened."

Ray didn't dwell on that any further, nor did he bring up the subject of the Rockoid woman who seemed to consume his thoughts more and more as time went on.

"I'm so sorry to hear what you're going through. I couldn't even imagine the pain you must be experiencing from all this," said Jennifer sympathetically.

"I'm really trying not to think about it too much. I realize there's nothing you or anyone else can do. Let's just get on with this session, and the rest of my life."

Major Grant paused for a second and looked into Ray's blue eyes, trying to convey her understanding of the situation. She had experienced her own episodes of lost love and tragedy in her lifetime, but didn't feel it appropriate to talk about it, at least not then.

"All right Captain Perkins," she smiled, a genuine smile and not professional at all. "Are you ready for the training session?" The Major's mood went from sympathetic to official.

"Sure. Are you just going to teach me with books, lectures or something like that?"

"It's combination of the two. You see, the educational process has, if I understand my history correctly, changed a lot. We find it's more efficient to feed the information right to your brain, without having it filtered by sights, sounds and the level of your concentration."

She barely paused before continuing her explanation with practiced efficiency.

"The headgear you see at the desks don't just educate you. They let you experience the lessons in three dimensions, so they really become a part of you."

She must have rehearsed this spiel. Ray could barely repress a smile as Major Grant continued.

"Normally, we'd have a few years to educate you, but time is short. We're going to have to cram that information into your head in the next thirty days."

"Now that sounds damned near impossible!" Ray smiled. "Back home my teachers couldn't do it in sixteen years."

Are they just brainwashing me, so I won't be a threat anymore?

Grant laughed rather charmingly.

"Give us the benefit of the doubt. We've gone very far in educating folks here."

Yeah, I bet!

"Just don't expect miracles."

"You may surprise yourself." She softly laughed again, and

resumed her spiel. "The first part of your lessons will bring you up to date on your world history. A lot more than technology has changed.

"For instance, Earth would probably still be recovering from the Third World War if it wasn't for the Alliance."

Ray's interest was immediately piqued. "What do you mean?"

"Our priority was rebuilding civilization after the war. We made some major discoveries on our own, but without the help of the Alliance, we'd be pretty far behind."

"So the aliens just gave us all this awesome technology?"

"Ray, we all know nothing comes free in life; there's always a price tag attached. The aliens didn't forget that. Don't think a Cettian ship happened to be orbiting Mars when an Earth shuttle arrived just to look at the scenery. The Cettian Alliance fully intended to make contact with the human race at that time. They did this for two reasons. The Cettians and the Tereaeans were intrigued by the fact we looked so much like them, so we all had something in common. Lots of Alliance corporations saw Earth as a great business opportunity, a way to make huge sums of money by selling us technology and buying out Earth-owned corporations.

"It's no big surprise Earth was flooded with alien capitalists and businessmen when we joined the Alliance. I think some people still feel they exploited us in some way, that we sold out our freedom to them in exchange for advanced technology.

"You can no doubt imagine people are still ticked off about that today.... You'll learn more about that during your lessons."

Ray wanted to ask more about this rather mercenary spin on the first contact scenario, but Jennifer continued without barely any hesitation.

"We're also going to have to retrain you so you can function as a military officer here. The training process has, as you can expect, changed somewhat, but not nearly as much as you might think."

Ray had to say what was on his mind. "This isn't some sort of brainwashing machine, is it?"

"Hell no. We don't...can't tell you what to think. You just receive the information more efficiently. How you use it is up to you."

Ray couldn't hide his skepticism.

"Ask anyone. That's how we run our education system here."

Her smile was genuine. Ray just sighed.

"I...I suppose it's all right then."

Ray continued to listen with rapt attention to the woman's description about his upcoming lessons. He couldn't help but look at her beautiful face, dancing eyes, and slim, athletic body, and his smile began to widen. This was someone who could help him forget his feelings of sadness and loss.

After she finished her brief lecture, Jennifer smiled. "We have to begin your training session. I've reserved the first desk for you. It's already been programmed."

"Are there any other students?"

"Not right now. You're in a class of one; you're unique."

Ray flashed a confident smile, sat down and dutifully put on the headgear. He was about to push a button when Jennifer added a caution.

"Hold on a second, please. I have to give you a special pill to let your mind accept the intense flow of information. Otherwise, frankly, your brain wouldn't be able to take it. You aren't built to absorb this amount of information so quickly."

"I'm not surprised." Ray flashed a sickly grin, wondering what might happen if the medicine was dispensed in the wrong proportions.

"Now, don't you worry. Dr. Johnson took care of that. Time will pass so fast, you'll barely be aware of it."

Strange how Dr. Johnson always managed to come up with something that could affect his mind. Ray wondered if it was deliberate rather than standard operating procedure. Regardless, he realized he must accept the inevitable, so he looked up with a passive expression. "Will I be aware of the learning process or just know the information when I need it?"

"It'll be an unconscious process, Ray," Jennifer exuded her

most confident smile to reassure her new student. "You'll know what you have to know, and by the end of the day, you'll probably be exhausted from taking in information. Now it's time to begin."

Ray dutifully donned the headgear as Jennifer walked over to him with a brisk, efficient gait, took out a small oval-shaped device, and touched his arm with it. He sensed a brief rush of energy through his veins and then felt relaxed. Jennifer returned to her desk and sat down. After a few minutes, to give the drug time to take effect, she looked into the small viewscreen in front of her and muttered some barely audible commands. The room darkened, and Ray heard some noises coming from his headgear. He adjusted the visors to fit his eyes better and sat back a little nervously.

The sounds became louder and he saw flashes of light. At first, everything proceeded at a very slow pace. He could see what appeared to be a three-dimensional newsreel, showing him events from his own history. The passage of information began to accelerate. Soon, the march of events and sounds moved so rapidly, he nearly became dizzy. At this point, the medication he had been given must have taken full effect because he lost consciousness in a whir of information he could barely grasp.

As quickly as the feeling arrived, it passed, and silence came in its wake. He felt someone removing the visor from his eyes and gently taking the helmet off his head. As Major Grant promised, he was seldom aware of how much time passed during the sessions.

For the next week, the process continued without letup. It almost got to be boring after a few days. Ray sat down at his teaching machine, accepted his medication, his lessons and his lunch breaks. Jennifer remained with him all the time, looking for all the world like she was actually interested in Ray's experiences while undergoing his rapid-fire schooling.

Well, I suppose she has to pretend to be interested. It's all part of the game!

Ray felt he had been doing physical labor for hours without letup. He'd slowly stand, feeling a little dizzy. At times there'd be a wave of nausea. Neither Jennifer nor the security people who came in from time to time seemed overly concerned. When Ray was escorted to his room at night, he was given another medication to make him comfortable before he went to sleep.

* * *

As Ray continued to be fed the intimate details of present day life, President Rogers met with Dr. Johnson in his personal briefing room.

A grave expression lined Rogers' face. "Now we need to assess the Rockoid situation. Show me the latest visuals from our scout ships."

Johnson nodded and gave a few commands to the viewscreen. Within seconds, the pictures appeared.

The oval-shaped Rockoid warships moved slowly. Six small, triangle-shaped Alliance scout ships, literally dots on the screen compared to the gigantic Rockoid cruisers, were trailing at a safe distance behind them.

After playback concluded, Johnson said, "I wish I had some news to report, Mr. President, but the fleet has barely moved in the past two hours. It's like an old rusty wagon or something. At the rate the Rockoids are going, they'll never get anywhere. And they're not responding to the hails from our scout ships or seeming to notice us. Luckily, they haven't shown any signs of aggression...yet."

"Exactly," Rogers broke in. "We still don't know exactly what the Rockoids will do, but one thing is clear: more and more ships are coming every day."

Johnson's eyes widened. "This sounds bad, Mr. President. I don't think I'm alone here when I say I think the Rockoids are coming here for something other than simple exploration. They could be out for blood. Maybe we should put our forces on alert... just in case."

"Henry, you know the Alliance has to abide by its codes of conduct. We aren't allowed to fire until we're fired upon."

Johnson rolled his eyes. "I've heard that excuse a million times already. I have a feeling we're all gonna live to regret that policy."

Rogers looked at his old friend sadly and said, "You know the political climate around here. They don't have the stomach for another war. We're just going to have to wait it out and keep our fingers crossed."

A serious look came over Johnson's face. "Mr. President, I hate to bring this up, but do you really think Perkins is right when he says we attacked the Rockoids first? Do you think it's even possible?"

Rogers seemed unprepared for the question. A look of consternation came over him, and sweat began to pour down his face. After straightening his collar and clearing his throat, he responded in a hoarse tone. "No, of course not, Dr. Johnson. You and I know that Thompson is one of the Alliance's most highly decorated military leaders! She would never risk doing something so terrible! You've been close to her and her family; how you could you even consider such a thing?"

Johnson sighed. The doubts began to pile up in his mind. In recent days, he had been thinking more and more about the disturbing information revealed in Ray's dreams. Rogers was right when he said Thompson was not the sort of person who would launch an unprovoked assault on an alien colony. He had known her since she was a child playing cheerfully in his backyard. She was like a daughter to him. He had to trust her, her honesty, her instincts.

Why can't I get that nagging feeling out of my stomach?

He managed to stammer, "I don't know. I mean, Perkins' dreams have been right all along, down to the very last detail. Could he be right about this, too?"

Rogers stood up and put a comforting hand on Johnson's shoulder. "Henry, think logically here. You've said it yourself many times; dreams are not literal descriptions of events. Some of the details in Perkins' dreams may have been distorted by his subconscious. I'm sure his impression that Thompson attacked the Rockoids first is way off target. How could anyone believe such a terrible thing?"

Johnson didn't press the subject. No use trying to convince the President without hard evidence. He did find it rather strange that Rogers' denial seemed to be forced. Unfortunately, he'd have to deal with that later; maybe Rogers was merely responding to political pressure, trying to maintain an even keel.

For now he could only pray the Rockoids didn't have conquest on their minds.

* * *

It was the end of the first week of Ray's training. After saying goodbye to Jennifer at the conclusion of his session and receiving his nightly dose of medication, he walked out of the room and back down the hall to the front of the building, where Gotlieb was waiting, nervously tapping his foot, glaring at him with hands folded.

"Where were you?"

"Sorry, Jennifer let me out late."

"I bet she did, old man," exclaimed Gotlieb with a smile on his face, a smile that looked almost like a leer.

"No, David, it's not like that. I barely even know her!"

"I know you're lonely, Ray, but you have to realize you've just gone through an experience unlike any other in Alliance history— at least any we know about. You've got to try to keep your feelings in check. I know it's hard, but personal involvements right now probably aren't a good idea...even if you do want to get laid."

"I guess so," Ray sighed. "I just wish everybody would stop trying to pry into my personal life! I mean, sure, leaving my home, my friends and family behind was traumatic, but I'm gonna have to settle down sometime."

"I get what you're saying, old man. What you're feeling is totally normal and Jennifer's a great-looking woman too. But there's something you gotta know about her."

"She's a lesbian?" Ray broke in.

Gotlieb looked at him quizzically. "A what?"

"You know, a woman who...uhh...likes other women...a lot."

Gotlieb's eyes flashed in recognition. "Ah, I see you what you mean, old man. No, we don't have a special name for anything like that. But these days, pretty much everywhere in the Alliance, you can get married to a man, woman, alien, whoever or whatever you want, as long as it's legit. Marriage is for love."

"That's good to hear," Ray smiled, feeling reassured that at least some of the discriminatory traditions of Earth's past had been eliminated.

Gotlieb continued, "This is the situation, Ray. Jennifer's had a pretty rough time these past few years. Five years ago, her husband died in that battle with the Rockoids on Dorton. She was on another assignment when it happened, and she blamed herself for Jeff Grant's death. Jennifer had a nervous breakdown, and almost left the service. For the next few years, she traveled around the galaxy in this old freighter she bought second-hand. She said she wanted to get away from it all. It's only in this past year she's been able to resume active duty. Please, treat her gently, okay?"

"Of course I will. God, I'm so sorry to hear what she went through. I'll try not to push her into anything too soon." Ray gave a faint smile, trying to conceal the thought he could find other ways to comfort her. If only the image of Zanther would leave his subconscious mind. At times, he thought he was married to Zanther and she was always around, watching over him.

No wonder my marriage never worked out!

Since the Rockoids entered Alliance territory, his feelings about their presence had sharply increased. It wasn't just due to those awful dreams, since the medication helped him rest without much interruption. Whenever he looked to the skies, he could imagine the fleet, closing in on Earth, coming there to...he just didn't want to think about it.

He tried to change the subject.

"David, what's the deal between you and Johnson? You're always bickering with him. I never fought that much with my ex-wife."

Gotlieb laughed and quickly turned serious, "Ray, old man, you need to understand Henry and I are oil and water. He came from a military background; he's a military brat, and he can trace his family tree to the American Civil War! He was different in a big way, a child prodigy. He got his first Ph.D. when he was twenty—twenty, can you imagine that?"

Ray nodded. "No big surprise there. Seems like he has his paws in just about every major discovery I've seen here so far."

"I don't think anybody had the right to stop him, since he went on to get another half dozen of those silly pieces of paper. His family didn't have any money. He worked nights, washed dishes, sold shoes, got scholarships, whatever it took to stay in school.

"Today he's a medical doctor, an engineer, a top-flight military strategist. He could have written his own ticket; instead he works for the goddamned Alliance government doing their dirty work for a pittance. He's the president's right hand man, cause he won't lie to curry favor with him."

"Why does he seem to hate you so much? Personality clashes or something?"

"To some extent, but there was something else. You see, compared to Johnson, I had it pretty easy as a kid," Gotlieb said, as if he didn't quite believe things had been so simple for him. "My dad was rich, he contributed to the right political causes, and, worse, he bought a spot for me at the Alliance academy, pushing me ahead of candidates who were a lot more qualified. Johnson knew that, and never let me forget it; he made life miserable for me in basic training. I had to work twice as hard to achieve the same goals as everyone else. You know what—I did it! I got through it and got my goddamned commission, honors, medals. By myself, not with my dad's cash."

"I guess things didn't turn out so bad for you after all. Why did you leave the military?"

"Old man, I was damn sick and tired of it. I was in the Alliance military for twenty years—can you believe that? At times I thought I wouldn't get out of that hell hole with my head screwed on tight."

Ray chuckled. "Tell me about it. I didn't last more than seven months when I had that goddamned accident in the Middle East."

"Listen, old man, I just got tired of the hassles and the changing political climate. I had a wife and kid and I needed a real family life for once. I took early retirement and got this job at the Vegas police force. It's great. Good pay, no serious crimes to worry about. I do my eight hours and head straight home. I don't have to worry about the money at all, really. My dad left me with this trust fund. I can sit home and watch the viewscreen and drink vodka martinis, or go out and play hovertennis. It's terrific, what a life."

Ray could see Gotlieb was not quite as pleased with his situation as he let on. Things had changed now; he was recalled to active duty via the personal intervention of President Rogers the day he arrested Ray. Gotlieb seemed to relish his status as a good friend of the President, and head of the task force set up to probe into Ray's unique situation.

When they got to the hotel, Ray asked Gotlieb if he wanted to join him for dinner.

"Sorry, old man, got to catch up on some briefing videos. Maybe next time."

* * *

That night, Ray had dinner alone, as usual—he was hardly conscious of what he ordered or the fact he consumed it so fast he nearly choked on it. He took a shower and plopped down into his bed, asleep with barely a moment's delay. The dizziness and nausea he occasionally experienced were long gone, and he fell into a quiet, restful sleep. He started to dream of Major Grant; those thoughts soon faded into nothingness. His sleep wasn't even interrupted by the image of space cruisers, battles, or Rockoids. He didn't dream at all.

Even better, the hauntingly beautiful Rockoid woman, Zanther, decided to leave him alone for once!

If only he knew that she too, dozens of light years away, often wished he would do the very same thing....

Chapter 11

For the rest of the month, most of Ray's training sessions consisted of the same tedious routine, though he was seldom aware of the passage of time. By day, he was educated in the finer points of recent Earth history. As time went on, he found he became accustomed to the nausea and dizziness he experienced at the end of each day; after a while he almost didn't need the medication anymore.

One afternoon Jennifer interrupted his history lesson.

"Hey! It's not time for lunch already, is it?" Ray said, though he was happy she had come in to visit him earlier.

"I think we should talk, Ray."

"Sure."

"I'm really happy to have gotten to know you over the past month, Ray. But here at the academy, we never really have any alone time. Now I think...well...maybe we could go out for dinner some time."

"Jenny, are you asking me out on a date?" Ray smiled.

"I don't know. It depends. It's your choice." Jennifer returned his smile with one of her own. "Either way I just thought you'd like to try real food for once. There's this really nice restaurant I like to go to and I think it might be a great experience for you... to try real food, that is."

"Major Grant, that sounds like a date to me."

"Then it's a date," she agreed, not too reluctantly, he noticed.

"What time?"

"Soon as we leave here. I'll let you off an hour early and I'll drive us over there. Sound good?"

"Just peachy." Ray smiled, as he began to ponder all sorts of possibilities about what might occur after their meal.

Before he got much of a chance to think more about such splendid subjects, Ray found himself thrust back into the middle of his teaching session, the last before he was to begin military training in a real barracks the next day.

Well, it looks like I'm going to have some fun tonight.

Ray's smile was big and obvious, though Jennifer didn't seem to recognize his enthusiasm.

* * *

That night, minutes after Ray's final retraining session, Jennifer drove him in her sleek black sports hovercar to London's old Soho neighborhood (which retained almost none of the low-rise brick buildings that had once defined it in the early twenty-first century), where the restaurant, François' Fralien Paradise, was located.

As they approached their destination, he saw the place was topped with a large green sign, with multicolored frames flashing on and off. Some strange music was played over a hidden loudspeaker system. He sensed an unfamiliar but pleasant odor, like broiled steak only a bit more pungent, filling the area around the place. It was evidently one of the dishes offered inside. Ray's appetite was whetted. As they approached the door, it opened automatically, and they entered quickly.

The restaurant was not unlike the fashionable eating spots Ray used to visit, with ornate surroundings, piano player, chandelier, and a real open kitchen in the rear. Ray was happy to see there were no signs of food replicators anywhere.

Something was strange about the creature playing that piano, though. First, of all, he, or rather, it, didn't look human; in fact, it wasn't even close. It looked almost like an elephant. Although it didn't have a trunk, only an enlarged nose, its rough skin was gray, and its ears were considerably larger than those of a human. It had thick arms, with three long, pointy fingers and a thumb, and two short, thick leg-like appendages. The only human-like attribute seemed to be the creature's feet, as it was wearing the same sort of boots fashionable in this era. Ray recalled from his teaching sessions that the musician was a member of a race called the Qverians.

The instrument itself, while having a conventional appearance, was quite unconventional in the way it functioned. There were two rows of keys, and the musician deftly moved its thin fingers across the many keys with incredible rapidity, revealing a dexterity that seemed way beyond what a common concert pianist might achieve.

The sounds it produced! They were unlike any piano or keyboard instrument with which Ray was familiar. The music was positively surreal, enchanting. The melodies were in no way familiar to Ray, yet he was so taken up by their majesty it seemed he was floating.

As he listened to it, he remembered from one of his teaching sessions that the music was a fusion of earth and alien styles. The piano was actually a holographic keyboard capable of duplicating any musical instrument or complete orchestra with perfect pitch, harmony, and timbre. This was quite an improvement from most of the synthesizers back in the twenty-first century, which sounded totally artificial in comparison.

Before Ray could ponder his lessons further, he and Jennifer were approached by a short, black haired man, middle-aged and somewhat rotund. Their host wore a silver suit, almost form fitting, which served to accentuate how truly out of shape he really was.

"Why, hello, Major Grant. It's so nice to see you again." The voice had a touch of a French accent. Ray didn't know if it was real or feigned, much as some of the waiters in a Chinese restaurant would affect an Oriental dialect in order to impress tourists.

"It's nice to see you again too, François. Sorry I haven't been able to get over here in a while. I've been very busy."

"Oh, that's fine. Would you like your regular table? It's available right now."

"Of course."

François led them to a round table with two wide, form-fitting seats at the back of the restaurant, from which they had a perfect view of the Qverian keyboard player.

Upon arriving at the table, François pulled out the chairs, and the couple sat down.

"Oh, Major Grant, you didn't introduce your new boyfriend!" he teased her.

"François, now stop! He's not my boyfriend, just one of my... students. We started class about a month ago."

"I see," Now François grinned from ear to ear.

Ray stuck out his hand, and François shook it.

"Nice to meet you. By the way, Major Grant, one month is more than enough time to get a boyfriend."

"François, just cut it out! You're always trying to play matchmaker!" She had a broad smile on her face now.

"I don't like seeing you alone all the time. That's all."

Jennifer changed the subject. "So we're starving, François. How about you bring us some Kodoki 2185 wine to start?"

He handed them their menus and walked away. After looking over a vast selection of strange and varied dishes, Ray took Jennifer's advice and got the Fralien crepes. While waiting for the food to come, they drank green wine, a popular import from the Alliance world of Kodoki. While waiting for their meal, the two talked about their pasts, especially their childhoods. They found they had more in common than either had imagined. Jennifer had also been born in the south, in Virginia, before her family moved to the Mars colony. Her parents both passed away in the last few years. As they got to know each other, they become closer. They seemed to be a good match. Perhaps they might have entered a deeper relationship earlier...if it weren't for the striking image of a certain alien woman that continued to haunt Ray.

Ray barely considered that, in his time at least, it wasn't appropriate for students and teachers to have a relationship. Besides, their ages were similar and his student status would soon end.

After a short while, François returned to their table, putting down two large dishes with silver covers in the center. He also set down a bottle filled with a strange green liquid.

François made a dramatic flourish as he lifted the covers and exclaimed, "Dinner is served!"

Ray looked down and saw two regular-looking crepes, and next to them an ordinary-looking salad. Suddenly, to his complete surprise, he noticed the lettuce moving right off the plate, sneaking its way off the table; he caught it with his fork before the living vegetable could escape and put it right back on his plate.

"What the hell is this? Why is the lettuce moving? Am I hallucinating or something?"

François laughed, holding his bulging stomach. "Ha, ha, I have tricked you! I forgot to tell you when you ordered that the lettuce in the crepe is alive! Alive!" He laughed heartily at Ray's obvious discomfort.

A sickening feeling suddenly came over Ray. The thought of eating living lettuce didn't sound so appealing to him. He braced himself, as he began to feel extremely nauseated.

He managed to stammer a response. "Why was the lettuce moving away from me?"

"I guess it didn't like you very much." François grinned.

Ray groaned. "Oh come on, lettuce doesn't have any personality!"

"Maybe it does, maybe it doesn't. We've never been able to figure it out for certain."

"What—where does this thing come from?"

"Oh, it's a long story. Some time I'll tell you. You'll really get a kick out of the tale. I have searched far and wide for the finest ingredients for the meals we serve."

François turned serious and said, "I want you to taste it now; you'll love it."

Ray was reluctant to devour something that was still alive when he put it in his mouth. He had a hard enough time eating sushi, and the fish were dead before being consumed.

He picked up his fork and poked it into the lettuce a couple of times. As he lifted it toward his mouth, he heard a tiny whine.

Shocked. Ray nearly dropped his fork. He began to put it back down, resigning himself to the fact he wouldn't be able to tolerate the living food.

"Try it, my alien friend, whoever you are. I had something quite similar to that dish last night, and I must admit, it was a meal I shall never forget," said the voice that suddenly appeared in Ray's head.

The words were in perfect English, but the voice had a peculiar musical lilt, one so pleasant he thought the one who uttered those words could comfort him with her voice alone. He was utterly entranced and yet totally surprised.

"Who said that?" asked Ray out loud.

Jennifer stared at him. "Ray, what are you talking about? Who said what?"

"It wasn't the lettuce talking. It isn't that advanced." François chimed in.

Ray shook his head. The voice had gone away, as he looked back at his dish.

"Sorry, I thought I heard someone talking to me from across the restaurant," he lied, though he figured Jennifer didn't believe a word of it.

With renewed confidence, he grabbed his fork, took a piece of the crepe, and slowly put the food in his mouth. He chewed it, slowly, deliberately, trying to force his mouth to make the usually instinctive motions. With a great deal of effort, he swallowed the first bite, trying as hard as he could to give a show of courage to

Jennifer and François.

He needn't have suffered the agony; it was delicious!

"Ha, ha! I knew you'd like it!" said François happily. "Now I have to go take care of my many other satisfied customers."

He strolled off again in his stiff manner, chuckling happily.

They both enjoyed their wonderful meal of colorful crepes, that living—well, moving salad, and sweet, non-intoxicating green wine. After they finished their meal, François came by with a dessert cart from which they each chose a piece of Fralien cake.

The cake did not exhibit any outward signs of movement while being eaten.

When Jennifer asked for the check, François had a broad grin. "It'll be my treat...this time."

"Thanks, François. That's so nice of you!" exclaimed Jennifer in mock sarcasm.

"Anything for you, my dear," said François as he kissed Jennifer's hand and started to move his way up her arm.

"Hey, don't bother my girlfriend!" Ray shouted in mock anger.

"Oh, I thought she wasn't your girlfriend!" François responded, feigning surprise.

"She is now, I suppose. Damn! I thought Frenchmen would have changed in this century." He tried to keep the last sentence barely above a whisper.

"I figured you'd know just what Frenchmen were like in the your century."

"What? How did...how did you know?" Ray couldn't conceal his surprise.

"Don't worry about it, Jennifer didn't tell me anything about you. You've become a legend around these parts; word has passed rapidly through the underground."

"Since you're Jennifer's friend, I suppose I can trust you," Ray lied. "We have to go now."

"Goodbye, François. With any luck, I'll see you next week," said Jennifer with a sly wink.

Jennifer and Ray then began walking toward the front entrance. François shouted, "Au revoir, Madame Grant, and you, too,

Monsieur Perkins!"

The restaurant's proprietor shook his head and said quietly to himself, "Quite an odd couple."

The so-called "odd" couple made their way out of the restaurant and returned to Jennifer's vehicle.

They weren't holding hands, at least not yet.

As he thought about taking her hand in his, Ray again saw the image of Zanther in his mind's eye. Would she approve?

"Oh, don't worry about me, my alien friend. Go right ahead," said that same, strange, musical voice inside his mind.

Ray nearly fell down in shock. Jennifer wondered what was going on, though she didn't say anything, figuring he had tripped on something.

As they neared Jennifer's sleek black hovercar, Ray noticed how it almost shone like a diamond in the moonlight. It looked even prettier than it had before.

So did Jennifer.

He got into the front seat, and Jennifer sat down next to him. The seat belts wrapped around their shoulders and waists. Within a matter of seconds, the hovercar gently rose into the air, and after a short delay, it shot off in a burst of speed.

After traveling through the city for a few minutes and gazing at the wonderful sights, Ray became tired simply looking at pretty architecture.

"This is getting boring. Can we go somewhere else?" he asked.

"Sure. Where do you want to go?"

"Where can this thing take us? Can it travel through space?"

"It can, but you have to turn on the life-support systems and activate the gravity fields before you're spaceborne; it won't leave the atmosphere otherwise. It's really fun. You could travel to Mars or Europa or anywhere in this star system. The engines aren't powerful enough for light—er, hyperspace!"

"I don't think I'm ready for space travel yet," Ray said quickly.

"Oh, come on, you'll love it!" argued Jennifer.

"Thanks, but no thanks." Ray protested.

"Okay, but you're missing out on a lot of fun. Besides, you are going to have to travel in space soon enough."

"Maybe so, but I'd rather remain Earthbound for a while longer."

"Okay. But since you said no to that option, I do have another choice to offer you."

"Where's that?"

"Atlanta."

"Sure, I'd love to see how my old second home has changed from when I knew it."

Without another word, Jennifer gave him a strange, almost twisted, seductive smile, pressed a red button on her side of the car and said, "Take us to Atlanta, U.S.A., Route 23-A."

"One moment, please," said a soft robotic voice in reply.

Suddenly the car sped forth with another burst of acceleration, lifted to a much higher altitude, and whizzed off into the night, toward the second largest city in the twenty-third century former United States of America.

As Jennifer's hovercar flew on through the night to the southeastern United States, light-years away in space, the pace of reconnaissance increased.

* * *

The Rockoid ships were still trailed by the half dozen Alliance scout ships, which maintained a respectable distance, attempting to show no action that would betray a threatening posture. Alliance command received moment-by-moment accounts of the progress of the strange visitors.

Attempts to communicate with the newcomers proved unsuccessful, as were efforts to decode their radio transmissions. The Alliance forces waited and watched, crews hoping against hope they would not be called to battle.

In the command module of the huge mother ship, Zanther knew she had to accept the consensus of her defense ministry. She gave the order for survey ships to scour the planets and moons in their vicinity to check for mineral deposits and bring back ore samples.

Once the mining ships were dispatched, the super cruisers con-

tinued their mission, but maintained radio silence. They communicated via telepathy, their accustomed means of private communication, beamed directly to the minister of defense for relaying
military orders. Zanther received regular updates about the mission's progress. She nodded her head in acceptance a few times,
but kept silent otherwise, lost in thought, her demeanor dour; her
doubts about the whole war effort wouldn't go away.

Her fleet had discovered the presence of the small Alliance
ships pacing them, transmitting sonar signals clearly designed to
determine the extent of the Rockoid defense system. But Rockoid
weaponry remained well hidden; their slow pace designed to convey the illusion the visit had a peaceful purpose. Although they
had been hailed by the Alliance communication center and by the
small scout ships, they maintained absolute radio silence and only
communicated with other ships via secured channels or mental
telepathy.

* * *

Barely an hour after the trip began, Ray and Jennifer reached
Atlanta.

As they got out of the car, he asked, "What do we do now? It's
getting kinda late. Maybe we should look for a place to stay for
the night." At the same time, Ray had an ill-concealed leer on his
face. Perhaps the implication behind his statement was a little too
abrupt.

Jennifer returned the smile for just a second, and put her shapely
hand on his shoulder. He felt a bit startled at the sudden touch,
since it felt so soft and pleasant. His feelings of nervousness began
to subside, though. His heart pounded. What would Zanther
think? Ray mused.

"*Stop asking me, Captain Perkins—that is your name, is it
not?*"

The manifestation of that strange musical voice stunned Ray
once more; by now he had identified it as belonging to Zanther.
This time he chose to ignore her.

"My uncle owns an apartment building here in Atlanta, and

and one of the units is for my use when I come to visit. Wanna see it?"

"Sounds great. Where is it?"

Jennifer pointed up and said, "Right here."

Ray looked up and saw a huge spiral building that must have been one hundred stories tall. His nervous feelings intensified. She was actually taking him to her apartment; she must have planned this trip. He felt excited, yet a little frightened; everything was happening way too fast.

Ray always had trouble with relationships; they were usually short-term, with abrupt but quiet breakups.

How long had it been since he had female company? Ray didn't dare to think. Months at least, even if one subtracted his passage to the future. He hadn't spent much time with Pat before that fateful trip; she had always been busy with work, he with his programming.

He made his decision.

"Let's go!"

"Come on in. I'm starting to get cold!" exclaimed Jennifer.

Indeed, the air was infused with the feeling of late fall, with a chilly breeze. His short-sleeved shirt didn't quite seem up to the task of keeping him warm and comfortable.

They walked together at a brisk pace through the entrance, heading inside the building. The furnishings in the large lobby were sumptuous, with rich white and brown carpets, fancy sofas, and comfortable-looking chairs and tables. The lighting had a sort of fluorescent look, but Ray couldn't see any source. No bulbs, chandeliers, nor fixtures anywhere.

He didn't have much of a chance to dwell on the nature of his surroundings, as Jennifer continued her fast pace to the open elevator, where they ascended to the eighty-third floor.

The elevator shot upward with a pace that jarred Ray. *When am I gonna got used to that?*

Luckily, this time at least, no song-like voice interrupted his thoughts, to his delight—or dismay?

Seconds later, they arrived. The elevator door opened and

Jennifer took Ray's hand, directing him through the long, curved hallway to a door that had the numbers 8334 on it.

Ray took a quick glance around, seeing the same thick carpeting that lined the lobby and lighting above.

As soon as they approached it, Jennifer placed her eye in front of a security beam emanating from the door and it slid open smoothly. They stepped into a nicely decorated, if somewhat small, apartment. Ray looked around and saw a bedroom with a king-size mattress in it, a small but inviting living room with bland, neutral-colored wood-like sofas and chairs, and a large viewscreen in front of the picture window. The bathroom was much larger than the one in his hotel room. The ever-present food replicator seemed no different from the others he'd seen.

The carpeting had the same relaxing motif as that lining the floors of the lobby, and there were some traditional-looking paintings of people, places, and flowers lining the walls.

The most striking aspect of the apartment was the fact that it didn't seem to be imbued with any of Jennifer's personality, at least that he could see. It was a nice apartment, but no fancier than a hotel, and with no sense of individuality. There were no signs of family portraits, custom embroidery, books, or any other signs at all that any individual truly called this place home.

He got a sense that Jennifer was reluctant to put down roots anywhere.

"Sit right down and I'll pour you a drink," said Jennifer.

"Sure," Ray agreed, vowing not to press this lovely creature for any unpleasant, uncomfortable personal details right now.

"I'll be right back."

Jennifer walked into the kitchen, and Ray plopped down on the sofa. He took time to notice that the multicolored fabric seemed to reflect all the colors of the rainbow, with patterns almost hypnotic in their intricacy.

As he sat down, he noticed the sofa seemed to mimic the shape of his body perfectly, as if custom-designed for him.

Jennifer opened a large sliding glass cabinet door and selected what appeared to be a regular wine bottle. She popped the cork and filled two large glasses. She strolled back to Ray in a smooth, studied motion, and he took the glass and drank from it perhaps a bit too quickly for his own good.

"I'll be back soon. I'm going to change into my nightgown," said Jennifer, flashing a seductive smile.

Ray seemed startled for a moment at the ease with which Jennifer made that announcement. He wondered just how many men had been invited to this apartment.

Jennifer had already walked into her bedroom. Ray briefly heard the sound of the sliding door on a closet and the faint rustle of garments being moved. Jennifer carried something into the bathroom, and the door closed.

Ray had to admit he had second thoughts. She was absolutely beautiful, no doubt about that, intelligent, and fun to be with. Yet uppermost in his mind was the image of his alien fantasy woman, a woman who consumed his thoughts more and more in increasing vividness, as the Rockoid fleet continued its journey. With Zanther's voice already beginning to intercept his thoughts, he wondered if she was truly aboard that craft, if he'd finally meet her very soon now.

At the same time, he longed for female companionship; if Zanther was real, would she consider an intimate relationship with the likes of him, a barbaric Earthman? Was it even biologically possible?

He received no answer, confirming his beliefs. No doubt she didn't understand or care what he thought.

So Ray readied himself for what he hoped would be a pleasurable evening.

Ten minutes later, Jennifer emerged from the bathroom. She wore a silk, nearly see-through shirt with frilly edges, with very little left to the imagination. She crossed her arms and glared at Ray with mock anger. "I expected you would be ready by now."

Ray grinned. "It's been a while since I last did this sort of thing."

Jennifer rolled her eyes. "Ray, don't tell me you've forgotten how to do this! Please don't make me have to teach you!"

Ray laughed. "No way, Jenny. I think I can remember the process...with a little help, of course..."

Jennifer gave him a knowing smile and grabbed his left hand tightly. "Okay, Ray, if you say so."

She guided him to the bedroom, slowly, with a warm, sensuous grin on her beautiful face. The door slid shut behind them. Jennifer began taking her shirt off as soon as they entered the room. Ray practically tore his shirt from his body. He slid off his pants and they got into bed, embracing, holding, touching each other tenderly, yet eagerly. It had been a while for Jennifer too.

Lips met, hands met, caressing, exploring, delighting one another. Ray was ready to savor each and every moment...soon the pleasure centers of his brain were working overtime.

* * *

Jennifer looked content. Ray stared at the ceiling as if something else was on his mind.

Jennifer observed Ray's faraway look with a little suspicion. "Ray, you look like you're a million light-years away."

Ray gave her a faint smile. "Considering the circumstances, I guess you could say that."

"What are you talking about, Ray?"

"I don't know...it's just those dreams...that woman..."

Jennifer interrupted. "What woman?"

Uh oh, I should have just shut my damn mouth!

"Jenny, maybe it's better if we just drop the subject..."

"If you're thinking about another woman, it'd be nice to." Jennifer now glared at Ray.

He couldn't...didn't want to lead her on.

"It doesn't make any sense. It's that Rockoid woman that I see in my dreams every night...I can't stop thinking about her...I think I'm obsessed with her..."

"Are you kidding me, Ray? You're obsessed with a *Rockoid* woman? A woman you've never even met? A woman that could very well be our enemy?"

"I just don't understand any of it, I really don't," Ray replied as he tensed up. "Her image won't leave my mind. Nothing like this has ever happened to me before...Am I going crazy?"

Jennifer barely let him finish before she angrily jumped out of bed, grabbed her shirt, put it back on, and stood staring at Ray with her hands on her hips for several tense seconds. She finally shouted, "Ray Perkins, I can't believe you! Don't you like me?"

Tears streamed from her eyes. "What else do you want from me?"

"Jenny, it's not that! You have to understand. I'm sorry...."

When he took her hand in an attempt to comfort her, she spun around and slapped Ray's face. He caressed the wound as Jennifer stomped out of the room, still sobbing uncontrollably.

Ray sighed, not believing what he had just done. He shouldn't have let his lust control his actions. He wasn't ready for any emotional entanglements right now, and it was a sure thing Jennifer wasn't either.

That damn Rockoid woman was ruining his life! He probably lost any chance he might have had at pursuing a meaningful relationship with anyone.

Ray's emotions were a whirlpool of contradictions. Part of him desired a continued relationship with Jennifer; part of him remained obsessed with the image of Zanther.

Ray attempted to apologize over and over again, but Jennifer wouldn't accept any of it. She sobbed uncontrollably and ran back into the bedroom, slamming the door behind her and leaving Ray to spend the rest of the night on the sofa.

Ray stayed awake until morning. He sat up and thought...and thought...and thought...for a long time.

Several times, he swore he heard a soft voice calling out to him from the bedroom, *"I'm sorry..."*

Maybe it's just my imagination working overtime...

Chapter 12

Over at the Alliance command center in Brussels, the progress of the alien fleet's arrival was being monitored on a minute-by-minute basis.

Scanning devices examined the Rockoid craft for evidence of hostile intent, but couldn't find any indication there were weapons aboard or defensive shields had been activated. There was a growing hustle and bustle of concerned conversation and movement among the Alliance commanders. As yet nobody had any inkling of what was to come.

Meanwhile, millions of residents of the Earth colonies of Mars and Europa continued their daily rituals. They worked, played, ate and slept. They did not sense the potential danger to their society from external sources. The economic downturn was enough of a concern to obscure other considerations.

Each month, the human resources division of RECOM issued new, impersonal layoff or early retirement lists. The employee simply punched up a directory on the viewscreen and checked to see if their name was there.

If it wasn't, he or she reported to work.

* * *

The next morning, Ray got dressed quickly and decided to take another stab at an apology. He found Jennifer drinking a cup of coffee in the kitchen. She was already dressed for work and got up as soon as he entered the kitchen.

Ray tried again to make her understand, "Jennifer, I'm really sorry about what happened last night. We shouldn't have made love. We...I wasn't...ready."

The little apologetic speech he'd practiced caught in his tongue, and he was left stammering.

Jennifer gave him a friendly smile. "Ray, I should apologize too. I totally overreacted."

"Jennifer, I feel like a total heel! I mean, it was all my fault. The problem is...I just can't shake the image of that Rockoid woman. She's been haunting me for so long, and I just..."

He sighed. "Do you understand what I'm trying to say, Jenny?"

She replied quickly, if not too believably, "Yes, Ray, I understand perfectly. You don't have anything to be concerned about. We had a good time. We just have a few things to work through, that's all." She gave him a warm smile, but Ray could swear he saw a tear forming in the corner of her right eye.

He went over to Jennifer and embraced her, holding her gently. She snuggled close to him; when they finally pulled themselves apart a few minutes later, he kissed her gently on her cheek.

She smiled at him, and they walked out of her apartment together, holding hands, heading back to the Alliance training center.

* * *

By Rockoid reckoning, some ninety timeframes passed before final decisions had to be made.

During that period, Ray Perkins obediently submitted to an

accelerated military training program. Teaching machine lessons were intermixed with live exercises at a military barracks. He welcomed the personal contact. At the same time, Jennifer was frequently called into conference with Captain Gotlieb to assess the Rockoid situation and report on Ray's uncanny knowledge of that battle on a far-off world.

* * *

Within a meeting chamber in the mother ship, an important session was about to convene. It was time for Empress Zanther and her ministers to reach a final, fateful decision concerning the battle plan

The initial plan was simple and direct: a full-blown frontal assault, a favorite method of conquering one's enemies.

They would attack the Alliance capital worlds, Earth, Taucon and Terea, at the same time. If all went as planned, their war of vengeance against the Alliance's terrorist attack would begin in thirty-five timeframes.

Zanther was already seated at a metallic, gray circular table, when the remainder of the council arrived. The defense minister, Xorax, strolled haughtily through a door at the end of the chamber.

Xorax presented an imposing figure, over six feet tall and somewhat portly for his race. Typical for a Rockoid male, his head was shaved bald on the top, with a crest of jet-black hair stretching across the back. His face was stern, with dark, glaring eyes, and a suspicious manner. His eyes darted rapidly around the room as he entered, always on the alert, planning for surprises.

The supreme commander of the Rockoid military followed him.

The Empress looked carefully at those present, waiting for the proper moment to begin. A sense of timing was an important attribute for a leader.

Zanther gave a regal smile that signified she was about to discuss the tactical situation.

"Supreme Commander Queksnar, please tell us your plan of battle. Remember, your decision will decide the fates of billions of our enemies," said the Empress matter-of-factly, even though committing troops to battle was still quite new for Zanther.

Queksnar, a thin, distinguished-looking officer with a long history of decorated service, stood and bowed. His stern visage bore a thick mustache, and the fringe of hair around the back of his head was considerably thinner than that of most males his age.

"I know, your majesty. It is my plan to place battle craft in close proximity to Earth, Taucon and Terea. We will give no clues as to our intent; we will continue to maintain radio silence and defensive shields will remain inactive.

"We will initiate the battle simultaneously upon all three Alliance capital worlds and their surrounding colonies."

The alien commander didn't seem to breathe between his words.

"We cannot give the Alliance any time to rally its forces or evacuate its cities. We must quickly destroy most of their fleet. It will be a mismatched battle and one of reasonably short duration. Once their military has been vanquished, we will land our ground forces upon their worlds and take their resources as our own."

Commander Queksnar remained smug in his assessment of his race's military superiority. Aside from the invasion of their far-off colony at Dorton, he had not lost a battle in his lifetime.

"The Alliance's edict, not to attack unless fired upon, will work to our advantage," a grim smile spread from his narrow lips.

Queksnar pointed to the large viewscreen above the table and delineated the various components of the Rockoid invasion fleet with a small pointing device that shot a bright yellow beam on the screen. Although his fellow commanders already knew the details, it was incumbent upon them to accept this sort of description as a formality whenever a final decision was made about a pending military engagement.

As each type of Rockoid ship appeared on the screen, Queksnar briefly summarized its configuration and armament.

Queksnar went on with a brief presentation using a battle simulator, which displayed several possible combat scenarios on the viewscreen. The tactics were the same as those the Rockoids used in most of their prior military campaigns; again this was done strictly as a formality, complying with law and tradition.

At the end of his presentation, Queksnar put his pointing device down and waited. Xorax breathed a large sigh of relief.

Thank Reka-danai that sobrac [a Rockoid epithet roughly equivalent to the term "dirty son of a bitch"] *is finished. I was about to nod off*, he thought, keeping his feelings blocked.

During Queksnar's report, Zanther tried not to look nervous. She couldn't keep from tapping her long, delicate fingers on the table from time to time, as she became more agitated over the implications of the upcoming attack on the empire's enemies.

Her inner conflicts wouldn't go away. On the one hand, she had visited some of the regime's young soldiers during their training to spur them on to greater heights of achievement. On the other hand, some of these very same soldiers came to her to tend their wounds or cure their illnesses. Now her proclamation of war against the Alliance would condemn many of them to their deaths.

She could not let self-doubt overcome her or display signs of weakness. She removed her hands from the table and placed them in her lap.

"Commander Ivarna, do you approve of this plan?"

A middle-aged, tall, almost burly Rockoid male arose and stared above the table with his dark eyes. His smooth countenance was devoid of expression. Unlike most members of his race, his eyes were deep blue, perhaps an indication that one of his distant ancestors had mated with one of the empire's sister races.

His words were slow and measured, careful not to say things that exceeded his level of authority. Ivarna knew he had some strong allies in that room, who were watching his performance under pressure very carefully.

"Yes, I do approve of the plan, with this concern: What shall we do with prisoners of war?"

"Minister Xorax, what are your feelings on this subject?" asked Zanther.

"We all know we have very little cargo space in which to hold prisoners; most captives will have to be executed immediately.

The rest we will torture so we can learn more about their defensive tactics. As you are all well aware, it is the tradition of our people to execute prisoners if they are of no use to us," Xorax reminded the group.

There was an air of menace to his comments. Shortly after Zanther ascended to the Rockoid throne, Xorax maintained that, having been educated as a healer, she was not qualified to assume the role as the leader of their people, a position that put her in charge of their armed forces.

Zanther's family, the House of Zophine, had held the Rockoid throne for many generations, and Xorax knew it was unwise to attempt to stage a rebellion against Zanther. As a result, his opposition was relatively low-key. He would bide his time, and if his Empress should make a misstep, he would use any mistake to his advantage to further the success of his own long-term plans to usurp the throne for his family.

Zanther wore the mantle of command well. She answered Xorax promptly and forcefully. She was not oblivious to the subtle political maneuverings in the Rockoid Council of Elders…some of which occurred under Xorax's influence.

"Xorax, you do not need to remind me of the manner in which we treat prisoners. You know I will uphold the traditions of our people. If prisoners of war need to be executed, that is what shall be."

Xorax never ceased to admire the manner in which the Empress expressed her wishes in public. He sensed her private misgivings about the upcoming battle, yet he saw no strategic advantage in bringing those doubts to the forefront. He had no proof, just a feeling. The Council of Elders would not accept speculation, considering the stakes involved in the coming war.

Xorax smiled obsequiously and made his excuses.

"Please do not take offense, my Empress. I merely reminded you for the sake of the Council, who will consult the log of our conference. Now that it is settled, we need not waste time discussing defensive tactics. Everyone knows that our firepower and ships are far superior to the Alliance fleet, as Supreme

Commander Queksnar has stated. The only circumstance under which our standard defensive tactics would be altered is in the unlikely event that the humans and their allies had somehow developed a secret weapon of enormous power.

"Now is the time for her Supreme Majesty, the Empress Zanther, to approve these plans of battle. Your Majesty?"

He knew the Empress was cornered now. No excuses would be tolerated. She must act clearly, forcefully. Any doubt in her words or manner would provide the ammunition he needed to question her ability to govern.

The Empress paused for impact.

"I originally agreed on the all-out attack plan, when Supreme Commander Queksnar first presented it to me. Now I have changed my mind."

Queksnar, Ivarna, and Xorax were caught off-guard by the unexpected pronouncement. A look of astonishment filled their countenances as tense centi-timeframes ticked by.

"I agree with Commander Queksnar that we should initiate simultaneous attacks on the colonies of the humans, Cettians and Terraeans," Zanther continued, totally in control of the situation. "We know that the Alliance has been aware of our presence for some time now, and I am quite sure that the capital worlds will be very heavily defended, perhaps more than we originally believed. We should make the Alliance capital worlds secondary targets and designate the colony worlds in those systems as primary objectives."

Queksnar broke in, "Yes, my Empress, I'm sure it would not be very hard to redistribute our forces to fit your new plan. In fact..."

"Commander Queksnar, I am not finished. I believe, instead of commencing an all-out frontal assault, we should take out the industrial and military production facilities on the colonies first. No direct attacks on civilian targets will be permitted. We will issue a warning to the Alliance: surrender or be destroyed. If their government does not give up within three Earth days...then we will conduct an all-out attack on their forces and population centers."

Queksnar nodded. "My Empress, I trust your decision fully and I do not wish to question your authority, but tell me one thing. What has caused you to change your mind?"

"Yes," Xorax broke in, "you know very well that a direct assault on their home worlds would provide the fastest route to success. It will allow us to display our full strength and make prospects for the Alliance's surrender more likely."

"Minister Xorax, an all-out attack is certain to cause unnecessary Rockoid deaths, exactly what I want to avoid. We suffered quite enough when the Alliance barbarians attacked Dorton," Zanther replied.

Commander Ivarna spoke up. "Empress Zanther, our statistics clearly show the Alliance fleet is, at best, only half as strong as our own. Victory is assured."

"Perhaps so, Commander, but statistics based on samples of data do not show how many ships the Alliance actually has. We also have no way of knowing how much of a fight the Alliance will mount. Furthermore, many non-aligned worlds in this part of the galaxy are said to be negotiating for membership in the Alliance; they may very well support our enemies in this struggle."

Xorax protested angrily. "Empress Zanther, anything less than an all-out attack would be seen as an act of cowardice. I warn you now that I do not support this change of strategy!"

Zanther stared imperiously at her defense minister.

"Remember for one moment what your grandfather, Emperor Sakoris, said when he learned the Alliance had refused to abide by the Teldra Accords. He warned us all that the Alliance represented the greatest threat to galactic peace and stability. If Dorton did not convince you, remember what happened to the Jintorians when they encountered the Alliance. Those incidents, alone, should be enough to prove how much of a threat our enemy represents."

Zanther's comeback was swift, assured, and emphatic. "Do not forget, Minister, that my grandfather and father tried to establish more neutral policies toward the Alliance because they believed it did not represent a significant threat. As you know, the Alliance was asked to accept a series of treaties developed when not one of their races had yet discovered interstellar travel. Its conduct prior to the attack on Dorton is subject to many interpretations."

Zanther gritted her teeth. "And furthermore, let me remind you that I am your Empress, and I *will* make the final decision."

Quickly, Xorax bowed, as obsequiously as ever. "Yes, my Empress."

Zanther turned to Ivarna before anyone else could protest. "Commander, I want you to take the super cruiser Indignant, along with fifty support cruisers, and head for Earth's colonies at best speed. You will be directly commanding the forces attacking those planets."

She turned to Queksnar. "Commander, you will stay here and take control of our remaining forces. When the time comes, we will go to Earth and command the main frontal assault on the Alliance from there."

Xorax observed the proceedings with renewed respect for Zanther. Despite his deepest hope she would reveal signs of weakness, he could not help but be impressed at the authority with which she took command, and the carefully thought out strategies she voiced. As much as he wanted to assume the Rockoid throne himself, he had to admire her courage and her intelligence. She would indeed be a suitable mate for him, despite the vast difference in their ages; his lust intensified the more he considered the possibility. Xorax would continue biding his time, expressing his criticisms with the proper degree of respect.

Xerox remained, however, unaware of the inscrutable outside forces that had even now begun to possess his mind and his soul.

"One more thing." Zanther interrupted his reverie. "Remember to take out the colonial production facilities only, Commander Ivarna. We are not attacking civilian targets unless it is absolutely necessary."

The commander nodded in reply.

"The attack is to begin immediately. You are now all dismissed."

Xorax, Ivarna, and Queksnar quickly walked out of the room. While she still had her private reservations about the need for such an invasion, Zanther knew that Xorax could use such doubts to his advantage. She had not accepted the mantle of leadership lightly. She often had to put aside her inner feelings and act in accordance with the needs of her people and requirements of the situation.

When it came to sending her people off to their deaths, she could not fully suppress her deep misgivings. Her late father shared the same sensitivities. She recalled how the Emperor often visited the family of a war casualty personally when he could or hold a private session in his chambers when large numbers were involved, to share a grief he accepted as his own.

Zanther knew he wasn't just putting on a show for propaganda or to impress the people. He refused to have such sessions broadcast across Rockoid space and didn't allow any journalists to interview any of the bereaved families.

Zanther's expression was stern now. Without the slightest hesitation she got up, walked boldly and briskly out of the chamber, returning to her throne room.

As the fleet sped toward the scene of the upcoming conflict that would determine the fate of the Alliance, she began thinking about the human she continued to see in her dreams. It was an enigma she knew she must strive to understand. As her ship approached Earth, the dreams intensified. At times, it seemed this alien being wanted to reach out to her; she had to admit she wanted to reach out to him as well. She playfully sent telepathic messages to the alien, feeling he somehow understood her. She ached to get to the bottom of this mystery soon. Zanther had the deep feeling that if she didn't understand the source of those dreams and deal with it, tragedy would result...a tragedy that could claim the lives of millions of beings from both civilizations.

Chapter 13

Ray remained in a bit of a funk over the next few weeks. His workdays were longer than ever, and he felt utterly exhausted by the end of the day.

His next task was the hardest of all. He had to qualify for a position in the Alliance military. Despite his extensive military background, that training barely counted for entry-level status in the twenty-third century. He had to enter the academy as just another cadet. They did agree to restore his rank of Captain if he successfully got through the intense training sessions and passed with a reasonably high grade. Although Ray acted as if it was a piece of cake, he knew he had to work harder than he ever had in his life to qualify.

Ray dove into the training sessions with an intensity he never knew he possessed. In short order, he began feeling strain in muscles he didn't think existed. His martial arts experience helped him here, as many elements of those disciplines formed the core of the hand-to-hand combat procedures every Alliance cadet had to learn.

One afternoon, to Ray's delight, Jennifer managed to get some time off work and arranged for him to be given the rest of the day off. She met him in the parking lot of the training center. As soon as they saw each other, they ran over to each other and embraced, like old friends who hadn't seen each other in years.

Ray raised his eyebrows. "You're sure I won't get in trouble for ditching class?"

Jennifer laughed. "Don't worry, Ray. I've already arranged everything with your instructors. The whole afternoon is ours.

"Now let's split or whatever you call getting the hell out of this place in your time."

Without a moment's hesitation, they jumped into Jennifer's hovercar, and sped off toward Atlanta. Ray drove this time, as he had finally gotten the chance to learn how to pilot a hovercar just a week or so before.

The hovercars practically did all the work for the driver. All one had to do was enter the proper identification codes to turn on the engine, reach cruising altitude, guide it with the steering stick once in a while, and the onboard computers would do the rest, assuming the car was on autopilot, a mode in which the craft practically drove themselves.

Before Ray actually received his license, Jennifer had to witness him enduring a successful driver's test and he had to fill out numerous forms that dealt with the equivalent of auto insurance in the twenty-third century.

Scientists said we were going to become a paperless society. Yeah, sure, right.

As they made their way to Jennifer's apartment, Ray's wrist-view device interrupted his train of thought and announced, "You have one viewscreen message, Captain Perkins."

"That's a surprise. Who's it from?" Ray asked.

"It is from Captain David Gotlieb. Authorization to play it?"

"Yes, go ahead."

"One moment please."

. The face of Captain Gotlieb appeared on Ray's wristview, but the message was clear without the need for his commander to say anything more.

"Hi, old man, I'm afraid I've got some bad news for you."

Ray's heart sank. He looked at Jennifer, and it was clear she was on the same wavelength.

"The Rockoids just arrived over the colony worlds in the Tau Ceti, Terea, and Sol star systems. I understand they've already begun firing on military and industrial installations."

Ray had to struggle to keep from losing control of the hovercar. His face stayed grim, his eyes showing an almost fearful look now that what he dreaded for so long seemed about to come to pass.

He tried to conjure up the image of Zanther, wondering just what sort of role she had to play in these attacks. Try as he might, no thoughts about her emerged in his conscious mind. It almost seemed as if the alien woman was otherwise occupied—in truth, she was, though Ray didn't know that.

He turned towards Jennifer and saw she, too, had nearly lost her professional composure. For a second, he saw the suggestion of a tear in her eye, but she turned her head quickly.

Ray barely had a second to think however, as the message continued, "I never thought this would really happen. We're gonna have to let you off training early. We need to know everything we can about your latest dreams, in case they affect the invasion, and our plans for defense. We're checking the status of the Rockoid attack from satellite stations here in Brussels, and also on Taucon and Terea."

Gotlieb continued his explanation with an impassive expression, but Ray could see worry in his eyes. Strange how he'd been able to pick up on the emotions of others so quickly. He wondered if those god-awful dreams had a role in it.

"You gotta come here to Brussels right now, Ray," Gotlieb acted as if he'd rehearsed the speech over and over again before he called. "Join us at the Alliance's military command center. We're already preparing for a full scale defense, so you better hurry."

Ray started considering the possibilities. "David, just how bad is it?"

"Let me say it's going to get a whole lot worse before it gets better, old man. See you soon."

The image of Gotlieb disappeared. Ray sat transfixed, wide-mouthed and wide-eyed. His worst nightmares were coming true, literally before his eyes.

* * *

A half hour later, Ray and Jennifer arrived at the Alliance command center in the outskirts of Brussels.

Once they left the parking area, they saw a large nondescript building looming across from them and far up into the sky above and quickened their pace. Once they were inside the building, they found their associates waiting impatiently for them.

Ray saw Captain Gotlieb and Dr. Johnson, who were accompanied by a blond-haired, blue-eyed woman with a dark silver uniform. They waved at their companions and walked toward them.

Ray realized the unidentified woman seemed very familiar, although he had no conscious recollection of meeting her before. He soon realized he had seen her in his dreams, but he couldn't remember the exact role she played. The woman's uniform had a large emblem on her shoulder that identified her as a commander. She also had a rather extensive collection of medals, no doubt reflecting the honors she had been accorded during her military career.

While she was tall, slender, quite attractive, she also radiated a level of authority that seemed far beyond her age. He guessed she was in her early forties at most, though her cream-white complexion made her appear much younger. Her steel blue eyes seemed penetrating, inquisitive and even a bit menacing.

Ray stared and a shudder of frightened recognition erupted in his spine. He tried to shield his reaction to the menacing stare.

Gotlieb introduced her. "I want you to meet Commander Elizabeth Thompson, one of the last remaining Alliance war heroes."

Ray nodded and stepped up to her. With a forced smile, he saluted her and said, "It's a pleasure to meet you, sir."

Commander Thompson, who only recently received a promotion to a rank just below Johnson's, appeared to accept the greeting as if it had been expected, customary. She nodded formally and replied. Her voice was husky, battle-worn, with a distinct, uppercrust British accent, "It is a pleasure to meet you as well, Captain Perkins. I have heard quite a lot about you."

"Positive, I hope, sir," Ray replied as his mind began to conjure up the visions of this highly decorated military commander portrayed in his dreams.

Ray could barely contain himself. His worst fears had been confirmed. Thompson was indeed the very person who led the Alliance forces in the battle over Dorton. He couldn't see her face in his dreams, but those eyes; he could feel their cold, calculating, menacing stare. For a moment, Ray wondered if she hadn't realized he suspected her of being the treasonous aggressor in that savage battle, the instrument that brought upon this present war with the Rockoids.

How could the Alliance commanders not know? Was it all a gigantic conspiracy, a conspiracy that extended to the president's office? Were they all hiding the truth from him and Alliance citizens?

A part of him still couldn't believe what he felt deep down in his soul to be the awful truth. Maybe he could read the mind of a Rockoid, but how could he possibly observe events that Zanther didn't see? The very idea seemed incredibly silly. He had always dismissed such prospects as superstition, the stuff of one's overactive imagination.

Fortune tellers, Ouija boards, precognition...impossible!

Ray tried to will himself to believe that these incredible visions were just psychological constructs, products of his all-too-vivid imagination, as Dr. Johnson suggested.

Yet almost every important detail of Ray's dreams turned out to be true. Was Thompson a hero or a traitor? Even if she betrayed the Alliance, she was also a highly decorated military officer; he wouldn't dare make accusations against such a person without strong evidence. Dreams would never be considered evidence. If

Ray didn't hold his tongue, at least for now, he'd face a certain court martial and an equally certain prison term.

He had to bide his time, watch, listen and hope for a chance to prove his case before this terrible tragedy went too far, assuming it wasn't already too late.

It was wartime and the fate of millions of beings on both sides hung in the balance. Ray didn't know why it was his lot in life to play a pivotal role in deciding issues of war and peace. The responsibility weighed heavily upon him. He wondered if he should have gone on that silly mission to Area 51. If he still lived in the past, he would be sitting at home in front of his computer, writing a new computer game or riding through the countryside in his old Mustang, not worrying one bit about matters of interstellar war. He wondered what Gonzales would have thought when he disappeared. Would he have left Ray for dead? Would Ray simply have remained unconscious on the floor of the laboratory in Area 51 until he either died of old age or was discovered and thrown in prison?

Jennifer stared at him. She could see the deep frown and creases in his forehead, signs of internal struggle, and she hoped he'd soon tell her what drew his attention away from the serious matters of war and peace.

Commander Thompson interrupted his thoughts, acting as if she suspected nothing. "Captain Perkins, we must get to the primary command center immediately. Time is of the essence, and our forces are rapidly being worn down by the Rockoid assault."

"Yes, Liz," Johnson broke in, "y'all need to find out what's going on with this situation since we last checked.

"Oh, I'm sorry, Ray, I suppose I should explain. Commander Thompson is a close friend of my family. Her late father, Rex Thompson, was one of my closest friends; when he died, Liz became a part of my family too. My wife Becky and I...we never had any children of our own. Becky asked Liz to live with us when she went into the Alliance Academy. She's really like a daughter to us."

Oh my god! For a moment, Ray experienced an intense wave of vertigo, but Thompson's voice interrupted him before his internal struggle led him to say something foolish.

"Excuse me, Captain, I believe it's time for us to go." Thompson broke in with a hint of sarcasm. "We really do not have any more time to waste."

With Thompson leading, Ray behind her with Jennifer at his side, and Gotlieb and Johnson taking up the rear, staying quite a distance from each other, they began walking briskly to the command center, where they would watch the progress of the conflict.

According to the latest intelligence reports, the six targeted colonies were still under heavy assault, and the Alliance defense forces in the area were having trouble keeping up with the enemy.

At the same time, he could hear Johnson barking orders into his wristview, though the specifics were a blur to him. Johnson consulted with the command team, en masse it seemed, and received a blow-by-blow account of the proceedings. At times, Johnson would also brief Thompson. They nodded agreeably and he gave further orders.

As they continued on their way to the main command center, Ray became lost in thought as he began to consider his prior dreams more carefully. He struggled to determine why they sometimes presented such odd perspectives; he came to a chilling conclusion, one he hadn't taken seriously before.

Some of his dreams had revealed the space battle as a Rockoid might have perceived it! When he saw Rockoid ships being fired upon, he witnessed the attack from what looked like a viewscreen aboard a Rockoid ship—or from the perspective of one of those humanoid creatures.

Surely, he wasn't a Rockoid in disguise, was he? The whole idea just didn't make sense, and didn't explain his ability to see what happened aboard an Alliance ship, involving Thompson, either. He didn't want to think about the implications of this mysterious ability to see events that occurred in places where he wasn't physically present. What did they call it on those late night radio shows back in the twenty-first century?

Oh yes, remote viewing.

At this point, Thompson, who stood right in front of him, turned around and demanded, "Is something the matter, Captain Perkins?"

Ray guessed that Thompson had a far more intuitive grasp of the situation than he would have expected, considering her somewhat cold demeanor.

"No, no. I'm probably just a bit tired from the long hours every day at the Academy," Ray replied quickly.

"Oh, that's quite all right; I perfectly understand the tension you must be under," sighed Thompson. She nodded her head agreeably, but it was clear to Ray she wasn't satisfied with his answer.

Ray also wondered if anyone had told this woman about his suspicions concerning her role in the Dorton affair. If she were indeed guilty of the barbaric acts for which the Rockoids no doubt blamed her, he'd soon find himself in deep trouble and possibly be in danger of losing his life. Maybe she'd dispatch him on some suicide mission to get him out of the way.

He returned to thoughts about his dreams. He knew the safety of the Alliance might depend on knowing the truth about what happened during their first encounter with the Rockoids, and why Thompson was considered the hero rather than the villain in that encounter. Only a fool would believe the Rockoids wouldn't retaliate some day. An answer nagged at core of his subconscious, but Ray didn't pick up on it.

* * *

In minutes, the party arrived at the main command center. The bright, off-white chamber stood thirty meters high and extended the length of a football field. The walls conveyed the clinical feel of an operating room rather than a top-secret military facility. Status viewscreens lined the far walls, and the hustle and bustle of activity proceeded at an almost dizzying pace.

Ray stared in amazement at the viewscreens, watching Rockoid ships attacking Alliance colonies from different vantage points.

Every so often, a technician handed Commander Thompson or Dr. Johnson a paper-thin portable viewscreen shaped like a large notepad that contained status reports; it reminded Ray of an iPad back in his own century, only this amazing contraption could be transformed clay-like into smaller sizes as needed. Johnson and Thompson nodded their heads or barked a few orders before returning the devices to their bearers.

The gloomy atmosphere hung thick like a blanket, permeating everyone's consciousness. Those present seemed to do their jobs quietly and efficiently, but their melancholic looks were hard to conceal. When Ray examined the surroundings a little more carefully, he saw some of those present wiping their eyes with a tissue or handkerchief.

Gotlieb struggled to maintain a confident attitude and began describing the purpose of the command room. "We can monitor the status of the Rockoid attacks on all Alliance worlds here, and stay in direct contact with all the fleet commanders. Updates to defense strategy can be communicated almost instantaneously."

Ray took a closer look at Gotlieb and saw worry in his eyes, a grim, determined expression on his face. He followed Gotlieb over to one screen where a black-haired woman, who appeared to be of Latin descent, was hard at work.

"Lieutenant Francesca, please show Captain Perkins the image we received from the Mars colony," instructed Gotlieb.

"Yes, sir," said Francesca.

The woman was young for an officer, perhaps in her early twenties, short, very slim, with long, curly black hair, big hazel eyes. She seemed to be wiping a tear absentmindedly with a finger. "Bring up image two hundred fifty-eight."

Ray couldn't help but notice the barest suggestion of a crack in her voice, a trace of huskiness.

The picture appeared on the screen. Ray gasped at the shocking image, one of absolute devastation, worse than anything he'd ever seen before, except for those awful pictures from World War III.

There were battered buildings and rubble everywhere. A few fires appeared to be burning in some sections of New San Francisco as Francesca panned around the city. Crushed hovercars lay on the ground upside down; sidewalks and streets were nothing but debris. To his horror, dead bodies, and body parts, were clearly visible.

Ray had seen the horrible aftermath of war before, but he never got used to such scenes. Part of him was inured to the grim reaper's presence on the battlefield, part of him was repelled; he found his emotions hard to suppress.

"How...how did this happen? When?"

"It came without warning...we didn't have time to mount a defense..." Gotlieb stammered, "the Rockoids just let loose on us. In...the attacks on the cities of the colonies, key production centers were taken out. Now most of them are running on emergency power reserves. Casualties were surprisingly pretty light."

"What about the atmosphere? All those cities are in self-contained domes."

"A backup system repairs any holes in the dome around New San Francisco and restores the proper atmospheric pressure in a little while. That's probably the least of our problems."

He listened intently as Francesca tried to explain the situation. "Sir, we lost contact with New San Francisco just before you got here. Our satellite network couldn't scan the city, as if the signals were being jammed."

She sat down at her console, picked up a tissue absentmindedly from her purse, and stared out into space.

Gotlieb took a long, deep breath, and tried to update Ray on the rest of the frightening picture.

He thought about his responsibilities to his family, his friends, and to the Alliance, who now depended on him for accurate information, presented dispassionately. He took another deep breath and then spoke. His voice began weakly, but soon gained strength.

"We sent some scout ships, but we lost contact with them. About an hour later, we managed to reestablish communication with one of the vessels. The others were destroyed. The surviving ship sent the image you just saw. If this is what these Rockoids plan to do to the other Alliance worlds then we're in...well, we're in for one hell of a time," explained Gotlieb, trying to keep his voice steady.

Ray stood wide-eyed and remained silent for several minutes.

He shook his head, tried to compose his thoughts, and found he had the voice, though he was barely conscious of the words.

"What are we going to do now? Are we finished?"

"I don't know, Ray. Unless we can come up with a powerful defense, fast, our prospects of turning back this invasion are pretty damn depressing," replied Gotlieb.

They walked over to Johnson, who still fumbled with the portable viewscreen image. He put on reading glasses and looked over the status report again.

A few minutes later, Johnson absentmindedly dropped the viewer on a nearby desk and put his glasses back in his pocket. He stood there fuming.

"What is it, commander?" Ray asked.

"I can't believe this. Alliance Intelligence says that enemy fleets have just arrived in at least three other star systems. Our forces are going to be spread extremely thin. A large portion of our fleet is at the other side of the galaxy, on various exploration missions. The Rockoids must have known that..."

Johnson was still the battle-hardened veteran. As much as he ached inside, he was able to rise to the occasion and perform the duties assigned to him without outward signs of the emotions raging within him.

"It'll take days or even weeks to recall all our cruisers. If the Rockoids continue their attack, we may be out of luck," said Johnson with only a trace of emotion in his voice. "The Rockoids knew how, when and where to stage their assault for maximum effect. They must have known the Alliance wouldn't fight unless attacked first."

"But we could have started calling back those ships when we first knew the Rockoids were coming, couldn't we?" Ray chimed in.

"Ray, if we had done that, there would have been chaos once the news broke. Billions would panic if they thought they were about to be attacked. It would be a political and logistical nightmare."

Gotlieb attempted to sound calm. "Sir, we should contact the leaders of all the threatened Alliance planets and colonies, send warnings to all the emergency centers there."

"Thank you so much for stating the obvious, Captain. Of course, we got to notify the authorities in those star systems now, and tell them to evacuate their major cities! Billions of lives are at stake!" Johnson's deep voice sounded almost like a bark now.

Thompson intervened.

"For heaven's sake, end this ridiculous conversation! We must be acting, not talking!" Her stern voice was clearly accustomed to command, dispassionate.

Without warning, Thompson raised her voice to an almost piercing level. "I warned you all these Rockoids were up to no good. You should have listened…you should have destroyed them when we had the chance!"

Johnson put his arm around her shoulder and said in a fatherly voice, "Liz, please, settle down. I don't want y'all to get too hyper right now. We need your command skills now more than ever."

She remained silent for a moment and stared at everyone.

At that moment, the images of the Rockoid ships hovering over the Alliance colony worlds were replaced by a symbol, consisting of a large circle in the center of which was a bird-like creature with its wings outstretched.

A booming voice came on the loudspeakers, interrupting the transmissions. "The Rockoid Empire demands your surrender forthwith. A response is required within three days. Failure to surrender will result in the destruction of the major cities on the Alliance planets Earth, Taucon, and Terea."

That same message was repeated at least twenty times, using the Alliance universal translation system to convert it to all known languages.

Once the warnings stopped, the symbol on the screen became distorted, and there was a loud rumbling sound, emanating from an unknown source. The screen went blank, and there was silence.

Chapter 14

Technicians worked vigorously to restore the viewscreens in the various Alliance command centers. It appeared the Rockoids somehow jammed the signals at their source, and the backup systems were unable to prevent the incursion. No Rockoid-based jamming signals could be detected, no radio waves at all on any known frequencies.

Ray, Johnson, Jennifer, and Gotlieb were struggling to devise a plan of action, though Thompson appeared to be thinking about something else.

Finally, the silence was broken. "This is insane!" Thompson shouted. "We should have returned all our forces to Alliance space as soon we knew the Rockoids were coming! We might have been able to save the colony worlds!"

"There was nothing we could have done, Liz," interrupted Johnson. "We couldn't have known. We restored all the reservists to active duty; we couldn't do much of anything else without setting off ten kinds of hell among the Alliance worlds."

"Look how they attacked us during our peaceful exploratory mission near the Dorton colony! Wasn't all that enough for you?"

Peaceful, yeah sure. Only a moron would believe that! Despite his misgivings, Ray held his tongue.

"We could have at least gotten our forces to the threatened colony worlds as a precaution. It's obvious any population or strategic center would be most vulnerable," Thompson barked.

"Our forces have been spread terribly thin," Liz. "Now there's not much we can do without further dividing our forces. In fact, the attacks on the capital worlds have just begun; at this moment we have just engaged Rockoid forces over Terea," explained Johnson.

Thompson's eyes widened. She frowned, her face transforming into a worried expression.

"What's wrong, sir?" Ray asked.

"Henry, did you just say my home world was being attacked?" asked Thompson.

"Yes, we received word of a battle taking place over Terea a few minutes ago. We did dispatch a fleet to defend..."

Without warning, Thompson became agitated, almost hysterical. The onlookers were at once surprised and shocked.

"For God's sake, save Terea! My sister lives there, my friends— what will happen to them?" screamed Thompson wildly. She broke down and started to cry.

Gotlieb walked over to Thompson and put his arm on her shoulder in an attempt to mollify her. Suddenly she spun around and Gotlieb found himself flipped end over end, lying on the ground. Thompson was a master at hand-to-hand combat, more powerful than most men.

Gotlieb merely sat there, blood streaking from his cheek, which struck a nearby desk as he fell.

She reluctantly reached out her hand and helped Gotlieb get up, rather forcefully.

"If you dare lay a hand on me again, Captain Gotlieb, I will demote you to the rank of private," said Thompson sternly with a hint of arrogance in her voice.

"I'm sorry, Commander Thompson." Gotlieb stammered. "Why did you attack me?"

She ignored his question. "I will forget about your misjudgment this time, but do not dare ever touch me again."

"Yeah, I get it, Commander, but I wanted to reassure you..." Gotlieb started to say.

"Shut up, Gotlieb! You may think you can charm me, but I am not the least bit interested in what you have to say!" exclaimed Thompson angrily. Johnson walked over to Thompson and talked quietly with her. She seemed about to argue with him too, but thought better of it. Johnson's voice remained a whisper, but Ray couldn't miss its meaning.

A few words caught his ear: "Liz, I'm gonna have to relieve ya of your command if you continue these fits. I can't continue to stick up for you like this! Please!"

A tense silence persisted for a few seconds until the technician, Francesca, stood up and exclaimed, "Dr. Johnson, Dr. Johnson!"

Johnson turned around and asked, "Yes, Ms. Francesca?"

"The satellite system is back online, sir! We've reestablished communication with our colonies!" she exclaimed.

"Show us the latest images."

"Yes, sir."

She ran back to her station. A few seconds later, it was clear their worst fears had been realized. Again there were audible gasps of shock around the command center, as everyone present stared at the ruins of the largest city, Ulara, on Loveer, one of Terea's colonies, as well as that of cities on other Alliance colony worlds.

"Oh, my God! First the production centers on Mars and Europa, and now this!" exclaimed Johnson, clearly shocked.

Ray sighed. This situation was deteriorating by the minute. But he had an idea. While he doubted anyone would take him seriously, he threw caution to the wind and motioned Johnson over to him.

"Yes, Captain Perkins?" Johnson asked.

"Sir," Ray whispered quietly, "I have to talk to you about

this situation."

He quickly glanced around, and his eyes locked on Thompson, who seemed to be glaring at Ray.

"In private."

Johnson nodded quickly, and together they went into a small adjoining briefing room. Once the door had closed behind them, Ray began, "Dr. Johnson, I know I've said this before...but I still think Commander Thompson was responsible for attacking the Rockoids first...."

Johnson sighed. "Ray, please, you know we can't talk about this. Do you know what she would do if she heard what you were saying? You'd be stripped of your rank, court martialed. I'm cutting you slack here, but you've got to face reality. There's no way..."

"What about my dreams? What if Thompson really did attack them first?"

The scientist shook his head. "Oh come on. That's crazy, just crazy. I've known Liz nearly all her life. She'd never betray the Alliance if her life depended on it!"

"My dreams clearly show..."

Johnson held up a hand. "I'm sorry, Captain, but just because you weren't born in this century doesn't mean you are exempted from following your orders and obeying our laws. I order you to stop this behavior this instant. Don't do anything rash or else you could very well sabotage our entire military operation."

He paused for just a moment to let his words sink in. Ray looked on in stunned silence.

Quite reluctantly, Ray finally replied, "Yes, sir."

Suddenly there was a knock on the door. Johnson gave an acknowledgment and it rapidly slid open. Francesca burst into the room, with a big smile on her face.

Johnson glared at her. "Lieutenant Francesca, what the hell..."

"I'm very sorry, sir, but we have successfully established a trans-space link with the Rockoid flagship."

Johnson's eyes widened. "How the hell did you do that?"

"It was Commander Thompson's idea, sir...."

Johnson did not let her finish her sentence; at that moment he rushed back to the main control center. Thompson stood in front of a viewscreen with a big smile on her face. She stepped aside to show the emblem of the Rockoid Empire. Looks of amazement filled the eyes of the onlookers.

"How did you do it, Liz?"

Her smile lessened a bit. "It wasn't as hard as you might think. You see, while you and Captain Perkins were in that room chatting away, I decided to make one last attempt to resolve this situation peacefully. I asked Lieutenant Francesca to test a few protocols. I realized there was a way to get around the Rockoid jamming frequencies by throwing a hailing signal at multiple frequencies from different locations."

Johnson smiled at her. "Thank you, Liz."

He turned to Francesca, who stood behind him. "All right, open all hailing frequencies. Y'all get ready for our first communication with the Rockoids...on our own terms!"

Everyone cheered in approval, but Johnson quickly quieted them down. Static filled the airwaves. The hailing frequencies were open and ready.

"Greetings, Rockoid flagship. I am Commander Henry Johnson of the Alliance. I don't know what we've done to offend your Empire, but I assure you our people only seek peace."

Johnson spoke in slow, measured tones, making sure each word was spoken clearly, so there would be no possibility of misunderstanding. The message was beamed through the Alliance's universal translation system, which instantly converted it to the speech forms of hundreds of different alien races. Since the Rockoids were able to tap into that system, he felt certain they'd have little difficulty deciphering his message.

"The Alliance is still willing to make peace with your people. It is not too late to stop this war. We are prepared to hold a conference in the next Earth day to discuss this matter. Please respond."

The image on the screen changed to that of the ominous flagship hovering in space not far from Earth.

An Alliance warship came into view on the screen, and it just as quickly exploded into millions of tiny fragments as the Rockoid cruiser destroyed it.

Dr. Johnson smashed his fist on the nearest table as hard as he could, nearly cracking the table in half. Although the table didn't split apart, a telltale crease was left in its shiny surface.

"This is it!" he shouted, "We've waited around long enough! It's time we took some action and staged a counterattack!"

Thompson chimed in, "It's about goddamned time!"

"All we have to do now is get President Rogers to sign off on the battle plan," said Johnson.

"Ms. Francesca, get President Rogers on the viewscreen!"

"Yes, sir!"

A few seconds later the Alliance president's concerned face appeared.

"Yes, Commander Johnson?" asked Rogers.

"Mr. President, we need your approval to begin military engagement with the Rockoids..."

Rogers interrupted Johnson with a bit of abruptness, tinged with sadness, "Yes. Begin the counteroffensive. We cannot waste any more time." Johnson nodded in agreement.

"If there's any good news here," Rogers continued, "it's the fact the Rockoid ships are moving very slowly. They're cruising in normal space, so we have a little more time to prepare."

Everyone hoped the Rockoids would truly adhere to their three-day deadline. A miscommunication among Rockoid commanders had already resulted in the premature attack on Terea.

"The evacuation forces are doing the best they can to get most of the populace in the threatened areas away to shelter. We have assembled six large assault groups from available personnel. Briefings are going on as we speak. Right now I believe we should focus our efforts on defending the colonies instead of the capital worlds."

Johnson couldn't conceal his shock. "President Rogers, I don't wish to question your orders, but we're leaving our three most important planets defenseless. We can't risk what would happen if the Rockoids break through the defenses."

"Commander Johnson, you have to realize the Rockoids expect us to send most of our forces there. Since they've left only a small portion of their fleet at the colony worlds, it would be more productive to attack the enemy forces there. It will force them to move the majority of their forces away from their real targets, and it might just give us more time to gather our resources. If they are really going to abide by this three-day deadline of theirs, then they will not attack any more planets until the time limit is up. Clearly they're hoping we'll surrender without putting up a fight."

Rogers continued to detail his well-thought-out battle plans, and as he concluded his presentation, he looked straight at Ray. "Captain Perkins, I have a special mission for you."

Once again, Ray was dumbfounded. "Me, sir?"

"Yes." There was a trace of a smile on the president's lips as he spoke. "You will be part of a fighter squadron defending the Mars colony. Commander Johnson will see you're escorted to the nearest base. That's all for now."

Ray tried to speak, but only stammered and mumbled away. Maybe he shouldn't have voiced his fears about who was really responsible for that battle above the Dorton colony so freely.

Before Ray could utter a coherent word, the President's stern image disappeared from the screen.

* * *

Cadets, crew members, pilots, and officers, an odd mixture of humans and non-humans, hastily put on uniforms, quickly boarded cruisers, and took their assigned stations on other Alliance worlds. Before departure, they ran through standard flight checks, and reviewed the final commands from Thompson and other military leaders.

Most of the troops were excited about going into battle at last, but they had all seen the destruction wrought by the Rockoids, and many of them harbored the same fear—the fear they would not return home alive.

Chapter 15

Tensions rose rapidly on both sides.

Within twenty-four hours, the Alliance's counterattack began in earnest. The Rockoid ships didn't have a moment's freedom to attack more colonial cities before they saw their adversaries speeding toward them.

As Alliance fleets approached their targets, most of them were forced to split their forces, due to the presence of enemy warships both out in space and in the upper atmospheres of the colony worlds.

The fleets themselves were quite impressive, even though they were clearly outnumbered by what they presumed to be the greater firepower of the enemy.

The enemy fighters, shaped remarkably like Earth fighter jets of the early twenty-first century, were incredible devices by any standard. They were ten meters long, six meters wide and had room for only one pilot. They were capable of limited hyperdrive travel, as the engines had to be recharged frequently. Due to the sometimes daredevil maneuvers they had to make while in combat and limited energy reserves, they were not outfitted with artificial gravity generators.

Armed freighters, sixty-meter-long wedge-shaped ships, supported the fighters.

The brunt of the battle was to be borne by light cruisers, huge, long, bulky craft with a circular appearance. These ships were massive, some two hundred sixty meters long and one hundred sixty meters wide.

Backup was provided by a small number of the most powerful Alliance attack ships, the heavy cruisers, thick, irregularly shaped vessels consisting of an assemblage of turrets and cylinders. These were some five hundred meters long and three hundred meters high.

The size of the fleet coming to engage their ships was not lost on the Rockoids, who were quick to react.

In the upper atmosphere of the Red Planet, above the ruins of New San Francisco, the Rockoid super cruiser spun at a dizzying pace. The maneuvering ability of that craft amazed the Alliance commanders. As it turned to face the incoming ships, the Alliance fired.

Large beams emerged from the huge guns at the bows of the Alliance cruisers, and torpedoes spun wildly toward the invaders. Everything seemed to hit its target head-on.

The Alliance commanders looked on with astonishment when they saw the Rockoids did not change their battle formation to avoid the incoming firepower. Ray knew the answer—his dreams told the awful truth. He just didn't want to believe it.

Soon the Alliance found out; when the torpedoes and laser blasts struck their target, they simply bounced off without doing any harm. The enemy's shields were clearly impervious to Alliance weapons. The commanders ordered that the Rockoid flagship be fired upon with renewed intensity, hoping to overcome the alien shielding by sheer force.

Multicolored beams shot forth and struck the Rockoid ship from all directions. Hundreds of torpedoes were fired. A fiery, explosive display almost obscured the target. Commanders watched in expectation and exasperation. They tried again and again to penetrate the Rockoid shields, without success.

Alliance commanders found they had to scurry back and forth to avoid the beams and missiles that rebounded from the Rockoid craft. In a few cases, they sustained minor damage from their own "friendly fire."

Ray watched the entire sad affair carefully, trying to cull details from his memory of the Rockoid fleet that would help his comrades get past those shields. He could recall practically nothing that would help the Alliance military tacticians.

Meanwhile, the situation looked increasingly hopeless. Thompson ordered the fighters to withdraw and directed the cruisers to stay on course, try again to penetrate the invader's defenses. Before the Alliance ships could complete these tasks, what seemed like hundreds of enemy ships of varying shapes and sizes, all smaller than the super cruiser, entered Mars' upper atmosphere, approached them, and started firing.

The Rockoid fighters were themselves quite impressive compared to the equivalent Alliance vessel. Ray clearly recalled developing animated simulations of those fighters when he created his computer games. Seeing them up close was still a jarring experience.

The fighters were saucer-shaped. Ray wondered if they might have been a source for some of those UFO reports back in his time. Measuring fifteen meters long and eight meters high, the silvery craft had an intricate design, with creases and curves flowing in incredible symmetry.

They were works of art, as were the larger Rockoid ships, which displayed equally impressive, almost beautiful designs.

Ray wondered about the society that could create such strikingly elegant pieces of machinery. How could a race, so obviously devoted to beauty and form, stage a barbaric attack on another alien race without provocation? The more he thought about it, the more it didn't make sense. If the Alliance were the aggressor, then the Rockoids would be acting in self-defense.

Nothing about the situation seemed logical, but Ray was in the thick of it now, struggling to defend himself against enemy fire. Yet, strange as it seemed, he didn't find the going terribly rough. It often seemed to him as if the Rockoids were avoiding him. He had the vague sense this was deliberate. He maintained a defensive posture; he made no overt effort to engage the enemy.

Could Zanther be responsible for any of this? Ray sensed she was someone in authority, and had the power to tell her soldiers not to fire their weapons. How could she possibly pick out his craft from among the fleet of Alliance spaceships, unless...unless she could read his mind, know precisely where he was.

The thought was frightening, yet compelling at the same time.

The Alliance ships fought back vigorously, bravely, against the onslaught. They renewed the attack, focusing mainly on the sleek Rockoid fighters and smaller cruisers. Fortunately, the smaller vessels did not have impenetrable shields. The Alliance began to inflict some damage. A few alien craft exploded into fiery debris. Some of the larger Rockoid ships also began showing signs of damage under the relentless attack of the Alliance fleet.

Although they managed to make inroads into the rampaging enemy forces, the Alliance just couldn't withstand the weapons. Thompson watched angrily as she saw cruiser after cruiser disintegrating in a blaze of fire and falling debris. There must have been millions of those alien ships. She remembered the battle on Dorton not so many years ago. There the Alliance had the tactical advantage of superior numbers. Those images sometimes came back to haunt her.

The Alliance fleet had to withdraw or be destroyed. They could only prevail in this war by discovering the secret of those shields, so they could destroy the biggest Rockoid ships.

She pondered the situation for several more seconds, as her commanders urged her to press on.

"No, we have to end this before we have no fleet to defend ourselves. Call back the ships!" she barked. "Mission aborted!"

Although there was no radio response to the command, within

minutes the Alliance formation started to break up.

The Alliance's withdrawal began.

Movement was observed on the Rockoid super cruiser. Large turrets began extending outward from the center of the ship. It appeared the enemy was preparing to fire their weapons again. She dared not consider how powerful the resulting explosive force would be.

Thompson ordered the withdrawal to speed up, but not in time. Small beams spewed forth from the guns on the Rockoid cruiser and began coalescing into one great beam.

Before anyone could react, a giant laser shot sprayed forth from the super cruiser and sliced through five Alliance cruisers. Each one was turned into space dust within seconds. One second, there was a massive explosion; the next, only a cloud of dust was evidence that an object had been present. Some of the captains of the other cruisers appeared to panic and retreated without thought.

The Alliance's defeat wasn't confined to the ships assigned to protect what was left of the Mars colony. Similar destruction was wrought by the aliens in battles elsewhere. The weakened Alliance forces retreated, leaving the Rockoids free to roam without having to fight off any defenders. There was one positive development in this engagement. The Rockoids temporarily halted the forward march of their fleet. Instead the enemy ships returned to the Alliance colony worlds to provide extra support for their ships orbiting those planets.

The forces attacking other major Alliance worlds stayed put, waiting for the moment when the order would be given to begin their major assaults, once the ultimatum had expired.

As the Alliance ships retreated, many of the Rockoid ships started to pursue them while the super cruiser stayed behind to finish off Mars' last intact cities, most of which had been evacuated. Many more Alliance cruisers and armed freighters were destroyed before the remnants of the fleet returned to safety. While the cruisers remained in position, fighters and smaller craft headed toward one of the seven main command bases on Earth. Finally, the Rockoids gave up the pursuit. Enemy fighters returned to docking stations aboard their command ship and smaller cruisers returned to space.

Although terrible damage had been inflicted on the Alliance fleet, the devastation on the colonies was far worse. Fortunately, a large network of shelters had been created to offer protection for the populations of these worlds, so most of the colonists escaped serious injury; serious casualties remained relatively small. Many of their possessions and large portions of the tourist centers, though, were reduced to smoke and rubble.

The RECOM industrial centers were laid waste. It was clear the Rockoids planned on destroying the Alliance's ability to build the machines of war.

The Alliance hastily returned their remaining craft to their command bases. The remaining commanders assembled in a private chamber far away from the center of the largest command base on Earth. Several were delayed, since they had to travel in hyperspace to reach their destination. Thompson knew there were at least fifty division colonels and commanders between the six task forces at the beginning of the counterattack; now that number had been cut nearly in half.

Thompson reviewed the latest casualty list. Unlike their civilian counterparts on the worlds below, early estimates of the number of dead were astonishing—thousands, perhaps even tens of thousands perished during the initial engagements.

A mood of doom and gloom infected the surviving Alliance soldiers and command personnel.

After Thompson broadcast the depressing figures via transspace radio to Alliance commanders throughout the galaxy, more bad news arrived.

The fleet of cruisers the Ilsad Confederation, a small group of alien worlds friendly to the Alliance, had sent to assist in the battle against the Rockoids ran into an ambush while en route. Ten Rockoid super cruisers and five hundred smaller cruisers, reinforcements for the main Rockoid fleet near Earth, passed through the system at the same time.

The two sides discovered each other and battled it out. Many of the Ilsad cruisers were destroyed. Survivors managed to escape into hyperspace before being attacked; the remaining cruisers returned to their home worlds to avoid further losses. It was devastating news, compounded by the revelation that the Alliance suffered the destruction of nearly a fourth of the defense fleet for its capital star systems.

They would have to find some way to bring in reinforcements or else Earth, Taucon and Terea, and their 17 billion inhabitants, might have to surrender to the rampaging Rockoid fleet.

"We must act quickly, and recruit more assistance! I don't care if we have to abandon the colonies. We have to gather all the ships we possibly can to defend the central worlds!" barked Thompson.

Ray glanced at her out of the corner of his eye. Once again he was reminded of the terrible role she seemed to portray in his dream. And again, he resisted the urge to speak out. He knew that he couldn't make unsubstantiated charges without suffering the consequences.

A blond-haired officer stood up and said, "Sir, may I remind you Alliance edicts state very clearly we cannot evacuate a planet except in the face of a world-wide natural disaster or imminent destruction."

"Yes, I know that! We have no alternative. If we lost Earth or any of our other capital worlds, the entire Alliance could come crashing down around us."

The blond-haired man was an experienced commander. He bristled under Thompson's verbal onslaught, which continued, almost without letup.

He held his tongue, and after a few moments, sat down.

Ray raised his hand.

Thompson acknowledged him. "Yes, Captain Perkins." She gave him a perfunctory glance.

"Commander, I was taking medication to block those terrible dreams about the battle at Dorton, but now that they've begun to return, I feel they may help reveal something about the Rockoids. I'm convinced I've been tapping the mind of a Rockoid. I'm fairly sure it's the female whose face I see in those dreams. I think she may be someone in authority. If I could somehow get in contact with her...."

Before he could finish, Thompson broke in. "There will be no contact with the Rockoids! Speaking to them at this point will be considered an act of treason. Anybody who associates with those barbarians is just as bad as they are." Her fierce glare became almost irrational at this point. Ray could see her neck throbbing as she spoke.

As with her previous outbursts, she seemed to recover almost right away. Her voice became more controlled after a few seconds.

"Am I perfectly clear, Captain?"

"Crystal," Ray said. Despite what Thompson said, Ray already knew there was no way to stop him from becoming an active participant in the events unfolding before them. He also suspected there was a lot more going on with Commander Thompson. Something about this situation affected her far more than one might expect of a battle-hardened veteran. Ray had known many commanders during his time in the Middle East, but he had never seen anyone caught up as emotionally as Thompson. She appeared to be cracking fast under the strain; he knew such a situation could become dangerous.

That night, the dreams took on a renewed intensity.

* * *

Halfway between Mars and Earth, her flagship anchored in the middle of deep space, an increasingly angry Empress Zanther became more and more concerned about the course of the invasion.

She sat in her throne room holding a portable viewscreen in her long, delicate hands. A recording of what her ships witnessed in the just-concluded battle appeared on the screen. Whenever the Alliance weapons bounced off her ships, she remained calm. A touch of a smile creased her beautiful countenance. When the viewscreen showed her fleet's smaller spacecraft sustaining damage from the Alliance weapons, however, her mood changed, and she seethed.

Xorax had assured her the shields of even the smallest cruisers were impenetrable. He claimed their finest engineers had tested them.

Finally, she beamed a telepathic order to Xorax.

The minister arrived a few seconds later and walked rapidly up to Zanther's throne. He bowed. "You called, Your Majesty?"

"Yes, I did, Minister. Here, look at this viewscreen and tell me what you see," explained Zanther as she handed the device to him.

He had been observing the battle first hand. He knew what to expect even before he witnessed the playback in Zanther's presence. As the Alliance's fighters and cruisers plowed through the smaller vessels of the Rockoid fleet, he saw the damage. "I do not understand how this could be happening!"

She grabbed the viewscreen away from him, pointed a shapely finger at him, and shouted, "No, Minister, you knew. You knew very well our smaller ships could not withstand a sustained assault from the Alliance forces! Fortunately our largest cruisers have impenetrable shields and superior weapons; if they didn't, the counterattack would not have just inflicted damage on our fleet— it could have been a massacre! You should have learned from the way the Alliance so easily wrought destruction on Dorton. They cannot be easily defeated. Before this battle, they put up a rather spirited fight against our forces at Terea, even though they knew they couldn't win."

Zanther's anger intensified, "Tell me, Minister, who dared launch an attack on Terea against my direct orders?"

Xorax gave her what would have been interpreted as a dirty look. She barked back, "Minister, I would be careful on the way you show respect to your Empress!"

He bowed down to Zanther, hands behind his back, and said quietly, "I am truly sorry, your majesty. I admit we have a problem here. I shall have our finest engineers examine those shields and see if we can fix them in the field. Do not worry. We have inflicted serious damage to the Alliance fleet and will soon destroy it completely. Soon our flag will fly in the capital cities of the Alliance and their worlds will become Rockoid colonies. As for the one who disobeyed orders, I will make sure he is dealt with...in the appropriate fashion. One of his close relatives died in the battle over Dorton; he must have felt he could take matters into his own hands...he was quite wrong."

Xorax did not have to spell out the measures he would take. She accepted his apology; though it was clear to her his sincerity was feigned. She also knew from the minister's words that the disobedient commander would soon be at Xorax's mercy. She didn't expect to be hearing from that traitorous officer any time soon... or ever.

"Very well, Minister. Now go and do your job and report back as soon as you have more information."

Zanther dismissed Xorax. After the Minister departed, she walked over to a large porthole and looked out at the image of Earth in the distance. From space, the world seemed serene and untarnished by war. She wondered how things might have been had they been able to make peace with the inhabitants of that planet.

The more she thought about it, the more the doubts of the wisdom of their policy of conquering alien races swelled within her. Despite heavy support for her actions, she knew she would soon have to consider a policy change.

She also thought about the human male whose image filled her dreams. As the Alliance ships engaged her forces, she could sense his presence, pinpoint his location to within just a few meters, even in the vast distances of space. On a whim, she secretly sent commands to the Rockoid strategic computers so that the human's craft wouldn't register as an enemy ship.

She wondered what her counselor, Yexin, would think if he learned what she had done, but there was no time for her to speak with him. He was busy working with the rank and file soldiers, to instill in them the renewed faith they needed to ensure the mission's success.

Maybe Zanther would soon discover who the human was, his secrets and mission, but there was a war to fight, and there was so little time.

* * *

As Xorax made his way through the vast hallways of the flagship, his thoughts turned to Zanther. His feelings about her were
mixed. There was little doubt he desired her, not just because of
her beautiful face and form; having her was a fast route to the
power and wealth he craved.

Since the fall of the Zigant dynasty, the surviving members of
that family had disappeared into the darkness. After a long period
of anarchy and civil war in the Rockoid Empire, the Zigants rose
again to briefly regain control of the empire from unstable war-
lords. With the violent assassination of Emperor Eronetus and his
wife by alien dissidents, the Zigant dynasty lost its power base for
good.

Xorax himself was a direct descendant of the great Eronetus.

He believed combining the Empress's regal beauty and great
popularity with his military expertise would fulfill the failed
dreams of Eronetus — create a new generation of leaders that
would assume greater heights of power and eventual domination
of the entire galaxy.

So far, Zanther had rebuffed him with laughter and derision.
Both he and Zanther knew traditions dictated that any Empress
or Emperor having no mate at the time of taking power would
have to choose one within seven kilo-timeframes, the equivalent
of seven Earth years.

He thought he was the ideal consort for Zanther. Xorax
believed it was his divine right to sit by her side on the Rockoid
throne, as it had been his family's right for generations. It was all
the fault of the Rockoid Senate, which forced his family to enact
a series of poorly implemented policies, resulting in economic rifts
between the rich, middle-class, poor, and slaves. All this, plus
events beyond their control, contributed to the near downfall of
the Rockoid Empire.

Indeed, Xorax's madness had become all-consuming. He had
long-since forgotten that he was once a trusted friend of the royal

family and not its adversary. He remained ignorant of the true cause of his slowly deteriorating sanity, his uncontrollable mood springs.

Chapter 16

While most of the troops at the military base slept in barracks like their counterparts in Earth's past, Ray got his own room off base.

He mind filled with doubts as he went to bed that night. Ray reviewed the situation over and over again. There were too many questions about all that had happened to him in the past few weeks. Ray believed he had tapped into the mind of a Rockoid, possibly the one he saw in his dreams. Although the idea repelled him, he was also intrigued because it gave him insights into those strange, delicately beautiful, extraordinarily intelligent creatures.

These insights were all the more confusing the more he considered them. He felt strongly the Rockoids were not a war-like people. The thoughts he believed were relayed to him by that Rockoid woman showed that the depletion of natural resources throughout the empire forced them to attack uncooperative worlds that refused to share the coveted resources. The tradition of conquering other races considered inferior to the Rockoids had been established eons ago by long-dead rulers with less-than-peaceful goals. Had it not been for the affair at Dorton, would the Rockoids have given the Alliance any attention at all, since the Alliance was so far from the Rockoid Empire?

Ray's thoughts became more and more unfocused. He was exhausted from a long day of travel and war. The anti-dream pills were gone; he did take a sleeping pill, with Dr. Johnson's assurance he would be deep in peaceful slumber soon. Ray drifted quietly, comfortably, into a state of near unconsciousness...

* * *

That night he dreamed again, as he feared. This time the visions were more frightening than ever, far more intense than the dreams he had previously experienced.

For some reason, the dream went beyond the point where it had always ended previously. There was Zanther and her expression of anguish. The image of the battle became dominant again. He didn't understand why. Was Zanther sending him those visions?

In this new sequence, portions of the Alliance fleet continued to bombard Dorton, while at the same time the Alliance ships engaged the remaining Rockoid defense forces.

His mind suddenly focused on two ships, of a class that Ray did not recognize. The ships suddenly spun off in different directions, completely out of control, with fire bursting from all sides and engulfing their hulls.

Ray found himself in a state of fear and confusion, considering how vivid the dreams were now. Without warning, he observed yet another image he had never seen before. The battle scene changed to that of a gigantic steel-walled room with a decorative circular bed, a large black chair, and viewscreen, as well as other strange objects.

He could make out lush tapestries and huge, almost three-dimensional portraits of Rockoids placed around the room.

In the dream, he walked up to a mirror. He looked into it and he saw, not himself, but...the face of a Rockoid.

Zanther's face...

Ray awoke in a cold sweat. He ran into the bathroom and looked into the mirror, out of paranoia. He sighed, calming down when he saw the face in the mirror was still his. He took notice of the bags under his eyes, the hollow, gaunt look he presented, due to days of little sleep and intense pressure.

Suddenly he heard a beeping noise from his wristview. He turned the device on. "Display message."

Dr. Johnson's face appeared. "Ray, I need you at the docking bay right away. I have some good news for y'all."

The conversation ended abruptly. Ray wasn't about to disobey his commanding officer, despite his exhaustion. He took a fast shower, and within minutes, he completed his preparations and ran out the door, but not before he downed a small cup of coffee in an effort to stay alert.

He walked rapidly, his mind filled with questions and contradictions. Again he thought of his strange experiences in space piloting that fighter. He played back the scene over and over again in his mind.

One thing was clear: The Rockoids deliberately decided not to fire on him. He knew that now, as certain as he knew his own name. It must be Zanther! She was responsible. He could almost see her standing before him, smiling a strange, angelic smile.

He stopped for a second, looking back and forth, expecting her to appear from behind a hallway, walking up to him.

Nobody was there.

When Ray arrived at the docking bay, he noticed something very different about it. Yesterday, it had been lightly filled, since many of the fighters had been destroyed in battle; now it was crammed with what seemed like hundreds of additional fighter craft.

"That's not all!" Johnson yelled from behind him. "Look on the viewscreen!"

Ray glanced at a viewscreen to his right and saw a portion of the Alliance fleet hovering over Earth. It seemed as if there were hundreds of additional ships orbiting the planet, a few of them at least three times larger than some of the light cruisers Ray had seen going into battle the day before.

Why do those big cruisers look so familiar?

Johnson joined him now, and he seemed almost elated. "We have ten of these babies and we'll have more of them in the coming weeks. They're supposed to be the best ships in the galaxy. They have much better weapons and shields than our ordinary cruisers. We're sure they'll be able to take out a Rockoid super cruiser with the risk of taking only minor damage. Several hundred regular cruisers arrived this morning along with these ten battleships. A lot of them are from Alliance exploration fleets from across the galaxy. Many are commanded by veteran captains. Believe it or not, the rest of the ships are part of the reinforcements we thought had retreated to their home world."

"I don't understand."

"We are finally one up on those goddamned Rockoids!" Johnson beamed from ear to ear.

"We originally believed an armada of reinforcements sent by one of our allies, the Ilsad Confederation, was intercepted by an armada of Rockoid warships. The two forces supposedly fought it out until most of the Ilsad ships were destroyed. At that point, they sent us a trans-space radio signal saying they were returning to their home planet; they had suffered extensive damage and many casualties. They didn't encrypt the message, figuring the Rockoids would easily intercept them. The Rockoid reinforcements turned around and followed the fleet supposedly going back to their home world."

"What do you mean, 'supposedly?' Weren't they retreating for real?"

"That's what we thought at first, but when we received an encrypted copy of their command logs, we saw their real intent. It turned out their destination was not back to the Ilsad home world, but here. King Borin, the Ilsad Confederation's monarch, has confirmed our hopes. He told us only a small number of his warships had actually been destroyed in the skirmish with the enemy."

Johnson was in his element now, rejoicing over an event that might turn the tide of this dreadful war in the Alliance's favor.

"In hyperspace, a ship's precise location can't be measured. The Rockoids went off on a wild-goose chase. They'll find out they've been fooled soon enough; right now we have the advantage. We're bolstering the Ilsad crews with survivors from yesterday's battle as I speak. With any luck, we'll blow those goddamned Rockoids to space dust before dinner!"

"When do we start the offensive?"

"In a just a few hours, Captain Perkins; if these ships work as hoped, we could end this war within a few months instead of a few years...perhaps sooner!"

Ray wanted to agree with him, but he didn't feel optimistic. Something about those newly arrived ships triggered the memory of the dream he had last night...

Those ships were of the same class as the ones destroyed at Dorton! He wondered if there could be a design flaw that might cripple those super battleships?

"Dr. Johnson, forgive me for speaking up, but something's wrong!"

"What do you mean, Captain Perkins?"

"I...er...two ships, similar to the ones before us now, were destroyed at the battle of Dorton. It appeared the Rockoids only fired a few shots at them."

Johnson nodded, but said nothing.

"I think there may be a serious problem with those ships."

Johnson suppressed a laugh and sounded almost patronizing, "That's impossible, Ray, just impossible! These ships were built by the finest engineers in the galaxy, by the Tereaean mega-corporation RECOM. Did you know Commander Thompson's late father, Rex, was the chief executive of that company?"

Ray nodded as Johnson continued, but alarm bells went off in his mind. *So that's it!* He finally had some clues about what was really going on.

"RECOM is famous for building the finest ships in the galaxy. They are the number one military contractor for the Alliance government. Over ninety percent of our warships and fighters are built by RECOM and its subsidiaries."

He sighed. Ray needed to do some fast investigating here, to confirm his suspicions.

"Dr. Johnson, in all due respect, we shouldn't take any chances. We should recheck the designs, make sure there are no flaws that could show up under the stress of battle."

"Captain Perkins, that is out of the question! Even if I wanted to have the ships rechecked, we simply don't have time. We'll be going into battle in less than six hours! If you knew exactly what this flaw might be, we might be able to examine it more carefully."

"I wish I did...I don't have the faintest idea what the flaw could be. It might be a defect in the battleships' shielding systems...."

Johnson cut him off by shaking his head. "I'm sorry, Ray, but a 'feeling' won't convince the Alliance to delay our next attack. Unless you can come up with some evidence..."

"Aren't his dreams enough? I mean, everything else in them has turned out to be true so far."

Johnson and Ray looked behind them to see Gotlieb coming toward them. Johnson groaned as he came forward, "Captain Gotlieb, we really don't have time for this...."

Gotlieb glared at him. "We have to find the time, sir. If there really are flaws in those super battleships, then we could be in for a hell of a time when they engage the Rockoids. We really should recheck those designs, like the old man here recommended."

Ray rolled his eyes at hearing his nickname. Johnson shook his head. "No, Captain Gotlieb, we just don't have the time. Captain Perkins doesn't know where the flaw is or what it is. I'm very sorry. There's no way to know those dreams are accurate in every respect. RECOM assures us this design has been thoroughly tested under the most severe conditions. There's no time for more testing. A renewed enemy offensive may occur at any moment. We need to get going."

They followed Johnson down the hall to one of the briefing rooms where hundreds of cadets were given the battle plans at one time.

They entered just as a session began. Ray seated himself next to

Gotlieb. This time Dr. Johnson himself gave the briefing, standing calmly before a large podium. Instead of showing images on a viewscreen, he described the battle plans verbally. He kept everything simple and basic.

Ray was used to Johnson's long-winded dissertations. He found it hard to realize this loquacious scientist was a battle-hardened veteran, one used to communicating the most complex strategies to his troops clearly and succinctly.

Johnson said the Alliance would have the majority of its battle cruisers surround the Rockoid super cruisers and keep them at bay, while the rest of the Alliance war fleet dispatched the remaining Rockoid ships. When most of the smaller resistance was overcome, they would pull forces together and then pound the Rockoids with a massive show of firepower to defeat them.

The briefing ended in minutes. There were a few questions, but everyone seemed to accept the new plan. Thompson stood there and scowled.

It took another five hours to complete battle preparations. The base overflowed with Alliance troops, all requiring thorough if concise briefings about strategy before being dispatched to their ships. During this time, Ray tried to recall the nagging problem with the newly arrived super battleships, the ships the Alliance counted on to turn the tide of battle in their favor. Somewhere, there was a deadly design flaw that could doom the entire fleet if it was not dealt with in time.

When the entire Alliance fleet departed, Ray began to believe what he thought was a winning plan would turn to disaster if he didn't remember the key details Johnson needed to act. It was clear the super battleships were the key to a successful campaign.

Ray was so deep in thought when he took off in his fighter craft he didn't even notice the autopilot had been activated. Space travel was far less intrusive upon one's consciousness in this century. One could often take off into space and barely notice that he or she was traveling at all, unless that person was in a real hurry to attain faster-than-light speeds.

The power of the little ship amazed him. Accommodations

were simple and comfortable. Instrumentation seemed sparse for such a complex vehicle. In fact, many of the controls were computer-generated. The sensation differed little from flying in an old twenty-first century airplane. In his own time, he had never had a chance to fly into space, but he also knew those who did had to deal with weightlessness as an overriding factor. He was securely strapped into the diminutive fighter, so weightlessness wouldn't be very noticeable even if there was no antigravity capability.

Ray looked at the near three-dimensional image displayed by his little viewscreen. There he was, surrounded by hundreds of Alliance ships. He traveled via a pre-programmed route.

The autopilot did its job efficiently, without protest. Ray needed to take over manual control only when making his own runs against the Rockoid ships.

Within minutes, the Alliance fleet closed in on six enemy super cruisers floating only a few hundred thousand kilometers from Earth. It was certain the Rockoids knew about the advancing Alliance fleet, but they didn't make any defensive maneuvers. They waited, as a large beast awaits its prey.

Thompson's voice boomed on the radio. The transmission was encrypted, to prevent enemy detection. Ray noted the return of that stern authority she had exhibited when he first met her.

"Attention fleet commanders. I'm sending our battleships ahead to surround the Rockoid cruisers. The enemy should be dispatching their smaller ships, so be prepared to carry out your specific battle plan."

Ray knew he had to speak. Although he doubted Thompson would actually listen to him, he had to take the risk. Rather than hesitate, he turned on the trans-space radio and stated the frequency that would connect him directly to Thompson.

With a trace of nervousness in his voice, he announced, "Commander Thompson, Captain Perkins here. I have to tell you something. My dreams reveal there is a possible design flaw on our battleships!"

Thompson's voice was laced with anger. "What are you talking about, Captain? That's impossible! These ships are among the best in the fleet. RECOM engineers tested them thoroughly, using the best tools available. Nothing could possibly go wrong with them!"

"In all due respect, Commander," Ray exuded a calm, rational posture, "my dreams clearly show something is definitely wrong, something about the way the weapons or shielding systems are designed."

"That's preposterous, Captain Perkins! We can't change the battle plan now; we're about to engage the enemy! It would be too dangerous to hold back our trump card. Those bloody Rockoids know what's going on. They've probably intercepted some of our radio signals. Secured channels aren't one hundred percent secure; you know that. In fact, we really shouldn't be spending this long talking. Now think very carefully about what you are saying. I know you have faith in your dreams, but that's all they are, not perfect viewscreen logs. This is reality...not fiction. I'm going to tell the super battleships to lead the fleet into battle. Do not bother me again with your dreams. Is that understood?"

Ray sighed heavily, but didn't betray his feelings.

"Yes, sir."

"Over and out."

"Over and out," Ray responded as he switched off the radio communicator.

His skin prickled at Thompson's stubbornness. He recalled the lessons drilled into him by the teaching machines about Alliance history. Rex Thompson had been a famous industrialist and a philanthropist, giving huge donations from his vast wealth to the right causes. He had also been active in the political world, an outspoken, charismatic supporter of rearming the Alliance.

Before he realized his dreams, he died in a freak accident at the peak of his power. At the time he was considered a potential candidate for president.

What is his daughter's connection to all this? Ray wondered.

Ray looked out from one of his fighter's portholes as he saw the large super battleships speeding up, readying themselves to engage the enemy in battle. He observed the smaller Rockoid cruisers and fighters emerging from behind the flagship super cruisers.

As he stared at the Alliance's super battleships, he enlarged the image on his viewscreen to pick out details of the weapon turrets. They were withdrawn into the craft and would only be extended when the ships were ready to fire. By then they'd be engulfed by the intense beams from the Rockoid weaponry and become hard to examine. The answer seemed to be right in his grasp, yet he couldn't recall any of the crucial details.

Ray began to relax, despite the fact he was about to go into battle and perhaps to his death. He struggled, trying to remember...

Suddenly an image flashed in his mind, an image likely received from the Rockoid vantage point, but a significant one.

He realized what he had perceived in his dreams wasn't quite -correct!

At the battle of Dorton, the two super battleships he had seen, the *Acclaim* and the *Reliant*, spun out of control and burned up in the planet's atmosphere as soon as their weapons fired while under direct attack. If the battleships tried to attack the Rockoids with weapons at full power with maximum defense shields activated, the gyrosystems aboard the ships became unstable. Thompson wouldn't like what he had to tell her. He knew he had to notify her immediately about his discovery.

Before she could voice more than a simple greeting, Ray screamed into the radio at the top of his lungs, "Commander Thompson, you gotta send back the battleships right now! I know what the flaw is. If we don't act on it, we're screwed!"

"Captain Perkins, do not shout at me like that. You forget to whom you are speaking. Now tell me what the flaw is," said Thompson, barely suppressed anger in her voice.

"When the battleships are going at full speed, everything works...until they fire their weapons with shields at maximum..."

"Are you sure of this, Captain?" She couldn't conceal her disbelief; in fact there was an obvious air of sarcasm in her response.

"It's in the weapons control systems." His voice seemed to get louder and louder by the second. "Something the engineers cooked up to make the ships maneuver faster, right?"

There was no response.

"It wouldn't show up under stress testing because real weapons weren't actually fired, not under a simulator. That's why the Ilsad never discovered this problem; they probably didn't...couldn't subject these ships to actual battle conditions. When the weapons are at maximum...with shields also fully activated, the circuits can't handle the load and the ships spin out of control!"

Thompson remained the unbeliever. She wanted to show Ray he was wrong; she had an intimate knowledge of the ship's engineering; she had been educated as an engineer before she joined the military and could identify every single part of those vessels, as if she had designed them herself. In fact, many modern RECOM designs incorporated key enhancements that she originated. Ray didn't know a damn thing about engineering...how dare he try to make himself sound like he did?

Instead of arguing with him, Thompson simply shouted, "Captain Perkins, the readings on those ships are absolutely perfect. Our condition is green. You forget I am an engineer, and you are not. I will not tolerate any further interruptions. We must start the attack now."

Thompson didn't wait for Ray's response. She pretended he didn't exist as she barked, "General, tell the super battleships to fire their ultralaser batteries at full power!"

There was static....

Ray could see the super battleships' turrets warming up, getting ready to fire.

For a moment all proceeded as planned. A confident smile appeared on Thompson's lips. *That primitive bastard from the past was wrong.*

Suddenly the large weapons atop the super battleships exploded with an elaborate display of multicolored fire. Before the shocked eyes of the Alliance fleet, the huge spaceships started to spin wildly, falling out of control back into Earth's atmosphere.

As the ships began to plummet toward Earth, they found themselves directly in the path of a contingent of Rockoid heavy cruisers. Despite attempts to take evasive action, there was a massive collision. Every other ship in the vicinity felt the impact, as shards of fiery metal shot forth. In seconds, a massive explosion not only took out the affected Alliance ships, but a number of enemy craft as well.

Hundreds of tons of wreckage burned up in the atmosphere, but some fragments managed to strike the surface, hitting homes, office buildings, and in a few instances, people as well.

Ray stared on with frustration. He couldn't tell Thompson "I told you so"—there wasn't time. Before he had a moment to think of the consequences of the disaster he witnessed, he was ordered aboard Thompson's command ship.

He hoped they would at least thank him for the warning, even if it had come too late. He directed his ship's computer to change course and reach the Alliance's flagship as soon as possible. He reached the ship's docking bay and was safely parked inside within minutes.

In his mind, he could see the image of Zanther. For a brief second, he sensed she was reaching out to him, to talk to him, but the image faded as quickly as it appeared...

Ray remained in a dark mood as he exited his ship. A contingent of troops greeted him and rushed him briskly to the ship's command center, adjacent to its bridge, where he saw Thompson standing, her teeth gritted, face taut.

She screamed, "This is all your fault! You knew and you didn't tell us until it was too late to verify the information."

"My fault?" Ray's face revealed his shock. He had never seen Thompson so angry. "I tried to tell you, but *you* wouldn't listen."

"Yes, it's your fault! If you'd remembered some of this information sooner, we might have saved those ships, and done some real damage to the Rockoids! We could have delayed the attack for a few hours to fix the problem. More than likely, it's a simple redesign of a processor circuit that isn't managing power properly and overloading."

Thompson conveyed absolute confidence that the problem could be easily solved, but in truth, the superstructures of the vessels required some heavy-duty reengineering and reinforcement before they would withstand the rigors of battle.

"But I..." Ray tried to explain. "Everyone is telling me the dreams aren't true. I begged you folks to listen."

"No more excuses, Perkins. If I could get my hands on you..."

Thompson tried to keep the conversation between Ray and her private. They were all alone in the small command room. One of the crew members, a security officer who had no great love for Thompson, overheard her piercing voice and relayed it to the communications officer. Soon the rest of the Alliance fleet knew what was going on.

They had thought of Ray as a hero, one who had used his knowledge of the Rockoids to help them. Most shocked were Ray's two closest friends, Jennifer Grant and David Gotlieb. Grant was too angry to say anything, but Gotlieb was ready to defend his friend. He contacted Thompson on his fighter's viewscreen. His anger seethed through every word.

Thompson accepted the call, but clearly didn't welcome the intrusion.

"All right, Commander Thompson. This is enough! Leave Captain Perkins alone! These dreams are as strange to him as to the rest of us. It's a no-win situation. We gotta use his information as best as we can. We gotta work together to deal with the Rockoid threat...not tear each other apart!"

"What? Are you arguing with me again? This is the third time this week! I demand an explanation!" shouted Thompson.

"I'm not arguing! I'm just trying to..." Gotlieb attempted to explain, but ended up stammering as he tried to reason with his superior officer.

"Shut up, Gotlieb! I have had enough of you as well. I warned you. You are hereby reassigned to desk duty in the information-processing center. You may not participate in any war-related activities! Return to your base immediately!" exclaimed Thompson angrily, a little bit calmer than she had been a few minutes earlier...though just barely.

"Commander, you're not listening...."

"Be quiet! Or would you rather face a court-martial?"

"Very well, sir," grumbled Gotlieb.

Ray looked outside a window displaying the scene of the battle in space. He saw Gotlieb's fighter plane breaking away from its formation and heading back to Earth. His anger boiled over. Thompson's bizarre behavior stunned him to the core. He could barely control his own temper.

Instead he held back his emotions, and tried to mollify her instead.

"Commander, you really shouldn't have been so hard on Captain Gotlieb. I mean, he was just trying to…"

"Shut up, Perkins, before I decide to court-martial you next! You have been a great help to the Alliance so far, despite the fact you have a horrible memory. I will see you are punished too, if necessary! Do you understand?" Thompson asked sternly.

"Yes, I do, Commander."

Word quickly spread throughout the Alliance. The near-universal reaction was shock, astonishment, and nobody was more upset than Johnson. While Ray received his dressing down from Thompson, the scientist/commander quietly reviewed some unexpected, enormously upsetting information from an important source. The information left him stunned, incredulous, barely believing the evidence of his eyes and ears. His eyes became misty as he made the fateful call to security. How could he tell his wife? She'd be heartbroken.

He steeled himself for an unpleasant encounter, and contacted Thompson on a specially encrypted radio band, ordering her into a private session, via viewscreen.

Ray was quickly dismissed from Thompson's command center and glumly walked through the large ship's passageways towards the docking bay, where his fighter was being serviced. His dark and angry mood dominated all other feelings. He knew Thompson was being unreasonable. He couldn't believe the Alliance's top command let her get away with it. He entered his ship and sat in the pilot's chair, silent.

He knew now he must return to Earth. Something about that private session between Johnson and Thompson didn't sit right with him. He broke his fighter off from the formation and flew, back towards Earth.

He knew that his departure and destination were obvious to the Alliance command, but he didn't care. He knew where he had to go. To his surprise, nobody made any attempt to stop him.

* * *

Thompson sat alone in her quarters after dismissing her security guards. Johnson greeted her with a strange formality, referring to her strictly by her rank. She stared at him carefully on the viewscreen. Johnson's face evinced absolute anger. She could see his hands shaking as he prepared to speak.

"You called for me, sir?" Thompson quickly saluted him, but her eyes betrayed her reluctance. Johnson could see it even on his viewscreen. She resented the intrusion. She wasn't through with Gotlieb and Perkins, and was about ready to pounce on Grant as well. Maybe Johnson would finally show his appreciation for her work at getting such incompetents out of the fleet. Maybe that long-sought promotion and its higher pay were about to be hers. She knew she deserved it. He seemed furious right now, so she wouldn't ask, at least this time.

She had never before tried to use her friendship with Johnson to get a promotion—at least not after he got her into the Alliance Academy when her father died. Even then, she figured she would soon get the position anyway.

Meanwhile, four security guards entered her command room and surrounded her.

"Commander Thompson, recently your behavior has become more and more erratic. Your actions against Captains Perkins and Gotlieb are particularly unacceptable. I have decided to overrule you on your decisions about them."

Thompson stared, without expression, into the viewscreen. She saw the security detail closing in around her, hands on their holstered weapons. Her eyes revealed her shock, yet there was a grim smile on her lips.

"We have also discovered you still have ties to the RECOM

Corporation, even though you agreed to shed them when you joined the service. We have signed confessions from the Alliance officials who received kickbacks to accept the contracts to construct more of those defective super battleships, and sell them to the Ilsad Confederation despite evidence of design flaws. The officials at RECOM were duped into believing the flaws had been fixed...obviously they weren't."

The revelation clearly shocked Thompson to the core. She had concealed her connection with RECOM, setting up a secret account to handle the financial and business transactions. She swore she'd kill whoever those moronic beam-spillers were. She never believed her cost-cutting measures would have such dire consequences on those new battle ships. Surely they couldn't blame her....

Johnson continued, without interruption, face determined, voice steady. "We also now know the truth about the battle of Dorton, Commander. You can't hide anything from us any longer. We know while you claimed to have severed your ties with RECOM, you still control a five percent economic interest in the company. You've retained more than a third of the voting power. We know you used that financial power to make sure RECOM's executives did your bidding. With RECOM's core spaceship construction business facing massive losses due to disarmament throughout the Alliance, you staged an unprovoked assault against the Rockoids. You deliberately massacred the population of Dorton in order to start a galactic war, where RECOM would stand to benefit greatly."

Thompson finally managed to stammer a response, "Henry, you know that's not true. I had no motive to attack the Rockoids. They're nothing more than fanatics who have a history of invading and conquering the territories of races they call inferior..."

"Ah, but y'all did have a reason to attack the Rockoids, Commander. We were lucky to find that out, too."

Thompson seemed about to faint but then her voice regained control, and she shouted, "Did Perkins tell you?"

"Perkins helped me see the truth, and prompted us to do a thorough investigation, that's all. I should have seen the warning signs long ago. The evidence was there, plain as day. Did you think you could keep me in the dark forever?"

Thompson seemed about to stammer a response, but stopped in mid-sentence, as Johnson continued to detail the charges and specifications.

"We learned that while y'all claimed to be on a mission of peaceful exploration around the independent worlds between the Alliance and the Rockoids during those two years, you were really traveling to those planets on behalf of RECOM to negotiate military contracts. When the Rockoid intelligence network learned what you were up to, the Rockoid High Command decided to stop you right in your tracks and negotiate mutual defense pacts with most of these races. In one fell swoop, they eliminated the need to buy weapons from RECOM.

"Then, during the last few weeks of the mission, you learned the Rockoid royal family was enjoying a holiday on Dorton, that they had minimal defenses, since they were in friendly territory. You took that opportunity to launch an unprovoked attack on the colony, killing millions, including the Emperor and Empress. The only reason you got away with this for so long was because you paid off all the right people and your hand-picked crew didn't fully comprehend what they had done until it was too late. Thank God some of them had a conscience, and confessed their crimes when confronted."

Johnson's face turned red with anger.

Thompson glared. "You have no proof of any of this, Henry. Whoever told you this lied! Those cowards were only trying to protect themselves. I swear on my father's grave, I never attacked the Rockoids! I would never do that to the Alliance!"

"Don't sully Rex's reputation with your lies. In addition to crew members from the ships under your command, forty-five different RECOM executives, who faced execution for high treason if they lied, signed confessions telling us the real facts. Our lie detectors said they all told us the truth. We suspected what you did for a long time—they gave us the evidence we needed to prove it."

"What evidence would that be, besides fruitless and unsubstantiated lies?"

Johnson's look turned to a fierce, infuriated stare. "Maybe this excerpt from your command log during the battle of Dorton will remind you of your deceit."

Thompson's eyes widened in fear. She had destroyed those logs long ago. There was no possible way anyone could have retrieved them. Even she no longer had access to a copy. The memories remained only in the darkest depths of her mind.

"Yes, I'm sure you're wondering how we did it. You thought you could hide those logs from us forever, didn't you? Well, thank God we managed to locate Captain Darbol, your old security officer from the *Star of Terra*. We subjected him to a Brain TV scan and discovered he was the only one besides you who had seen those logs. We managed to extract his memories of the logs and we have those images here for your viewing pleasure. Enjoy."

Johnson's face was replaced by the image of an all-too-familiar command deck on a warship...none other than the *Star of Terra*, Thompson's flagship at the battle of Dorton. The events transpired just as she remembered them.

* * *

There, standing before her on the bridge of the heavy cruiser, was a tall, young, muscular man with light brown hair and hazel eyes, her second in command, Colonel Jeffrey Grant....

A heated argument ensued between the two. Colonel Grant's face was twisted in anger and frustration.

"We can't do this, sir. By firing on the alien ships, we violate one of our most sacred edicts. It could be considered grounds for a court martial!"

Thompson's steel blue eyes narrowed, her face taking on a dark look. "If we do not fire, they will destroy us. Would you risk genocide? How dare you suggest...."

"Sir, you're not listening..."

"That's enough! If you continue with this insubordination, I will remove you from the bridge and throw you into the brig. Is that clear?"

Sweat poured down Grant's face. His eyes widened, and his face twitched nervously. He did not answer for a moment, but then finally responded with almost no expression at all, "Yes, sir."

"Excellent, I'm glad you see it my way," Thompson said, with the hint of a sneer.

Without a sideways glance, the command was given in Thompson's loud, imperious voice. "Weapons officer, target the primary enemy ship and fire!"

The weapons officer looked nervous for a second, but she nodded and complied with Thompson's orders.

Thompson watched, as the command ship moved slowly, deliberately, to the front of the huge Alliance fleet, and closed in on what appeared to be the Rockoid flagship. As soon as it came within range, the weapons officer, tears streaming down her eyes, opened fire on the unsuspecting opponents. Lasers of bright green and yellow shot forth, hitting their targets relentlessly.

* * *

As soon as the recreated log entry left the screen, Johnson reappeared, a grim, accusing look on his face. Thompson had been rendered speechless, her eyes vacant, lips pressed tightly together. Thompson seemed to get increasingly angry at each word Johnson spoke; her eyes seemed to blaze with fire. She knew she had been caught red-handed, and there was no turning back.

Johnson wouldn't give her the opportunity to think about her future plans, as he announced, "There is one last thing I must show you, another excerpt from your personal log as viewed by your security officer."

Thompson's entire life seemed to pass before her eyes as she listened to Johnson.

"How could you? How could you do such a terrible thing to Jennifer Grant? You said her husband died from wounds sustained shortly after the battle, while trying to recover wounded soldiers from a damaged ship. The logs betray you."

For a moment, it seemed to Thompson as if her heart had stopped. Her breathing came in quick gasps; she had trouble keeping her -balance.

This isn't happening to me, this isn't happening, this isn't happening...

* * *

Johnson's image was replaced once again, this time by a scene of Thompson's private quarters aboard her flagship. She sat in a chair, seemingly calm and collected. Colonel Grant stood before her, a stern look of disapproval on his face.

"General Thompson, launching an unprovoked attack against an innocent civilian colony warrants drastic consequences. You had no reason to attack those aliens first. When we return to Earth, I will be reporting you to the Alliance High Command. Until then, I am hereby relieving you of command and taking control of this fleet."

Thompson stood up, catching Grant by surprise, a fierce glare on her face. That glare was suddenly replaced by an evil smile. "I'm very sorry, Colonel Grant, I am afraid you won't be able to do that."

A suspicious look came over the Grant's face. "Why is that?"

"I am afraid you will be taking a leave of absence from your service in the Alliance military...a permanent leave of absence."

Without warning, Thompson pulled a laser pistol out of her pocket and aimed it at Grant's heart.

The move came swift, unexpected. Grant had no time to defend himself, no time to pull out his own weapon and fire. Thompson's face took on an evil sneer as she fired.

There was a loud thud as Grant's lifeless body fell to the floor...

* * *

Thompson nearly fainted, her eyes glazed over.

Johnson's face returned to the viewscreen for the last time. In a strong, authoritative voice, he said, "I promised your father I'd take care of you. I also took an oath when I agreed to serve the Alliance, to put aside personal considerations when the circumstances required it."

Despite his almost overwhelming sadness over this turn of events, Johnson gritted his teeth firmly as he recited his decision in his rich, baritone voice.

"It is my sad duty to inform you I am relieving you of your command. I have asked the security detail to take you to Bethesda Memorial Hospital and submit you to a psychiatric examination. When the examination is over, you will face a court-martial for high treason, conspiracy to commit treason, war crimes, conspiracy to commit war crimes, murder, conspiracy to commit murder and bribery. In addition, there are hundreds of other minor charges, which you can find in the indictment I just sent to the Alliance Court of Justice on Qveran. Due to the extreme nature of these crimes, you will face a death sentence if you are found guilty. We're also going to investigate the possibility you may have been collaborating with enemies of the Alliance to plan and execute this present attack. I'm sure we'd very much like to know everything you been hiding from us all these years."

Johnson paused long enough for the impact of these pronouncements to sink in. He was simply amazed that he managed to keep his emotions in check under such painful circumstances. Just when he thought he had succeeded completely in blanking them out, he found himself wiping a small tear from his eye.

"Now take her away!"

As Johnson spoke, Thompson's face remained frozen with disdain. As the security detail prepared to escort her from the command center, she twirled around and kicked the security chief in the face with a speed and force that seemed almost inhuman. As the officer fell unconscious, she grabbed his weapon and pressed it against the forehead of another guard. "If you and your associates do not come with me, I will make sure you do not leave this room alive."

Thompson glared at Johnson.

"I'm sorry, Henry, but I cannot let you do this," she said in a measured voice. "I am not going to let you and the others destroy my career. I should have been supreme commander, not you. What I did to destroy the Rockoid colony proved that! And Grant? He was the guilty one, trying to usurp my authority. His death was too simple, too fast. He should have been tortured, slowly, painfully...and now I'm terribly sorry, but it is time for me to leave."

With the weapon still snug against the officer's head, Thompson directed the still-conscious security guards to a small freighter she had kept in waiting should she ever need to stage a fast getaway from her command ship. In just a few minutes, the renegade commander had taken her hostages and boarded her freighter. There had been no warning. Before the Alliance commanders could act, her vessel jumped into hyperspace and sped off to an unknown destination.

The destruction of the Alliance super battleships and Rockoid heavy cruisers did little to reduce the intensity of the battle. If anything, each side redoubled its efforts to defeat its adversary.

The Alliance, however, had not been badly hurt by the destruction of their battleships. Most of the crew members managed to leave in escape pods before explosions claimed their ships. In a sense, the Alliance actually benefited from the experience. They knew now those cruisers weren't capable of functioning in a combat situation, and took steps to get other classes of warships into combat as fast as possible.

The Rockoids had been dealt a heavier blow than anticipated. The Alliance commanders optimistically estimated that over ten percent of the Rockoids' heavy cruisers had been destroyed in the collision, when in reality only five ships had been lost.

The Rockoids were not deterred by their losses. If anything, they seemed much more determined to gain the upper hand as the battle quickly intensified. They threw all they had against the Alliance fleet.

Over each of the three threatened Alliance worlds, the atmosphere was filled with fire, smoke and the deafening sounds of explosions. Metal fragments fell randomly across the landscape. Had it not been for the fire-repellent materials developed as a result of World War III and the Jintorian wars, flying debris would have caused serious damage.

Despite these precautions, there was structural damage to some smaller buildings, though most of the affected cities had been evacuated long before the attackers arrived.

While many more Alliance cruisers and armed freighters went down in the first stages of the Rockoid attack, the Alliance started to learn how to deal with their enemy's weapons.

Ray remembered many of the most intimate details about the Rockoid ships, information he had always seemed to know, now pouring into his consciousness. The dream sequences had become so vivid that he was now able to recall many specifics at will. He was certain the source of those dreams was close, that he could tap that knowledge somehow.

No doubt it was his inexplicable mental link with Zanther that caused him to see the battle of Dorton from the perspective of a Rockoid.

The Rockoid lasers worked best with fixed targets, but they would still hit anything in their path. Moving targets were more difficult to handle, especially smaller fighters that flew at the edge of the weapon's firing range. The Rockoids depended on the maneuverability of their ships, rather than moving weapons turrets, for accuracy with larger targets. The giant ship-busting lasers could not be fired very often. Each time they were used, massive amounts of energy were drained from the ship. It took a while for the system to recharge sufficiently to allow regular weapons to be used. As a result, the giant lasers were only activated as a last resort, since the main weapons of the cruisers could function quite well in holding off enemy assaults and destroying enemy warships.

Once the Alliance learned of this weakness, they were able to dodge the lasers. Casualties were greatly reduced.

After failing to knock out the Alliance fleet with their bigger ships, the Rockoids decided to use smaller ships to overwhelm and destroy their adversaries. However, the Alliance was ready for them.

The smaller ships were far more maneuverable than their larger super cruiser counterparts. Although the Alliance fusillade was intense, the Rockoid cruisers were able to get out of the way before they were hit. Still, several of the enemy light cruisers exploded under the weight of heavy Alliance firepower.

As both sides began to learn each other's tactics and weaknesses, the battles over Taucon, Terea, and Earth slowly moved into a stalemate.

The Rockoids, realizing their strategy needed a major revision, reluctantly started pulling back to their front lines around the colony worlds in these star systems.

* * *

Zanther grew extremely upset with the fleet's mounting losses, particularly the deaths of so many of her subjects in a war that was supposed to inflict relatively light casualties. As she felt the death cries of her fellow beings in her mind, she grieved for each and every one, praying for a more peaceful existence in the afterlife. She felt the deaths so deeply, it was as if her parents had died all over again.

So when Xorax visited her in her private chamber, Zanther surrendered all semblance of calm. She didn't wait for his customary greeting before confronting him with a harsh dose of reality. In fact, she practically screamed at the top of her lungs.

"You told me our victory was assured. How could you be so misguided?"

Xorax looked at her with a sneer. "Your Majesty, there are some things that happened that we did not, could not, predict! We did not estimate the extent of their ability to repel our invasion!"

Zanther broke in, "I do not care what you estimated! Thousands of our people are dying as we speak. We must take the battle directly to their capital worlds! I want ground troops immediately dispatched, starting with Earth itself. Inform our forces to abandon their attacks on other Alliance planets! We must force surrender before we suffer any more losses. We must not show the Alliance any mercy; we must destroy them!"

Xorax replied again with that same sneer. "As you wish, Your Majesty."

He turned to leave the room. As he walked away, Zanther quickly regretted her outburst. She wondered once again if perhaps there was another way to resolve this conflict at the bargaining table, maybe find a means for the Alliance to pay reparations for their original unprovoked assault and massacre against her people. Why was war the only answer? Why must more people die? What about the citizens of the Alliance who had nothing whatsoever to do with the business of war? Why should they suffer because of the acts of ruthless military commanders?

Is there no other way?

And those dreams…their vividness only intensified. Every night she imagined she was immersed in that strange desert battle, witnessing events she could not explain.

Even stranger was the dream she had earlier that day. The human male whose mind she'd tapped into, actually seemed to be trying to communicate with her, trying to convey an important message, a message that delivered a totally unexpected slant on this dreadful situation.

Zanther's suspicions turned out to be correct. Day and night, Ray tried to visualize the truth about the Dorton battle and somehow beam it spaceward to Zanther.

If he could talk with her directly, show her the truth, produce the logs that indicted Commander Thompson as the true aggressor. Maybe then, this terrible war could end.

Was it already too late? Ray felt consumed with anger and frustration; he somehow had to take matters into his own hands.

For Zanther, the news was simply too incredible to believe. If the messages she received were true and not deceptions, it would mean the human commander who ordered the attack on Dorton did so in violation of Alliance doctrine. That commander was now a fugitive from justice.

Maybe it was just wishful thinking; could it be that this entire war was a gigantic, tragic mistake?

The idea was inconceivable!

Thousands of lives and untold amounts of property had been lost on both sides...it was all a waste!

And in the worst case scenario, what would happen if the Alliance defeated the Rockoids...what would be the consequences?

* * *

Returning to an Alliance base outside Brussels, Ray's fighter quickly and deftly skirted the perimeter of the landing field, and set down. As soon as Ray exited his ship, a crew of officers escorted him to the Alliance's command center, where he saw Dr. Johnson seated in front of his viewscreen, a wounded look on his creased face.

Johnson hastily greeted him with a brisk salute, which Ray returned.

"Captain Perkins, you were in pretty hot water back there!"

"Tell me about it. What happened to Thompson? You said she was a decorated war leader! I warned you all over and over again, but nobody would believe me!"

"Liz's story is terribly complex," Johnson said, with the sort of understanding that came from a father talking about his rebel daughter. He gave Ray the details of Thompson's arrest and escape, speaking slowly, gravely. "I have to tell you putting her under arrest was one of the most painful things I've ever done. Damn it, her dad was a classmate of mine. He inherited his father's business, RECOM Corporation. Rex Thompson died eighteen years ago in a freak accident while on vacation. I was godfather to his daughter."

Johnson sighed, as tears filled his eyes. "She was never the same after Rex's death. As heir to the RECOM fortune, she dove head-long into running that company. She was one of the youngest corporate executives in the Alliance, but soon got embroiled in corporate politics, and was finally ousted from its board of directors. She remained the largest single stockholder, though. She had the inside track on big contracts awarded to RECOM. Liz begged me to get her admitted into the Academy and adapted to the military life fast enough to attain a command rank at a much younger age than anyone expected.

"Liz was supposed to have severed her financial ties to RECOM when she joined the Alliance military. It's a requirement. She even gave us a financial statement, signed by her accountants, to show the money had been placed in a special trust fund, a fund she couldn't access. She lied to us, all of us…"

Johnson closed his eyes and breathed deeply, as if to calm himself.

"Liz retained control of that money and secretly ran RECOM as well, recently firing the executive who managed the company's day-to-day affairs. She wouldn't let him carry out his plan to turn RECOM's core business from the production of war materials to civilian vehicles. She'd have none of that."

Ray sat down and waited for a long, long story, eyes narrowed, trying hard to keep from interrupting.

"We've had decades of peace since the end of the Jintorian wars. The war machine was being scaled down. Contracts for RECOM were no longer something they could depend on. Despite their political connections, they began to lose money. Employees were laid off with little or no notice. Even the hefty profits being made at some of RECOM's other divisions could not completely cover all the losses. When the Rockoids offered to defend the worlds from which Thompson tried to get lucrative military contracts, that simply pushed her over the edge and so…"

"Thompson started a war. I guess some things never change. The old military-industrial complex is still alive and well," Ray broke in.

Johnson took a few deep breaths and nodded, wiping tears from his eyes, "Our worst fears were confirmed when we discovered she gave the order to fire on the Rockoid ships, against the objections of her second-in-command, Colonel Jeff Grant. She later murdered Grant when he tried to relieve her of command for her actions."

Colonel Jeff Grant! Jennifer's husband!

With difficulty, Ray tried to quell his anger, think logically, reasonably. Thompson's betrayal didn't surprise him. Political corruption was a constant throughout history, and he never doubted more than a few twentieth century wars were started to enrich certain powerful industrialists. The commander's escape was another matter entirely. What havoc could she cause if she wasn't brought to justice?

As all the scattered pieces connected in Ray's mind, he realized he couldn't hold his tongue any longer. His voice croaked, as he tried to keep himself from screaming at Johnson. He pointed his finger angrily at the scientist.

"The only reason the Rockoids attacked the Alliance was out of self-defense. They believed we attacked them first! Damn it all! If you had listened to me, all this death, destruction; it wouldn't have happened."

Johnson ignored Ray's insubordinate behavior. He knew Ray was right. All Johnson could do was sigh. "I'm so sorry I didn't believe you. After all this...well...after all this I can believe anything about Liz. I knew her when she was just a child. I held that little girl in my arms...cared for her when she was sick...this, well..."

"For God's sake, Dr. Johnson, how can you let this war continue? It has to stop right now!"

"Ray, how can we turn back? It's impossible! The Rockoids think of us as butchers, mass murderers. They're right; we attacked them first! The die is cast."

"There has to be a way..."

"What do you propose to do, whisper sweet nothings in your Rockoid girlfriend's ear and everything's gonna be all right..."

"Please sir..."

Ray wanted to say more; the conviction grew within him of what he could do, what he had to do, what he was meant to do.

He began to believe he was brought to the twenty-third century for a reason. Perhaps fate existed after all, and this was his to achieve.

"Dr. Johnson, please listen to me," Ray never sounded so sincere, so much in control of his emotions. "I have to speak with President Rogers. I think...I know...I have a plan."

Johnson seemed about to respond. Instead, he looked directly at Ray's determined blue eyes and nodded. It was crazy, foolhardy; he suspected just what Ray was about to suggest. It was outlandish, suicidal, but it may just work...

"Come with me, Ray. We don't have any more time to lose."

Contacting the President by viewscreen was too risky; the enemy had probably tapped into Alliance security systems.

With scarcely another word between them, they rushed out of the base and boarded a private hovercar for Stockholm, where the Alliance president was meeting with leaders of several other threatened Alliance planets.

Johnson and Ray caught Rogers moments before the session was to start. He waved them inside his office quickly, drumming his fingers on his desk as they came over to him. He seemed very tense, bags under his eyes as if he hadn't slept in days. The ridges in his head seemed to throb.

Johnson quickly explained the situation.

The president seemed lost in thought. He stood up from his desk. "It's all true, then, What in God's name are we going to do now?"

Rogers' reaction seemed rehearsed, as if he had prepared a statement like this all along. Ray, trying to concentrate on the situation, did not pick up on the suspicions lingering at the back of his mind.

Finally, he received his cue to speak. Without a moment's hesitation, he announced, "I think I have an idea of how to stop this war."

Johnson just smiled. The faith he'd put into this stranger from another century was about to bear fruit. Maybe there was a god after all.

"I have to go to the Rockoid command ship myself." Rogers looked startled; Johnson began grinning from ear to ear.

"If I've somehow tapped into the mind of one of the beings there, maybe that same individual has tapped into my mind. I feel this person is a leader, maybe their ruler. Don't ask me how I know this because I have no idea...I just feel in my heart that she isn't really our enemy, that's she an honorable person, and as much a victim of this tragedy as we are. Maybe I can reason with her. I'm sure my telepathic communication with this Rockoid would be enough to convince them of Thompson's betrayal and end the war."

Ray omitted the detail that he had already been trying to radiate his thoughts into space, hoping this alien would somehow answer him and put a stop to this carnage.

Rogers seemed to be weighing the pros and cons for a moment. He sighed, sat down, and put one hand on his head while he began drumming his fingers on his desk again, in what had become an irritation rather than an interruption. Johnson and Ray stared at him impatiently for a few minutes, waiting for him to say something.

The President finally lifted his head, leaned back in his chair, and said, "Listen, Captain Perkins, I want to tell you this mission of yours may be the equivalent of a death sentence. If you get aboard that Rockoid command ship, you could be captured and tortured to death. This woman may be trying to deceive you. You don't have to go on this suicide mission; maybe we can find the road to peace some other way."

Ray smiled at Rogers. "I know the danger, Mr. President. But I also have access to information you don't have. If anyone has a chance to get in there safely, it's me. It's hard to express in words, but I feel she can somehow read my mind, and I can sense hers too. I know if I can meet her, I can show her what we say is true. There has to be a reason I got here in the first place. I can't believe it's a stupid accident."

The Alliance president knew Ray was right. Whether by accident or design, he was the only person who could pull this fool stunt off and live to tell about it.

"Do you wish to have any of our special forces accompany you on this mission? We could spare a small shuttle to aid you..."

"Thanks, but no thanks, Mr. President. I feel the mission will only be successful if I go alone. It's not as if I don't appreciate any help I can get. It's just...something in the back of my mind is telling me not to take anyone with me, something I can't quite explain. Must be another one of my weird hunches, I guess."

The president simply nodded. He wasn't going to be the one to doubt Ray's gut. His political instincts took over. If one person was lost, so be it. To him, Ray Perkins, as valuable as he might be to the Alliance, was expendable. He had no choice.

Why risk an entire crew if this turns out to be a fool's errand?

He gave Ray a rushed briefing, to prepare him up for the mission that might save them all.

"I received word just before you arrived, that the battle was starting to break up, that both our fleet and the Rockoids were retreating to rearm and refuel. This will give you a little breathing room to rest a bit, and prepare for your journey.

"The Rockoids' original ultimatum is going to expire in less than twenty-four hours, although skirmishes have continued. We have just intercepted a radio signal that indicates at least a dozen large transport-class ships are on their way to Earth for a ground assault. We are in for one hell of a fight!"

"Can't we intercept them before they arrive?"

"No, hyperspace travel doesn't work that way. Once a ship exceeds light speed, we can't pinpoint its precise location. We can only detect the disturbances it creates in the fabric of space. You can't fire weapons in hyperspace without destroying yourself."

"What about the moment it returns to normal space?" Ray knew the answer before Rogers reminded him of his brief lessons in faster-than-light travel. The point at which a vessel exited hyperspace couldn't be predicted in advance. The Rockoids could use such uncertainties to their advantage, as would the Alliance in a similar situation.

"When will this battle start?"

"We don't know exactly. It depends on how fast those transports are and how long they'll take to get here. Maybe they need time to prepare their troops—we can only speculate. Yet I fear what we've experienced so far is just the beginning. Unless we find a way to stop this war now, many more lives will be lost. This could be the bloodiest war we've ever fought, worse than either of the Jintorian wars."

Ray chimed in, "If I get my mad scheme to work, this could also turn out to be the greatest opportunity for peace the Alliance has ever had."

Rogers nodded in agreement. "Okay, Captain Perkins, go get some rest and maybe enjoy yourself a little bit. We'll meet together tomorrow morning, for your final briefing. Do whatever you want tonight. Between you, me and Dr. Johnson, go ahead and try to make contact; tell her you're coming. Beg, plead for an audience, whatever it takes to convince her to see you. We're depending on you now."

Rogers had a broad grin on his face. He almost believed a miracle might happen.

"Thank you, sir."

Ray's emotions turned numb, as he began sensing the task to which he had committed himself. It had all come down to...this!

The door slid open, and Ray turned to leave. He wasn't a bit surprised to see Jennifer and Gotlieb waiting by the door. Evidently they had been dispatched to Stockholm soon after Ray and Johnson departed.

"Hi, Ray," Jennifer said.

Ray stared at her, shocked. She was clearly distraught. Her lovely face was marred with tears. He wanted to embrace her, comfort her. He realized Jennifer now knew the truth of her husband's death.

"Nice to see you again, old man," said Gotlieb. He tried to act casual, but he, too, clearly felt the impact of Jennifer's grief.

They became silent as they left Rogers' office. Ray knew he needed to talk to Jennifer, but tried to remain casual; he didn't want to do anything that would make her even more upset. He also felt he had to apologize to Gotlieb.

"Listen, David. I really should have backed you up when Thompson started to get on your ass. I mean, it was my problem, not yours."

Gotlieb waved his hand at Ray. "No, I wanted to do it. She pissed off both of us and I thought it was time we gave her a taste of her own medicine. Besides, Johnson gave me back my rank and command as soon as he issued the arrest order for Thompson. Damn! I don't even want to think about how much somebody's brain has to be messed up to do what she did."

Ray nodded. "I wish we could figure out where she escaped to."

Nobody would say a thing. As a military commander, Thompson was the equal of anyone in the fleet. As a fugitive, she was a threat not only to the Rockoids, but to the entire Alliance. There was no telling how many supporters she had gathered. If she knew how to bribe the Alliance Fleet and lie her way into military contracts for RECOM, she knew how to play the political game, big time.

Jennifer stared at Ray. She gripped him in a tearful embrace. "Ray, if I had the chance, I'd rip that bitch's head off."

As Ray held her, he didn't respond to her remark. Jennifer became nearly hysterical, sobbing uncontrollably. Ray tried to comfort her, with little success. He whispered soothing words, finding within him what he needed to say. It still took several minutes before she finally recovered enough to wipe the tears from her eyes.

"Don't you worry, Jennifer, I'll see to it that she doesn't do any more damage. I swear it. Please, trust me."

Jennifer stared at Ray, disbelief in her misty eyes. She couldn't bring herself to believe that one man might be the instrument of their salvation. Still she sensed his determination, and began to half believe it herself. Jennifer managed a faint smile.

"If you ever find Thompson, bring her back to me alive. I want the pleasure of killing her myself."

Ray nodded and stared at both his friends, realizing this might be the last time he would see them.

* * *

Several hundred light-years away, a Rockoid super cruiser escorted eight huge oval ships. These transports seemed to dwarf the super cruiser in size, but were no less maneuverable. Their primary cargo consisted of thousands of ground troops; they were now closing in on the solar system where Earth was located.

They had stopped at a small planet, in an uninhabited system, a world rich in raw materials, to replenish propulsion systems. After recharging the crystalline generators used to power the hyperspace engines, the ships took off once more.

The trip to Earth would take about a day at the immense speeds at which they traveled. They flew on toward the scene of what might prove to be the most intense, most destructive, battle yet in the war.

Chapter 18

That night, Ray returned to the base with Jennifer. They both went off to their own rooms when they arrived, but not before one last embrace. They held each other, clinging to one another. Jennifer sensed Ray's worry.

Deep in his heart, Ray still wondered whether he might have, in another life, fallen in love with Jennifer. She seemed like the perfect woman. A guy would be blessed to have someone like her. Yet he couldn't shake the glorious image of Zanther from his mind. For some reason, he felt drawn to Zanther more deeply than he'd been drawn to anyone in his life. Maybe he would meet her at last, in the flesh.

As soon as he entered his room, Ray grabbed the viewscreen from his end table and sat down on the bed. He felt it was time he recorded everything he remembered from his dreams, hoping some tidbit of information would help the Alliance—in the event he didn't come back from this mission.

He turned on the viewscreen, using its logging mode to capture his comments. He was amazed at the flexibility of twenty-third-century computers. A soft female voice prompted him to enter his description in an organized fashion. The contents of the log were forwarded to Alliance command, so they could evaluate his information.

After he completed the last section of his report, he went to sleep, but woke a few hours later, barely refreshed, despite having taken medication to calm him down. He was about to go into the bathroom for a desperately needed shave and shower when he got an urgent call from Commander Johnson.

Johnson's face looked ashen. He looked as if he hadn't slept all night. Ray noticed the bags under his eyes, that he hadn't yet shaved. "Commander, you look awful! What's the matter?"

"We have received reliable intelligence that several large space-ships are about to exit hyperspace close to the moon. We still can't pinpoint their exact location. The time for the great battle is almost near, Captain. It is going to be a very long day, indeed."

Ray looked shocked, barely able to reply. He stared at Johnson for a few seconds, and stammered, "I guess I'd better get ready to leave then."

Johnson nodded in return, and managed a lame response. His image disappeared from the screen a second later.

Ray put down the portable viewscreen and got up slowly. He haphazardly grabbed a freshly cleaned Alliance military outfit from his closet and ran into the bathroom. Ten minutes later, fully dressed, he walked out the door.

Breakfast was served in one of the briefing rooms. Ray was surprised to see President Rogers there, as well as Commander Johnson.

Rogers waved him over. "Come, Captain Perkins. Sit down, we'll talk while we're eating. I ordered pancakes for us. Is that all right?"

"Yes, sir. That's fine," Ray replied absentmindedly, as he sat down.

Over breakfast, they began to talk. Ray didn't begin to consider the possibility this might be his last meal.

"Captain Perkins," the Alliance President said with studied efficiency, "Commander Johnson gave me a voice recording of everything you told us about your dreams last night.

"We really should have paid more attention to this before, but you know dreams; we've never thought of them as anything but subconscious images. How do you propose you're going to get onto the Rockoid ship?"

"That's the hard part. My dreams tell me Rockoid ships use some sort of grappling field to capture objects and bring them to the docking bay. It's run by a computer that reads ID codes, and decides whether or not to open the door. I may know just enough to help you fake those codes. At least I hope so."

Rogers sighed. "You're betting your life on this, Ray. You better be right or you'll be a dead man and we're gonna be in for one hell of a fight."

"I feel I'm right; I know I am. What other choice do we have?"

"I've heard about those grappling fields you're talking about. We have something like them in the testing process right now. If you get aboard their ship, though, how will you keep from being captured as soon as you land?"

Ray sounded more confident than he felt. His voice betrayed his nervousness; he did his best to keep his feelings in check.

"The Rockoids feel they are the superior race. They don't post guards in the docking bay because they don't expect there would ever be any intruders. Plus, the Rockoid female I'm in contact with will let me aboard; I believe that, completely," Ray lied.

Ray didn't want to reveal his belief that she already helped him in some fashion, by diverting the firepower away from his fighter when he was immersed in that first battle above the Mars colony. He felt certain the Alliance would begin to suspect his loyalty. He couldn't help but remain a little paranoid; it was his nature. Ray also knew that if he didn't take on this mission, he'd never know the truth about this Rockoid, why he was drawn to her and, he suspected, she to him.

"All right, Ray. The battle will commence sometime this afternoon or evening, which is when we expect the enemy transports to arrive. You'll have until fifteen hundred hours, when the Rockoid ultimatum expires, to get to their command ship and in touch with your alien girlfriend." Rogers' voice was as much serious as sarcastic.

"When the war resumes, we won't be able to stop it. The pressure is on you, old man." Rogers smiled slightly when he used Gotlieb's nickname for Ray. "You're going to have to produce. We're depending on you now."

"I know, sir. Should I leave now?"

"Yes, there's no telling how long it'll take for you to get on board their ship and find this female. I would suggest you get your ship ready and be off as soon as possible. Fly slowly and directly to your destination. Be casual, as if you know where you're going, one of the crowd; don't make any threatening moves. Otherwise, the Rockoids may think you're trying to attack."

"Yes, sir, I understand."

Rogers and Ray got up and shook hands. Rogers stepped to the side. Commander Johnson delivered the message he'd clearly been preparing for this moment. His craggy face seemed more lined than usual, seeming to buckle under the pressure of what might be the Alliance's final hours as a free society.

"You know, Ray, from the time you started enduring all those painful tests and interrogations, when you had to get used to our way of life in so short a time, I knew you had potential."

They shook hands quickly. Ray started to walk out of the room. Rogers came over and stopped him.

"Captain Perkins, I need some way to ensure that if you contact me you're not being held prisoner. We'll use code words. When I ask you if 'The sun is shining,' you'll respond 'Yes, but the ice is slippery.' Do you understand?"

Ray thought the phrase was utterly silly, but figured it was unexpected enough that the Rockoids wouldn't catch its meaning.

"Yes, I do, sir."

"If you are a prisoner, give any other response, understand?"

"Yes, sir."

"To make sure you're not doing it under duress, I want you to record that statement now, so our voice analyzer can compare it with the one I hope you'll make when you're aboard that ship."

That's the reason!

Ray looked straight at the president and calmly said the silly little phrase intended to confirm he was safe and sound once...if he reported back from the Rockoid ship.

"Very well, Captain Perkins. You can go now."

Ray saluted President Rogers and Commander Johnson before turning on his heel, finally walking out of the room.

The first step in getting ready for his mission was modifying the computer system of his fighter craft, using Ray's recollections of communications protocols and some of the identification codes that had been intercepted from a downed Rockoid ship. Memories of his dreams provided enough additional information to let the Alliance engineers adapt the system to Rockoid communication protocols.

Once the programming was finished, Ray entered the command codes designed to generate the bogus signals that would allow him to enter the enemy flagship's docking bay.

The Alliance commanders were informed the battle would commence at 15:00, when the ultimatum expired—that is, if Ray didn't return by then, or send a message. Intelligence indicated the Rockoids would begin landing their troops around that time to stage a ground assault. There was no doubt about it. Based on the estimated forces involved, the space and ground battle would result in catastrophic losses on both sides.

Ray realized again there was little prospect of him surviving this insane venture. *What do I do once I get inside that ship? Well, might as well make it up as I go along. That's what I've been doing so far.*

Ray looked up with a start. He felt a presence, in his mind. He struggled to concentrate, but it faded away as quickly as it appeared. Was someone...something...calling out to him? Zanther?

Help me, please, Zanther!

He repeated the message over and over again in his mind, trying hard to send it...somewhere...in the unlikely event she could pick it up. He knew he had to get under way, confront his fate... whatever it was. At least he'd die a hero! Quite a far cry from his hermit-like existence as a computer programmer.

After making some final modifications and checks on his fighter craft, Ray jumped into the sleek ship.

He engaged the pre-flight computer scans with efficiency. Once systems were pronounced to be in battle-ready condition, he took off. The ship flew off with hardly a sputter; it accelerated rapidly and was soon heading toward deep space.

Earth receded swiftly. Ray swung his craft over to the moon, making a beeline toward the dark side, now hidden in shadow. Intense feelings led him there.

If the enemy appeared where he suspected, Ray planned to use the cover of the Rockoid exit from hyperspace to get close to the flagship, hoping he wouldn't have to fire on any ships in self-defense.

Not that he would be able to inflict any damage on those huge ships. They could destroy him with just one shot; very reassuring when one was trying to stop a war.

Before long, Ray's computer alerted him to a disturbance in the fabric of space near the moon; the signature lasted just a few seconds. A dozen Rockoid cruisers popped into normal space as if by magic. His little craft was now immersed in the disturbance field. His instruments were rendered temporarily useless as the ship was buffeted sharply by the field's impact. He could hear metal groaning, stretching.

For a second, he feared he would be blown apart. Just as quickly as the pounding started, it stopped. It would be a short while before his instruments could function again. Ray had to proceed on dead reckoning alone, hoping he set his course properly to intercept what according to Alliance intelligence reports was the approaching flagship.

The super cruisers passed him in about thirty seconds. He didn't have much time. The battle would be raging in full force soon, if he wasn't successful.

Ray wanted to reach the docking bay of the flagship as quickly as possible, but he knew if he flew too fast he might draw unneeded attention. In minutes, he reached the entrance to the landing bay.

* * *

At the same time, the Alliance armada, having swelled with the addition of forces from other Alliance planets, began approaching the Rockoid super cruisers and the fleet of smaller battle cruisers. Both sides started to warm up their weapons. The Alliance troops on Earth commenced final battle preparations in the great Ardennes forest of northern France, historically known for major ground battles during all prior world wars.

The giant ships, transporting millions of Rockoid troops, began entering Earth's atmosphere and couldn't be stopped. Trying to shoot them down wasn't possible. The intensity of firepower needed to make a dent in the shields of those ships was enough to destroy everything on the planet's surface within one hundred miles.

President Rogers, Commander Johnson, the entire Alliance command and the troops preparing for battle, as well as worried civilians, stared at their viewscreens in nervous, fearful anticipation.

Chapter 19

A press of a button here, a touch of a viewscreen there, and Ray started sending the stolen identification codes to the Rockoid flagship.

The silence seemed deafening. Every second appeared to tick by with the most incredible slowness. Ray became more and more impatient. He wanted a response, any response.

It wasn't long in coming.

After thirty seconds, he could hear strange words being spoken in an almost musical tone, the Rockoid language, coming from his radio. He didn't attempt to answer, but waited patiently for long, suspenseful moments.

He began to fear his ruse wouldn't fool the Rockoids; he wondered if they'd just fire on him, destroy his little ship where it flew.

He looked aft and saw an opening appearing, as huge doors began sliding slowly apart, revealing a gigantic entranceway. In less than a minute, Ray found himself staring at that dark, gaping hole, as if the mouth of a beast had opened to consume its prey.

Ray's craft began to move slowly, unerringly, toward the powerful Rockoid ship, and down into a long, cave-like tunnel.

Ray realized trying to control his ship was useless and turned off the engines; he put life-support systems in low power just in case they were monitoring his ship's computer. The invisible force field continued dragging his fighter craft into the command vessel.

What seemed like hundreds of Rockoid craft flew around him. As the other ships sped past his tiny fighter, Ray became more and more nervous, hoping they wouldn't recognize the ship of an intruder. A few times faint, untranslatable voices could be heard on the trans-space radio; he ignored them.

Was Zanther trying to find him? Did she know he was now within her flagship?

Help me, Zanther! Take me to you! His mind cried our her name, over and over again.

* * *

Still seated in her huge throne room, Zanther was ready for battle. At the same time, she felt there was another force at work. She prepared herself for what the gods willed. Though reluctant to confer with her defense minister, she realized she had to summon Xorax to her chambers for a final briefing. His response was swift, almost obedient; he practically marched into the throne room only seconds later.

"Yes, Your Majesty?"

"Minister, make the final battle preparations. I wish to be alone, in contemplation, before the attack begins."

"Very well, Your Majesty. Shall I tell our commanders to start landing troops?"

"Yes, tell them to proceed with the surface assault."

Zanther kept her tones measured, deliberate, but there was a faint touch of husky emotion she could barely conceal. She hoped Xorax hadn't noticed.

Without a further comment, Xorax bowed quickly and left the room.

The young warrior Empress knew something Xorax could never anticipate would soon occur.

As Ray's fighter craft drifted slowly through the bowels of her ship, Zanther sensed his arrival. He had been calling out to her; of that she was certain. The human male was summoning, beseeching her to allow them to meet at last.

Zanther sat in deep contemplation, praying for inspiration from the gods to help her make the right decision that would save them all from more useless bloodshed.

Before her mind entered its meditative state, Zanther deliberately adjusted her computer system to allow Ray to enter. She surmised he had used forged identification codes, but allowed admittance, assuring passage went unimpeded.

* * *

At 13:45, Earth time, the first stages of the battle began. Both sides started to release their fighters, and the Rockoids brought their smaller cruisers to the front lines. At first, the ships came toward one another warily, firing occasional warning shots, but as they came closer the weapons' fire became more rapid. Before the ultimatum expired, a savage battle commenced.

Laser shots went off everywhere, ships dodged opposing firepower. Between the gaps in the Alliance and Rockoid formations there were small explosions, telling each side another ship had just been lost.

The Alliance battered the Rockoid front lines with all they had. Whenever the Alliance put a gap in the opponent's lines, the Rockoids filled it with more ships. The Rockoid plan of battle was to hold positions and not let the opposition break through until bigger ships were ready to be placed into battle.

There was one serious flaw in the Rockoids' strategy. With all of their ships in front of the super cruisers, it would be nearly impossible to get a direct shot at the Alliance warships without blowing up their own support craft.

At 14:40, the Alliance destroyed a heavy cruiser at the right flank of the Rockoid line. The enemy tried bringing in reinforcements to fill the gap, but there were no more smaller ship reserves except for ones already in battle. Only the bigger ships were left and they wouldn't be ready to engage the Alliance for another fifteen minutes; by that time it would be too late. The rest of the Rockoid fleet would not arrive until then.

Suddenly the Alliance turned its battle plan upside down, and launched a direct assault on the Rockoid lines. The enemy, unprepared for the maneuver, was completely surprised, and in a few minutes they retreated.

The Alliance kept ratcheting up the pressure on the Rockoids, attacking their lines, breaking up their intricate formations as well as placing fighters behind the bigger Rockoid ships to scare and confuse them, to disrupt their communications. This action was designed to effectively stop repair ships and fuel tankers from reaching the front lines.

By 14:55 a number of smaller Rockoid ships had fled behind their super cruisers or tried to escape through hyperspace. Others had been destroyed. The enemy now prepared their largest weapons systems to engage Alliance ships.

In response, the Alliance dispatched the Seventeenth Fighter Division to test a new tactical technique devised by Commander Johnson, based on engineering studies of downed Rockoid vessels. The plan was to fire a fusillade of lasers and torpedoes at specific locations on the enemy ships.

The fighters shot their load, two torpedoes for each fighter, and within seconds, the torpedoes struck their targets. The fighters retreated rapidly, as larger ships provided firepower to cover them. The enemy fought back, but their quarry escaped with only minor damage.

The Alliance commanders watched their viewscreens, tense, expectant, fearful at the same time. Slowly the Rockoid shields were penetrated, and Alliance commanders could see huge gaps in the hulls of two enemy super cruisers. The hull breach seemed to start a chain reaction among the ships that were hit, and Alliance officers could see large explosions in segments of the Rockoid craft.

At this point, the fighters' continued assault was reinforced by ultralaser blasts from larger Alliance ships supporting their attacks.

The combined weaponry did its job. In a few minutes, the damaged ships collapsed together in a terrible explosion, giving the Alliance attack ships seconds to get away before being engulfed in the resulting debris.

In moments, there were loud cheers resonating aboard Alliance ships. The command centers on Earth were filled with applause and congratulations.

But no one could get carried away with excitement just yet. The expected ground assault was still to come; the outcome of that battle was not as clear. And there was Ray Perkins, who had not yet communicated his status to anyone.

Regardless of Ray's fate, the Alliance commanders knew they had to get the upper hand. They redoubled their efforts to take out as many Rockoid ships as they could. By 15:05, three super cruisers had been destroyed, three more were damaged, and others still tried to fire undamaged weapons.

Meanwhile, the rest of the Alliance and Rockoid fleets jumped out of hyperspace. Thousands upon thousands of ships faced each other.

* * *

Some time earlier, Rockoid transports hovered over the plains of northern France. Panels opened up on the fore compartments of eight of the vessels. Out of these entrances came shuttlecraft, each holding thousands of troops, which rapidly descended toward the ground. There were millions of combatants on Earth now, all ready to do battle.

Once a shuttlecraft landed its passengers, its pilot returned it to one of the transports to bring down more troops. The transports used their own weaponry to keep Alliance ships at bay, firing to protect the shuttle squadrons.

At the same time, platoon after platoon of Alliance ground assault forces slowly made their way through the Ardennes until

14:00, when they came out into the open. They sped up, hoping to catch the Rockoids before they finished landing their troops and preparing their equipment.

The Rockoids were more experienced at ground combat, and quickly set their armored units, fighter craft and personnel in position. The Alliance's armored units rumbled over the Seine River at 14:50, two kilometers from the Rockoid landing site.

Both sides advanced and aircraft and armored units started firing at each other. The strange, circular Rockoid armored vehicles were outfitted with a vast array of firepower for craft so small. They were more than a match for the slower, rocket-driven Alliance tanks, which also had a smaller amount of weaponry.

There were virtually no casualties by 15:05. Only the armored vehicles and aircraft fought, while the troops advanced slowly.

Within a few minutes, full frontal assaults on both sides would commence. Both Rockoid and Alliance commanders made final preparations for the upcoming battle.

Chapter 20

Ray finally reached the docking bay doors at 14:15. His scanners were unable to glean any information on the sort of metal being used on the ship. He wasn't able to pick up more than general details about its structure. It was clear from the readings, though, that the doors had tremendous strength because of their molecular density. At first, he saw the doors opening for other ships, rapidly closing after they had entered. When his craft first reached the entrance, he was surprised he wasn't destroyed by a Rockoid weapon.

Once inside the ship, Ray watched as his lithe fighter craft was drawn slowly toward a docking bay several hundred meters from the entrance. He looked around and was lucky to discover very few Rockoid ships in the vicinity, nor did he see any living creatures about.

Ray took the occasion to get a careful look at the docking bay. The main landing area was a huge chamber similar to a typical Alliance landing base back on Earth. A control center was situated in its center, where he noticed several brightly uniformed Rockoids performing tasks of one sort or another.

Closed hangars with empty landing spots lined the sides. From his cursory glance, it appeared most of the ships had already departed.

Ray's fighter was deposited by the ship's computers at the center of the docking bay. Once the ship touched down, the grappling field was switched off. He discovered he was able to use the radio again. Ray did not want to inform the Alliance of his status, in fear the Rockoids would intercept the signal, so he kept radio silence.

He sat in his ship for several minutes, thinking about what to do next. He didn't know whether he should jump out of his craft and scream, "Hey, Rockoids! Come and get me! Take me to your leader!" or wait for someone to find him.

He knew he had to locate the being with whom he was in contact. He concentrated, looking for a clue as to what he should do next. Ray's solution came to him in a subtle, unspoken voice with clear intent. He knew where he had to go and how to get there, as if he were intimately familiar with this ship.

Ray had the intense feeling Zanther was near, watching his every move. She seemed to be trying to speak with him, though the words weren't audible...

Before exiting his vessel, he took a few quick readings of his environmental control system, pleased to discover the Rockoid ship's atmosphere was breathable.

Slowly, he walked to his fighter's aft section and slid the hatch open. He pulled himself out warily, watching carefully for any lingering Rockoid troops. His heart beat rapidly, and sweat dripped from his brow. He tried to breathe deeply for a moment, and attempted a meditative state.

Luck was on Ray's side. Except for the Rockoids working at the command console, nobody was present. He concentrated on the directions sent to him by that supposed telepathic command. He noticed a long, narrow chamber at his right: his destination.

Deliberately, he walked into the dim, cylindrical chamber. He struggled to see his surroundings. He realized the larger eyes of the Rockoids were accustomed to the darkness, but it was challenging for him.

He had been given some infrared glasses by the Alliance; in his haste he'd left them in his fighter.

Ray tried to stick near the walls, in case he ran into an enemy soldier. He hoped years of training in physical combat and mental discipline would take control if he were forced to attempt hand-to-hand combat with one of those beings. For a race inured to combat, he was certain they were physically formidable.

Ray pulled out a small control module from his pocket and pushed a few buttons on the scanning device the Alliance gave him. A few faint lights glimmered in the darkness. He made a few adjustments to home in on the Rockoids' life force.

He was shocked at what he discovered. Ray nearly dropped the contraption: There were so many Rockoids near him he could hardly count them.

He looked about, saw nothing, and stuffed the device back into his pocket.

Ray felt he was deliberately drawn down this route to his destination and depended on intuition to guide him. He walked more briskly, realizing he was closing in on the Rockoid leader's throne room.

He would meet Zanther at last. He knew it now.

His fears kept rising to the surface, as much as he tried to hide them. Could it be a trap? Or could it be the meeting that would save both their races from further bloodshed?

How could he know?

Suddenly strange music began playing in the background. The sounds almost seemed to lift his spirits, giving him a feeling of great contentment. He could not describe the melodies. They were so beautiful. Just as quickly, his mind returned to the task at hand, though it remained difficult to ignore the music playing in the background.

He looked back at a long pathway to his left, and saw a band of Rockoid soldiers marching toward the docking bay. Ray's eyes had become more accustomed to the unusual, almost faded red glow that served to light the ship. He could actually make out the creatures better than before.

At last, he saw the Rockoids as they truly were, not dreams. They seemed no taller than humans, but slender physiques gave the illusion of greater height. In the dim light, he couldn't see the color of their skin; they all seemed uniformly drab and under-nourished, as if anorexia was a way of life in their society.

And their eyes! They seemed huge and penetrating. This was mostly an illusion based on their dark pupils. Their heads seemed so human-like in shape; their noses were uniformly small, per-fectly shaped, as if they were all spawned from the same cookie cutter.

So human, yet alien at the same time, and even handsome by any traditional sense. They all seemed to have a look of refine-ment, superior intelligence.

What if they could be persuaded to become...friends?

Zanther, help me! Weeks ago, he felt she actually tried to speak with him, but once the war began, such communication abruptly ended. As he expected, there was no verbal response this time either, just the image of her calling out to him. He felt she was now attempting some sort of response.

Ray watched the procession in growing fear. They marched right past his docked fighter.

Standing to the side of the procession was a black-caped Rock-oid, who seemed to be directing the marching. He was large for a Rockoid, over six feet tall, nearly Ray's height, and portly, rather an anomalous sight among this throng.

The black-caped being appeared to be addressing the crowd. After a few minutes, everyone raised their hands in front of their heads, and brought them rapidly together and then apart. This appeared to be a military salute. Within seconds, the procession began to disband, and troops marched toward waiting ships. Their leader, whom Ray realized was male, stayed behind. Ray thought the creature was about to join his comrades; instead he stopped short and stared right at Ray's fighter.

He looked behind him and discovered Ray. He called out in the strange language; more than a dozen soldiers joined him. The commander and his soldiers began approaching the intruder.

His presence on the Rockoid flagship had been discovered!

Chapter 21

As soon as Minister Xorax became aware of the presence of an alien intruder, he sounded the alarm. Ray started moving at a near run as the soldiers began chasing him. He was unable to hear any sound, but he felt it. The high-pitched whining in his ears was painful. He staggered to his knees and covered his ears.

Finally, the alarm stopped. Ray felt dizzy. Sweat dripped from his forehead, around his face, over his eyes. His head throbbed.

He looked around, but the lighting was so dim he couldn't see beyond a few feet. He decided to sit and concentrate for a second, struggling to focus on the directions to Zanther's location. Ray thought long and hard, but felt nothing. He decided to take the advice of an old martial arts teacher and use mental disciplines he had practiced for many long, boring hours.

He relaxed, letting the energy flow into his mind. Within seconds, he had gotten an instinctive knowledge of destinations and routes once again. His headache seemed to have left him. Ray now felt calm, serene. With amazing accuracy he deftly traversed winding chambers, moving from one to another, as the intensity of the mental instructions he received became stronger.

Zanther, help me! Take me to you!

He felt he was close, but as Ray turned toward the dark chamber that would bring him to the Rockoid leader's throne room, he heard the march of running feet in the distance.

* * *

Minister Xorax knew nothing of Zanther's contact with a human. He was astonished to find an Alliance ship sitting unguarded in a secured landing dock. Whoever allowed this outrage to occur would shortly be dead. His entire being felt violated.

Xorax grabbed his weapon. He checked a small light that flickered above its trigger, saw it was fully charged and ready to fire; he hoped he'd have the pleasure of killing that wretched, barbaric human by himself, but was willing to share the honor.

Xorax summoned members of his elite security detail and alerted them to the threat at hand.

As they planned to go after the human, he suddenly disappeared from sight. Xorax just stared dumbfounded, his hopes of a quick capture of the intruder ended. He ordered his troops to spread out.

They fanned out and began searching every nook and cranny of the huge ship. Rockoid and human genetic structures were similar, so it would be difficult to detect a single human life form with their own scanners. They hoped there were more alien beings aboard.

Ray's instinct to come alone may well have saved his life.

The minister had the suspicion the visitor had a specific destination. He took his contingent of troops and headed straight for Zanther's chambers.

Privately, he viewed the possibility the Empress might die at the hands of a human with mixed feelings. On one hand, he wanted desperately to mate with the beautiful warrior Empress, who was young enough to be his daughter. On the other hand, he felt the chaos that would follow her death would not only intensify the war effort and ensure the victory the Rockoid gods had willed. Zanther's murder would also give him the opportunity he needed to usurp the throne. Still, Xorax had to put on the façade of saving Zanther. If there was any doubt about his intentions, he could be charged with treason, and face a death sentence. His troubled mind retained much of the logic of the cold, calculating military commander he truly was.

* * *

It would only be matter of time before the advancing troops caught up with Ray. He ran as fast as he could, hoping he could reach Zanther's throne room before it was too late.

Voices and sounds of many feet running toward him grew louder. He decided to focus more intently on Zanther's directions. As he started pondering the throne room's location one last time, the noises behind him grew fainter. Within a few minutes, he couldn't hear any sound at all. Ray's senses seemed to fail him and he could feel himself losing consciousness.

No, not now!

He tried hard to resist, but soon gave up as he realized he must surrender to the mind-numbing force that engulfed him.

Ray Perkins blacked out.

* * *

When his eyes opened, Ray briefly thought he was still unconscious. Darkness filled his eyes. After a few minutes, his sight returned, and he saw...what? An apparition?

Before him, a Rockoid female, wearing a long purple robe, sat on a large, black throne in the dark gray chamber. Ray couldn't miss the wide smile on her face, so incredibly infectious it seemed to draw him in.

There, in the flesh, was the woman of his dreams...Zanther!

She seemed taller than he imagined; he could see the shape of lithe muscles beneath the form-fitting garment.

Everything Ray had seen in his dreams was reality...in this

room…in this time and place. He could hardly believe it.

Zanther was surely dressed for the occasion. While she usually eschewed jewelry, in accordance with the warrior code, she now seemed bedecked in a ton of it.

Her wrists were covered with thick bracelets, encrusted with jewel-like materials that reflected all the colors of the rainbow in the dim light.

It seemed as if she had deliberately chosen to dress in this fashion only for him! He knew it to be true.

The room itself had an ethereal beauty to it, and Ray felt in some fashion it reflected the essence of its owner. There was a faint odor of many flowers, something akin to what he had seen in a botanical garden on his own world. He saw no flowers, nor plants about. Or at least anything that looked like any plant life he knew.

As Ray looked around in amazement, Zanther began probing his feelings. She confirmed what she sensed from afar.

Zanther saw only his good heart, and felt his loneliness. She knew he was attracted to her and she to him. At the same time, the shibboleths of Rockoid tradition were uppermost in her mind. Zanther knew the consequences of having a forbidden romance with such a person.

Entranced, they regarded each other, eyes wide.

The moment they longed for had finally come to pass.

Zanther spoke, or seemed to speak, though she made no sounds. In his head, Ray heard a sweet, almost musical female voice, filled with a richness and vibrancy that rivaled that of any performer he had heard in his lifetime: *"Greetings, Ray Perkins. I am Zanther of the Royal House of Zophine, Empress of the Rockoids. It is agreeable to finally meet you."*

"Wait, I don't understand what's going on here. Please just…" Ray tried to say.

"No, Captain Perkins, you do not have to speak. You only have to think of the words and I will understand them, despite the difference in our languages."

Ray was about to say something out loud again, but concentrated on his words instead and thrust them back into his mind before they flowed out to Zanther. "*It's great to meet you too. Now what about those guards that were after me?*"

"*Do not worry about them. I have already given them the order to allow you to come here.*"

Ray frowned. "*Are you sure they're going to agree?*"

"*Probably not. Right now, you are safe under my protection.*" She smiled again. "*For some reason our minds share the same frequency, the same wavelength; they are synchronized. That is why you were able to see the battle of Dorton from our perspective, and I was able to experience your ordeal in the desert from yours. You have seen the depths of my heart and soul, and I have seen yours as well.*"

Ray almost blurted out a question, but he thought it instead. "*You dreamed about...me?*"

Zanther's thoughts were calm, reassuring, "*Yes, Captain Perkins. You have come to me in answer to my deepest wishes, my heartfelt desires. The greatest battle between the Alliance and the Rockoids has already begun, but we still have a chance to end this war for the good of all. We must share our souls utterly, completely, so I can discover the truth about you.*"

"*I don't quite understand what you mean.*"

Her face flashed its glorious smile and he smiled back. He couldn't help it. He felt overwhelmed yet strangely comfortable in her regal...yes, divine...presence.

"*Let me explain. I need to ascertain whether the thoughts and feelings I sense from you are genuine or implants. That requires you to reveal all of your thoughts and feelings to me. You will not mind, I hope.*"

"*I guess not. I want to stop this war however I can. I think after all I've been through, a little invasion of my privacy is fine. I don't think anyone else would be crazy enough to even try something like this...*"

Zanther interrupted and flashed her glorious smile once again. "*Then, perhaps, that is your gift; you are capable of accomplishing the impossible.*"

"If only that was true. So please tell me; what do I have to do?"

"I believe it would be prudent if we delay my probe of your thoughts for a few moments. I hope you will accept my own thoughts....so you will better understand me and our motives for attacking your Alliance."

Ray interrupted. *"Your Majesty, is that really necessary?"*

"It is necessary, Ray Perkins, very necessary. If we are to stop this terrible war between your people and mine, we must both trust each other completely, absolutely. It would not be acceptable at all if I trusted you, but you did not trust me; trust must be shared. We must also understand the truth concerning the conflict between our peoples, why it occurred and who was behind it... that can only be done by understanding both sides of the story. However, we must do this quickly. I apologize for having to rush this delicate process, but time is short, and more and more die as we sit here."

Ray sighed and nodded in affirmation. He knew he had no choice. If he wanted to help end the war, this was his only chance.

He stood there and again tried to use the concentration techniques his kung fu master had taught him. After a moment, he felt himself getting slightly dizzy. The feeling left him almost as quickly as it came.

Suddenly a black and white blur appeared inside his head, and he realized he had forged a different link with Zanther. The blur slowly assumed all the colors of the rainbow. The colors spread out, became scenes, scenes of events in the past, in the present, events Ray knew he never personally experienced.

In the next moment, Ray felt an onrush of memories and emotions, some so compelling he was nearly swept up by their intensity. He saw a small, beautiful Rockoid girl frolicking in a huge forest, playing with friends and family—Zanther as a child, a lovely being who beamed with happiness and joy.

He saw a regal-looking Rockoid male and a Rockoid female, who bore a strong resemblance to the adult Zanther, standing behind their young child, smiling, as she performed what appeared to be a ceremony of ascension. He saw Zanther as an adult, proudly receiving something that looked like a metal.

The onrush of events almost overwhelmed him, but he strove hard to sort things out.

There was a large planet that looked quite a lot like Mars, where millions of beings lived in peace and harmony.

Without warning, a great, silent terror from space arrived.

He saw that which he had dreamed about, the battle of Dorton.

Alliance ships opened fire, and Ray sensed the wanton massacre of millions of creatures. He understood the nature of the Rockoids' hive consciousness, where everyone grieved in unison over the deaths of their fellow beings. He understood how the entire Rockoid race had been devastated by the deaths of so many of their people. He was appalled at the barbaric action Thompson had taken against the Rockoids, and realized why they sought revenge.

His eyes were full of tears, and his ears ringed with the sounds of long-ago explosions as he came to realize intelligent beings throughout the universe were very much alike, even if their external appearances were different.

The process of receiving Zanther's thoughts, up until now, seemed to proceed rather slowly. It suddenly sped up and images poured into Ray's mind, almost literally, at the speed of light. He was able to get glimpses of a few scenes; most of them went by too fast for him to tell what was really going on. He was overwhelmed, but at the same time, the feeling of love stirred with greater passion.

He knew the truth now. He truly loved the glorious creature that sat before him.

His feelings about Zanther overwhelmed all else at this point. They slowly blanked out the images received from her mind, and they quickly disappeared from his consciousness....

After a few minutes of silence, Ray managed to get his senses under sufficient control to speak to Zanther again via telepathy. *"I grieve for you and your people, Empress Zanther. What Thompson did to your people is the most horrible thing I've ever seen. When I tried to contact you before, I tried to tell you she was a* traitor, a renegade who fled after our authorities tried to arrest her. We have to stop this madness right now!"

"*We will get to that shortly, my very dear friend. First, do not forget there is still one matter of business left. You must reveal your own thoughts to me...so I can confirm what you have said is the truth.*"

Ray wondered whether Zanther sensed how much he really cared for her. What did this glorious creature think of him? Was he just an alien curiosity, one to be dismissed with a flick of her royal hand?

For now he had to push such selfish feelings aside. This meeting was the best hope...perhaps the only hope...the Alliance had for peace with the Rockoids.

He closed his eyes and relaxed his mind.

Suddenly he felt an odd tingling inside his head. It was as if soft fingers touched his brain, gently massaging it. It felt good and it made him comfortable, almost drowsy, and he felt like he could fall asleep right there and she would protect him. Within seconds, the feeling had passed, and another one entered his head: love. As Zanther probed his mind, he realized she, too, was deeply in love with him. He felt it and her smile radiated that love whenever she looked at him.

At the same time his heart leaped with this knowledge, his feelings of happiness were tempered with the awareness that theirs was a forbidden love.

He was human, she a Rockoid. Her society didn't recognize such relationships, forbade them. That, too, was implicit in the images that came to him.

The thought saddened him. Ray felt their love was strong enough to survive against the most impossible odds. He knew that; she told him so, body and soul.

By the time she was finished, they were transfixed, gazing longingly at each other, as Alliance troops marched to the Rockoid landing site on Earth and the battle in space became fiercer than ever.

Zanther looked at Ray for just a moment, with a glance of

understanding and care. He remained transfixed by her eyes. They struggled to brush off the almost hypnotic influence one had upon the other.

The feeling was so intense, Zanther couldn't help but speak out loud in her native language with words that seemed to come from another person, words that Ray could not understand. "It is you, Ray Perkins. You are he. You have a destiny; we have a destiny..."

They returned to the real world....

Zanther's intoxicating smile faded, and she turned serious. Other matters required her attention right now.

"I now understand the truth about this entire situation, Captain Perkins, just as you tried to relay it to me. I understand how one of your corporations put its own interests before those of Alliance citizens and started this war to further those interests. I must contact the Alliance president on your trans-space radio system so we can stop this war immediately!"

She pointed to her viewscreen and said to him, in his mind, *"You know the secret codes you must speak to reach him; even though I have seen them in your mind, I cannot speak them because voice prints will be checked. Please do it now, for time is of the essence."*

Quickly, Ray uttered the numbers that would activate the secured trans-space channel. President Rogers' worried face appeared on the viewscreen.

The President's eyes widened at the sight of Ray and he exclaimed, "Captain Perkins, Ray, is that you?"

"Yes, it's me!" It wasn't lost on Rogers' eyes that Ray beamed from ear to ear, never seeming happier.

Rogers thought to himself: *Just what happened over there? I sincerely hope he didn't...no, he's not that kind of person! What am I saying? This man is a hero!*

"Let me ask you a question, Ray," Rogers said, as if he didn't believe it was him.

"Yes?"

Rogers grinned and asked, "Ray, is the sun shining?"

Ray smiled back and said, "Yes, but the ice is slippery."

Zanther stared strangely at both of them, but she smiled, almost chuckled, knowing Ray had given the right password.

Rogers examined the voiceprint Ray made before his departure, and he smiled broadly. "Ah, then you're not a prisoner, are you?"

"I'm here of my own free will, sir," smiled Ray.

Rogers turned serious and said, "I must speak to the Rockoid leader right away! Can she speak English?"

Ray heard Zanther's voice in his mind. *"We have a translation device and I am sure we can synchronize it with the trans-space radio so your president can understand me."*

Ray repeated what Zanther had said to President Rogers. For the first time, he saw Zanther's face, and the look of amazement appeared square on his countenance. The President could not have imagined such a young and lovely creature being the supreme ruler of a civilization of billions of intelligent beings.

Seeing this woman as a flesh and blood creature, he knew why Ray was attracted to her. May his wife forgive him, but he could imagine Zanther winning a beauty contest with ease, if he were the judge.

Zanther spoke aloud to him through the translator with a serious expression, her voice changing subtly, accustomed to the mantle of leadership, "President Rogers, I am Zanther of the Royal House of Zophine, Empress of the Rockoids. It is agreeable to meet you at last. It is with deep regret this state of war has existed between our peoples. I see now who is to blame for this conflict: your traitorous commander named Thompson. I am ready to stop the bloodshed this instant if you are willing to do the same. I also pledge the work of our people to help you rebuild your colonies if you will help us rebuild our settlements on Dorton."

Rogers looked into the large, expressive eyes of the Rockoid Empress and her ever-widening smile. He stared at Ray, confirming she was, indeed, telling the truth. Ray just smiled. There was an unmistakable look of relief in the President's eyes. His response was measured but sincere.

"Yes, I believe you, Empress Zanther. I am giving the order immediately to cease all hostilities. You have my personal assurance the Alliance will help you rebuild the Dorton colony. In addition, I pledge our help in relocating the citizens still left homeless by this unprovoked attack. I also assure you we will use any means necessary to bring this renegade commander to justice."

With great relief, the two leaders spent a few more moments exchanging the details of what was intended to become the beginning of a formal peace agreement between the Alliance and the Rockoids. They both expressed the hope this would be the first of many such agreements that would ensure a lasting peace between their governments.

The conversation ended, and with it ended the war as well. For many people, their hopes of peace had finally been fulfilled, but not before vast destruction had been inflicted on both sides.

Zanther was especially pleased at the turn of events. She was certain now the ancients were right. The Rockoids were not meant to be a war-like people. It was time the barbaric policies that had gained supremacy were halted. They must acknowledge their true heritage, open themselves up to the younger races of the galaxy as they had already done to other great powers.

Zanther realized that while the races the Rockoids had conquered were treated far less harshly than they had been in years past, distinctions keeping them from becoming further integrated into Rockoid society had to go. All beings were equals in the eyes of the gods. Lots of work for her and her ministers to deal with in the weeks, months and years to come. Zanther realized there would be severe opposition from some quarters, from ministers who preferred the old ways. Despite the anticipated political conflicts, she eagerly looked forward to the process of change. She could also sense that a divine will was at work here.

With the tentative peace accord between the Alliance and Rockoids, she strongly suspected there would yet be tasks for her military forces as well, for she knew there lurked even greater dangers in the galaxy.

This was one thought Ray picked up, but he never had the chance to question Zanther about it then.

Meanwhile, the trans-space radio signals quickly reached the

Alliance and Rockoid fleets across the galaxy, as well as ground troops, as they were immersed in battle.

One moment there were the loud sounds of gunfire, flashes of light, and death cries of Alliance and Rockoid troops.

And the next...

The troops stared at each other in surprise and relief. With the command to "stand down," they slowly set aside their weapons and retreated to fallback positions.

The war was over!

After a few tense minutes, one Rockoid soldier smiled a strange half smile; a human soldier did the same. The soldier walked over to the Rockoid, who did not retreat any further. The soldier gently grabbed the alien's hand and shook it. Rather than be repelled at the gesture, the Rockoid smiled even more. They tried to exchange words, but the universal translation systems were not equipped to translate the alien tongues. Only the translation system in Zanther's throne room had been reprogrammed.

Once the new codes were generated, temporary translation devices were quickly set up, allowing the Alliance and Rockoids to communicate. While tensions were sharply reduced, it would take time for the two to warm up to each other. There was still a pall that hung over the entire episode. No peace treaty could bring back the many thousands who had perished in needless conflict. The political realities of the situation were certain to create obstacles to a lasting peace on both sides for some time.

In time, it was hoped the Alliance and the Rockoids could truly live together in peace and friendship.

As news of the end of the conflict spread across the galaxy, Zanther sat back on her throne and observed the proceedings with a confident smile. Suddenly, without warning, Minister Xorax burst into the room.

When Xorax entered, he started speaking Rockoid. The translation device was switched off, and Ray could not understand exactly what they said. He could read the words in his mind, deliberately relayed to him by Zanther, although the tone of their voices was more than sufficient to convey the sense of their conversation.

"What is the meaning of this intrusion, minister?" Zanther asked, angrily.

"I thought you were in danger, my Empress. I thought this... this...this outworlder was trying to make an attempt on your life."

"Minister Xorax, how dare you think such a thing! This human would never dare harm me...now that the situation has changed!"

To Ray's surprise, she actually winked at him.

"What do you mean, my Empress?"

"Minister, I have contacted the President of the Alliance and we have agreed to a cease fire. The war is over."

Xorax replied calmly, but there was a clear look of disdain and betrayal in his eyes. "With all due respect, Your Majesty, our traditions are never to make peace with enemy races, especially... lesser ones."

Ray bristled at the suggestion he was some sort of barbarian primitive. On the other hand, when he had first arrived in this century, everyone else seemed to consider him as such.

Zanther responded curtly, "Minister, may I remind you in the years after the reign of Emperor Eronetus, the government made it a policy to enter into peaceful relationships with all other intelligent beings if they did not represent a threat to us, and now that is no longer the case with the Alliance. You will accept the cease fire and assure it is enforced. Am I correct?"

Xorax stopped to stare at her for a few seconds. Ray couldn't detect an expression, but he knew the minister was none too happy at the turn of events. Yet this particular Rockoid official was a savvy politician and did not wish to disagree in public with the Empress. Xorax felt his time would come, so he simply said, "As you wish, Your Majesty."

Without another word, he turned and left, with no further hint of his reaction to the unexpected turn of events. As soon as the chamber doors closed, the translation device was switched back on. Ray said to Zanther, aloud, "He didn't seem very happy, did he?"

"No, he was not pleased at all, Captain Perkins." Zanther

flashed him her amazing smile again. "Do not worry. I will deal with him further at the appropriate time."

Ray sighed and said, "I just hope he doesn't develop into a problem."

"The only problem we have with him is his own. Once he was a trusted friend. But a strange madness appears to have possessed his mind. Now he regrets how my family took the throne from his two thousand of your years ago and he wants revenge. He only wishes for his dynasty to again rule the Rockoid Empire, and he does have supporters within our government, a significant minority that may yet threaten the peace process. However, I am sure logic will prevail in the end, and Xorax will realize this decision is for the better."

Ray and Zanther spent a few moments longer in deep conversation. The extended period of telepathic communication had given these two a very clear understanding of each other, and the shared exchange during Zanther's mind probe had, in effect, let each live the other's life for a few moments, sharing their most intimate thoughts. As a result, they'd now look upon each other as the closest of friends, perhaps even…lovers.

Such a strange combo we make. Could a relationship between us ever work?

Ray could tell Zanther knew what he was about to ask, but nevertheless she sat there waiting for him to voice the words. Finally he took a deep breath and asked her, "What about us, Zanther?"

Zanther sighed, and tears began falling from her eyes. She wiped them away quickly and replied, "Captain…Ray…I…I have to tell you something, but it is not something you wish to hear, nor something I can say without the most incredible pain in my heart.

"While the genetic similarities between Rockoids and humans make a physical relationship possible, it is forbidden by the edicts of our race. There is nothing I can do to change that. I…I have my duties and my obligations. I must soon return to our home world of Aeronautas."

She smiled faintly, trying to put a cheery outlook on a sad situation. "I have quite a few reforms I'd like to present to the Rockoid Senate. I believe the way we treat other races could use a little... tweaking or fine-tuning...that is how you say it, is it not?"

Ray was very surprised to hear her using Earth slang and simply nodded. Perhaps she picked it up during their mental union. However, he continued without hesitation. "Will I ever see you again?"

Zanther's smile grew even wider. "Ray Perkins, you and I are linked forever. I shall always be in your heart, and you in mine. Our souls are one. The laws of my people will never change that.

"We shall always be able to share our thoughts, no matter where we are located. In a sense we shall always be together, and maybe -someday..."

She trailed off, though Ray understood the meaning of her words.

The conversation ended for now, but he still wasn't quite sure how one said goodbye to an Empress, even one with whom he was in love.

Before he could do anything more, she surprised him once again by walking over to him and hugging him tightly. They remained locked thus for several minutes, holding on for dear life with tears in their eyes. Neither wanted to let go.

He wanted to kiss her and she him. Their lips suddenly met. Two lovers, always together, forever apart.

Finally, they both pulled away reluctantly. Ray smiled at Zanther and left her chamber. As sad as he felt, he was also happy he had, at last, found his true love.

Maybe someday...

He had to keep that hope uppermost in his heart.

As Ray left the royal chambers, he had an escort of Rockoid guards, who walked at a respectable distance behind him, treating him as an honored guest.

Within minutes, he boarded his fighter craft, warmed up the engines, and sped off back to Earth. As his ship rapidly flew away, the smile remained on his face, his eyes filled with tears.

Goodbye, my love. Perhaps we will meet again soon....

Chapter 22

Ray's return trip to Earth came to an abrupt end when, suddenly, an Alliance heavy cruiser appeared behind his ship. A few lasers struck the bow. His ship stopped dead in its tracks.

He had no time to act; he anticipated what he was about to hear. Sure enough, a familiar, husky, battle-worn female voice barked orders to him on the radio, "This is the Alliance heavy cruiser *Star of Terra*. Perkins, if you wish to live, you will come aboard this instant."

"Thompson! What the hell is this about?" Ray shouted, trying to make his voice sound surprised.

Thompson's voice seethed venom and she yelled at the top of her lungs. "You have just destroyed the balance of power in the galaxy! You have let those bastards get the upper hand, and you will pay dearly for that!"

Within seconds, his fighter docked with the *Star of Terra*, and the hatches of the two craft were linked. Ray tried to remain calm in the face of this reality; he knew he may not be able to get out of this predicament.

Just then, a thought occurred. He said nothing, but his mind sent a powerful message out into the depths of space.

Zanther, please help me!

It was a long shot, he knew, but perhaps it was his only hope of survival.

Suddenly the hatch burst open and several armed troops entered.

The troops confiscated Ray's laser weapon and conducted him directly to the ship's bridge, where Thompson was seated. Her hair was disheveled, her face drawn. There were rings around her eyes. It looked as if she hadn't slept in days. Her face had no expression at all, and she barked commands with an unexpected ferocity. When he walked up to her, she barely noticed at first. When she finally spoke, he could feel the hatred in her voice.

"Perkins, you have destroyed my career, my life, and probably destroyed my father's company because they won't be able to build any more ships for wars that are not to be. So you've probably wrecked the economy as well."

Ray sneered back at her.

"Okay, I've destroyed the universe. Soon you'll be telling me I've made you sterile too," he laughed.

"Shut up, old man." She glared at him. "Where you're going you won't have time to consider any more frivolous jokes."

Ray kept her talking, and slowly maneuvered himself toward one of the armed guards. They clearly feared their irrational commander, a fear that overwhelmed them so they had grown careless. Ray gave the guard a judo chop to his neck and grabbed his weapon in a single flowing motion. He pointed the weapon at Thompson.

"I'm going to take you back to Earth. You've killed millions of people, you lunatic. It's time you paid for your crimes!"

"How dare you!"

There was no warning. All it took was a well-placed karate kick. Ray's weapon dropped out of his hand.

Ray jumped on Thompson, smashing his fists on her shoulders and face and she fell. As quickly as she dropped to the deck, though, she was up again and raised her foot in front of Ray, who ran toward her.

He couldn't halt his forward motion in time. His face struck the leading edge of Thompson's foot and he fell with a resounding thud. His head felt groggy and he struggled against the darkness, feeling he was about to lose consciousness.

"I have had enough of you, Perkins!" Thompson drew her own weapon, glaring at him.

Before Thompson had a chance to fire, Ray heard a huge explosion as the cruiser dipped out of control. Everyone was thrown to the deck. Thompson's head smashed against a console, and she fell unconscious.

Ray managed to get to his feet and stumbled into an aft chamber. He fought his way, slowly, toward the main hatch, in an effort to reach his fighter before the *Star of Terra* crashed into something or exploded.

As he neared his ship, he heard a familiar voice in his head. *"Ray, Ray, are you all right? Ray?"*

His telepathic response came quickly. *"Zanther, I'm heading back to my fighter right now. You fired on this ship, right?"*

"Yes, all members of the Rockoid royal family are required to take military training. I was...how do you say it in your language? Ah yes! A pretty damn good shot!"

Ray laughed out loud, as he was once again amazed by how she so quickly adapted to Earth slang. By this point he approached the hatch of his little fighter. The larger ship still spun around, nearly out of control, as its crew tried to recover its balance. It was almost impossible to get the hatch open to reach his craft. With a great force of will and with all his strength, he managed to pry it open and felt relieved to find his fighter still attached, the airlock secure.

He ran straight to the pilot's seat. A few controls were activated, and the little ship slowly drifted away from the still-spinning cruiser. Ray set his course as quickly as he could, and fired the main thruster rockets.

As the fighter's speed accelerated, Zanther's warning rang loud and clear within his mind: *"Ray, you must get far away from that cruiser as quickly as you can."*

"As you wish, my lovely Empress. I guess I owe you one."

Ray couldn't help but smile as he thought about an Empress who meditated, healed the sick and was an expert spaceship commander.

He was eight hundred thousand kilometers away from Earth when he looked out the porthole and saw the Rockoid flagship firing at the *Star of Terra*.

On the bridge of the massive Rockoid vessel, Zanther stared out into space, tears steaming down her face.

"I take this action in the memory of Zikath and Counar. May Reka-danai forgive me."

She closed her eyes and breathed deeply while silently chanting an ancient Rockoid prayer used during times of war. She opened her eyes again.

She pushed the button to activate the ship's powerful weapons.

Suddenly several lasers poured forth from Zanther's ship and coalesced into one. The giant laser struck Thompson's cruiser point-blank, causing a great explosion that disintegrated it, leaving only small bits of debris and tiny particles of dust in its wake.

Ray breathed a huge sigh of relief as he saw the ship exploding. He sensed Zanther's complicated feelings of anger, sadness and relief.

Within seconds, the Rockoid flagship was out of sight, but her voice in his mind was crystal clear: *"I do not think your people will mind that Thompson's ship was destroyed. I only wish the problem with our defense minister was so easily resolved."*

"What's wrong?"

"He fled in his own private ship, with a few supporters. We are searching for him right now. He has sympathizers in our government who will no doubt protect him..."

Ray interrupted, more and more amazed at how easily this telepathic ability worked now that he knew how to use it. *"Does that mean your government is threatened because of this guy?"*

"Not us. However, there are greater threats in our galaxy and it is always possible the minister will try to make an accommodation with them. Next time we meet, I will give you the full story. In the meantime, I will send the intelligence information we have over to President Rogers. Now I must return to my throne room before they wonder where I went. They expect their Empress to be well guarded. While our leaders are traditionally expected to be intimately involved in the art of war, I doubt many would approve of their Empress being on the bridge of a warship, directly in control of weaponry.

"Remember, I shall always be in your thoughts. I love you, Ray Perkins. Be well and someday you will return to me. I swear it."

Ray sat back, relaxed, relieved, and hopeful his "forbidden" relationship with this alien woman might indeed have a future.

After a brief communication with the Alliance command, he made a beeline to the Alliance's landing strip in central Brussels.

* * *

Upon his arrival, he was amazed to find his friends on hand to greet and congratulate him. He didn't envision himself as any sort of conquering hero.

As they talked, some other folks recognized Ray from pictures shown on the news reports and went to meet him. Soon the group swelled rapidly. Before long there were thousands of people surrounding him, a mix of journalists and spectators asking Ray questions. There was also a procession of high-ranking officials from across the galaxy who came to congratulate him. The crowd clogged runways and caused a huge traffic tie-up.

Ray barely knew what to say, and though he tried to answer all the questions the best he could, it was just impossible.

He started thinking what it must have been like for a celebrity to try to travel around like a normal person. He wondered if things would ever be the same for him again.

Fortunately, the hustle and bustle began to subside as Alliance security guards quickly surrounded Ray and his companions and led them toward a waiting hovercar.

Within seconds, the hovercar took off and headed straight towards the White Palace.

Ray wanted to rest, but before he could shut his eyes, Jennifer asked him, "Ray, what about Zanther; do you..."

However, the content look on his face told her just what she needed to know. "You love her, don't you?"

Ray smiled. "Yes, more than anything in the universe."

"What about her?"

"I think so. She says she'll always be in my thoughts...we can speak telepathically now, as clearly as I can talk to you. I've never felt like this before about anyone."

There was a tear and a smile on Jennifer's face. "I envy you, Ray." The meaning wasn't lost on him.

That night, Ray made a brief effort to celebrate with his friends before crawling off to a nearby sofa and falling fast asleep.

* * *

Ray woke up early the next day, feeling refreshed for once. He hadn't needed to take any medication the night before, and his dreams about battles with the Rockoids were apparently over. He knew he would always have a telepathic link with Zanther.

"I am in your heart always, Ray Perkins."

He smiled.

A signal flashed on the viewscreen. A quick voice command and he saw Gotlieb's grinning face before him.

"Hey, old man, guess what? We've got thirty days shore leave. Time for fun and frolic."

"I'm open to suggestions. I've been aching to explore this brave new world."

"I've got a great idea. Let's examine those old Area 51 labs. They're right under the shopping mall, sealed away for decades. Maybe we could finally find out how you got here."

Ray had an inkling of dread. Though he usually trusted his feelings, this time he decided to ignore them, a serious mistake he would later realize. He figured there was nothing to fear from a long-abandoned laboratory.

"Sure I'd love to see what's really going on down there. We'd need some way to clean it out, right? There ought to be dust, insects and..."

"Not on your life. That place is sealed up tight. Nothing could grow in there. It's frozen in time. Don't get me started on the techniques we use to preserve ancient artifacts. We can keep things in their original state indefinitely."

"Wow, when do we get started?" asked Ray. "Can we have anyone join us?"

Jennifer's smiling face appeared on the viewscreen right next to Gotlieb's. "Ray, I'll be glad to join you folks. I'm looking forward to finding out what's down there."

* * *

The trip back to the shopping center seemed like déjà vu to Ray. He felt his neck hairs tingling as he walked through the huge mall. For once, he actually had a little time to inspect the stores and the strange offerings of products still unfamiliar to him. However, he was there to explore ancient artifacts, not window shopping, so he didn't keep his companions waiting for very long.

At last, they entered a service area, where a large door loomed before them. A small security panel was situated at eye level. Gotlieb walked over to it slowly. His retinal pattern was scanned and the door slid open with loud, grating noises. Clearly, this place wasn't visited very often and perhaps hadn't been in years.

Inside there was a small room with recessed lighting overhead. At one end hung a large viewscreen and some control panels. Otherwise, the room remained bare. Gotlieb punched a few codes, and the viewscreen lit. Gotlieb said "Unseal," and he waited.

After a few minutes, Ray heard the sound of air rushing all around him. The sound vanished, as the computer's voice returned with the announcement, "Chamber unsealed. You may now enter."

At the end of the small chamber, Ray saw the elevator, *that* elevator!

Within seconds, the doors slid open and Ray and his two friends entered the very elevator that took him down to the bottom of Area 51 over two hundred years earlier. Gotlieb pushed the button at the very bottom, and the elevator door quietly slid shut.

Nobody had said anything since entering the secret chamber. Ray tried to remain calm, but his feeling of dread became almost oppressive. He had never been one to ignore his instincts, but he thought his fears were senseless, so he decided to suppress them and continue on his journey.

The motion of the elevator was slow at first, but it eventually accelerated downward at an almost dizzying pace. Ray felt a tightening in the pit of his stomach as the elevator came to a stop and the doors opened.

The scene inside astonished him.

They entered the same laboratory he'd trashed when he first visited Area 51 in his own century. The machines had been reconstructed; there was no sign of the destruction he wrought. He was even more amazed when he saw huge flickering lights, and heard a loud grinding sound. Gotlieb looked around and saw a master switch. He slowly walked toward it and raised his hand.

"Hmm, I wonder why this was left on. Oh well, might as well conserve energy..."

At this point, Ray had a sudden revelation and tried to warn Gotlieb not to turn off the switch...he was too late!

Gotlieb switched off the power supply and Ray stood there, staring at everyone in dumb amazement.

At first, he felt dizzy. Suddenly, as when he first traveled to the future, all motion around him seemed to stop. White flame began to engulf him and he started falling toward that horrible silver tornado again, seeing his life spinning before his eyes once more.

He struggled to get away from that awful turbulence. He breathed harder and harder and felt as if he was about to suffocate.

Everything went black.

* * *

It was a while before he could see again, but the voice was very familiar. "Ray, Ray what the hell happened to you? Are you okay? Do you need help? Wake up! Wake up!"

The fog before his eyes lifted and he looked up. Apparently he had fallen. He stared at the concerned face looming above him.

Ray panicked. *No, it can't be! It's impossible...this is all a dream...a nightmare. This couldn't possibly be happening!*

Manny Gonzales looked at Ray with growing concern. He had followed him down into the lower chambers deep within the Area 51 complex after Ray failed to return the following morning. When he entered the secret laboratory, he saw it filled with a strange, smoky mist, and within that mist lay Ray's unconscious body. Without a second's hesitation, he lifted the larger man over his shoulder and slowly stumbled out of the laboratory, into the elevator, out of the facility, and back to Ray's car, where Ray was now lying in the back seat.

How he had accomplished the task continued to amaze the old soldier. Somehow he found within him the reserves of strength sufficient to drag Ray to safety.

Gonzales had had to cash in many favors to get inside the base, and steal his way out, with Ray in tow. He feared they had been discovered by others not privy to their little "arrangement," but there was no time to consider that now.

"You had me worried sick, Ray. What happened in there? Did something explode?"

Ray struggled for a few seconds before he could get his voice to work. Finally he stammered, "The Rockoids, Jennifer, Gotlieb... where...what...were they all part of my dream?"

Gonzales stared on in wonder, but finally managed to say, "Rock who? What? I don't know what the hell you're talking about, but..."

In his haste to rescue his friend, he had not paid much attention to what Ray wore. The strange, multicolored garb was completely unfamiliar to Gonzales, yet it appeared to be a military uniform of some sort. An insignia representing one's rank, similar to a captain's emblem, adorned the left shoulder. He noticed strangely shaped medals, apparently honors for meritorious service in battle.

It was made of a material totally unlike anything he'd ever seen, a form-fitting, shiny fabric that was soft, yet gave the impression of incredible resiliency. It was the sort of uniform one saw in a science fiction film. There was also a strange watch on Ray's hand.

It looked a lot like he came from an early Halloween party.

"Ray, what's this stuff you're wearing? Where'd you get it?"

Ray finally recovered enough to look himself over. "I thought they captured you."

Gonzales laughed, "Me? No way! They just arrested a soldier who made a ruckus after going out for a night on the town."

"Where am I?"

"I found you unconscious in that strange laboratory. I brought you back here to your car, before they spotted me."

Ray got up with a start and cried out, "I have to go back there!"

Gonzales looked puzzled. "What do you mean? Back where?"

Quickly, Ray told him about his experiences in the future, about his friends, the battles with the Rockoids...about Zanther. As he told Gonzales about his amazing adventure, a look of increasing shock came over Gonzales' face and his eyes widened. He simply couldn't believe it. The entire thing seemed impossible, fodder for a silly science fiction novel.

"Come on, man, you must have been dreaming. Maybe you had a little too much to drink in there..." Gonzales laughed.

Ray glared at him. "Manny, it was real! I've really been to the future. I have go back...to her! I belong there now!"

Ray started to become hysterical. Gonzales talked calmly. "Listen Ray, I don't know what any of this is about, but you've had a terrible ordeal. Maybe you picked up that clothing in the laboratory, maybe..."

"Yeah, but what about this?"

He pointed to his wristview. Ray played back scenes that showed him and his companions from the future. He also displayed the log he made of his encounter in Zanther's throne room. Gonzales looked at the holograph-like images and heard the sounds, which, for a moment, made him feel as if he was seated in a large movie theater. He had a confused look on his face, as he searched for the source.

Gonzales marveled at the amazing little machine for a moment longer, until he realized the truth of what he had just seen. The very last image was one of Zanther seated on her throne with a huge smile on her face, recorded just before Ray had left her ship.

"Then this...this thing...it really is from the future. You've been there, haven't you? Is that Zanther? She's so beautiful. No wonder you've been so obsessed...."

Gonzales was struck speechless.

"Manny, I've got to find my way back there. It's my home now... my life is waiting for me there. Help me, please!"

"Ray, I really don't know what to say. But we've got to get away before we're both caught and arrested. The only way you can get back to wherever you went is to remain free."

Gonzales picked up Ray's keys, which had been left conveniently on the front seat, and started the old Mustang. Ray sat in the passenger seat, dazed, as he put on his seatbelt. For a second, he almost believed it would wrap itself around him automatically.

Ray stared at his little viewscreen as the car accelerated. Her picture was still there, unmoving, as he pushed the Pause button.

As the sun rose, the car sped away in the early morning light.

Exhaustion overtook Ray and he soon fell asleep. He dreamed about a world of wonder, friends and love. A world he feared he'd never see again...

The great battle was history, but Zanther stood plain as day before him. Instead of anguish, he saw the bright gleam in her eyes and a big smile. He could feel her deep love for him.

He smiled back...

About the Authors:

Gene Steinberg discovered the magic of writing while still a teenager. He edited his own science fiction and New Age fanzine, and began writing a science fiction novel about an Earth man who finds himself in an unknown land faced with life-threatening situations.

In the 1970's, several of his science fiction/science fact articles appeared in *Saga UFO Report* and *Beyond Reality* magazines.

In 1984 Gene began to work with the original Apple Macintosh personal computer and never looked back. Over the next few years, Gene finally decided to follow his dream and become a full-time writer, but he also devoted extra time to work as a computer software/systems consultant, partly to provide material for his books and magazine articles.

Gene has written more than 30 books on computers and the Internet, plus hundreds of articles for such industry publications as *MacAddict, MacHome, MacUser and Macworld.* He has also written for CNET, ZDNet, Gannett News Service and usatoday.com. Gene's computer news and support Web site, The Tech Night Owl (www.technightowl.com) receives over 1.5 million hits per month, and he hosts two weekly syndicated radio shows, *The Tech Night Owl LIVE* (www.technightowl.com/radio), focusing on personal technology, and *The Paracast* (www.theparacast.com), which is all about UFOs, the paranormal, and what Gene describes as "things that go bump in the night."

As for that science fiction novel Gene began as a teenager, he and his son, Grayson, have expanded that original story and used it as the basis for the exciting new science-fiction adventure series, *Attack of the Rockoids.*

While not saying just what's being planned for the future, Gene admits that the first novel is just the beginning. There are more stories to be told about the characters he and Grayson have created. The best is yet to come.

Grayson Steinberg first began to write while still in grade school, beginning with short plays performed by his classmates. He also wrote a number of short science fiction and fantasy stories, both for his schoolwork and on his own time. His writing abilities grew over the years until he decided to put them to good use and join forces with his dad, Gene Steinberg, to create *Attack of the Rockoids*.

In addition to his versatile writing talents, Grayson is a die-hard music lover, guitarist and violinist. He listens to everything from alternative rock to free jazz.

Grayson graduated from Arizona State University in 2008 with a BA in journalism and mass communication.

He also completed reporting internships at several publications in the Phoenix metropolitan area, including The Arizona Republic, the region's biggest daily newspaper, and the Phoenix Business Journal.

These days, Grayson lives in Madrid and teaches English as a foreign language to both children and adults. He continues his writing career in his spare time.